Hel
Copyright © 2

No part of this publication may be reproduced, stored ...
or transmitted in any way by any means, electronic, mechanical, photocopy,
recording or otherwise without the prior permission of the author except as
provided by USA copyright law.

This novel is a work of fiction. Any similarity to actual people or events is
entirely coincidental.

Scripture quotations are taken from the Holy Bible, King James Version,
Cambridge, 1769.

Author photograph © Jerry Teets Photography

AP
Ancient Path Publishing Inc.
PO Box 648
North Liberty, IA 52317
Visit www.ancientpathpublishing.com for more information and
submission guidelines.

S.C. Sherman is available for book signings and speaking events.
Bulk order discounts and to learn about fundraising opportunities visit
www.hellandbackbooks.com

Printed in the United States of America

AlphaGraphics
720 Pacha Parkway Suite 1
North Liberty, IA 52317
www.us639.alphagraphics.com

ISBN: 978-0-9845133-0-7
06.15.10

Dedication

This story is dedicated to my wife, Amy, for enduring my idea of the week and living a life that has tended to wrench violently up and down.
Thank you and I love you.

To my children, Mollie, Cole, Brock and Sariah, you are truly the crowning glory of my life. I love you and I am so very proud of you. May whatever you do in life lead you to the Kingdom.

To the King of all Kings.
Thank you for the breath, the sword, the shield, the helmet, and the way home.

Special Thanks

I would like to thank the following for their encouragement, advice, editing, and friendship. Your support has been invaluable.

Bruce and Ruthie Lengeman
Dan and Nicole Irlbeck
Doug and Annie Pudenz
Gene and Mabel Bontrager
Craig and Lori McConnell
Jamie and Carmen Bontrager
Alicia Dawson
Mary Palmer
Kalyn Durr
Jeanne Marie Leach
Kelly Mortimer
Rose Irlbeck

Hell & Back
The First Death

A Novel by
S.C. Sherman

Lake Michiansa!
Thanks,
SC Sherman

Index

Part I
Life and Death

I	Old Warrior	1
II	The Sum of Life	15
III	Unexpected Visitor	31
IV	Knocking Down Death's Door	49

Part II
The Kingdom of Heaven

V	Eyes to See	55
VI	The Throne Room	73
VII	To the Mountains	91
VIII	Forgotten City	107
IX	Plan of Attack	127
X	The Armor of God	145

Part III
The Realm of Hell

XI	The Lake of Fire	169
XII	The Woman in the Wilderness	183
XIII	The Catacombs	199
XIV	The Woman and the Dragon	207
XV	From the Pit	225
XVI	Race to the Lake	241
XVII	Last Rites	251

Author Disclaimer:
This author being of sound mind and healthy fear of the Lord makes this claim. This book is a work of fiction and nothing more. It is by no means an addition to or manipulation of the written word of God. I heed the warning found in the prophecy of Revelation 22:18-19. I pray this book be an enjoyable read that sparks discussion and spiritual thought.

PART I
LIFE AND DEATH

I
OLD WARRIOR

Joe Rellik slipped through the jungle like a shadow. Training and experience allowed him to disappear. It was easy, like breathing, he didn't have to think about it. Death followed at his heels, ready to reap the harvest. Eyes focused on the bamboo and thatch hut, dead ahead. Joe held his breath, listening for anything unusual. He heard nothing but the sound of rain falling on water and blood pumping in his ears. In spite of the downpour, the awful heat of the bush permeated everything. Sweat and rain ran down his body into the thigh-deep water. Almost there, he wiped the back of his hand across his face as light poured forth from a window of the target. One last check of the heavy weapon assured Joe, locked and loaded.

A red and yellow snake swam directly between his legs. *I hate snakes! I hate this place!* No time to worry about that. Movement inside the hut forced Joe tight against a moss-covered tree. Raised voices argued in some Asian tongue, he couldn't tell for sure, either Vietnamese or Cambodian. It didn't matter. He'd been sent here for one reason. Kill everyone in and around the hut found at these exact coordinates.

He was ready, both excited and nervous. As soon as the lead started flying and the people started dying, he knew he'd feel all right again. It was his specialty. The knack for killing was the only gift he'd ever discovered about himself. It didn't matter anymore whether it was right or wrong. It was just what he did, and he was anxious to get on with it now. Joe leaned against the outer wall of the hut. He closed his eyes for a second or two to clear his head. The warm rain bounced off his cheeks.

Joe clenched his teeth and opened his eyes. In one fluid motion, he kicked the door hard, and stepped inside, the M-16 firing on full auto. His ears rang from the deafening roar as hot lead sought out flesh to destroy.

He released his trigger. Acrid smoke filled the air and empty shells littered the ground. Something was very wrong. No one was in the room, alive or dead.

He moved forward. The door slammed shut behind him. Joe whirled around and hit the deck, firing back toward the entrance. Again, nothing, no one was there. When he stopped firing, silence choked the heavy air. Then he heard it. He couldn't quite make it out. Could it be English? It sounded like a woman or a child.

He heard it again, "Daddy."

The word tugged at his heart. He didn't like to kill kids. They hadn't told him who his target was. Just to kill everyone here. When he reached the back of the hut he found something strange - a hallway. On full alert, he slowly stepped into the passage and slid forward. Red flags went off in his head. *This is wrong!*

His boots made a strange sound, and he noticed smooth concrete. The icy-cold hand of fear tickled its way up his spine. Concrete, in the jungle? *Where am I? I have to get out of here!*

Light streamed into the dim hall from a perfectly rectangular, metal-framed door. The kind found in a hospital or a school back home, not in a hut behind enemy lines. He inched his way toward the open door. Without looking, he replaced the empty magazine with a full one, showing skill and precision obtained from years of practice.

He heard it again. Joe paused and held his breath, straining his ears. It was definitely a child or a woman calling, "Daddy."

The voice felt familiar. His fear deepened as his breath came quickly.

"Daddy!" the voice cried loudly. There was no mistaking it now. His heart sank into his boots. It was his daughter's voice.

He burst through the doorway. The blinding flash instantly

turned to darkness and his eyes struggled to adjust. A musty smell assaulted his senses, and a lone beam of light cast eerie shadows on a stone wall. The steady sound of dripping water echoed through the dank room. A little girl sat in the corner with her back toward him. Her fine hair just hit her shoulders and had a tint of red to it. She wore white clothing, like linen, but dirty and unkempt. Her size told Joe she must be about ten years old.

His gun fell from his hands as he rushed toward her. The faint sound of a chopper reverberated overhead. He knew his time was limited.

"Sweetie," he said in his most gentle voice. "What are you doing here?" The girl didn't answer, and continued rocking her body back and forth.

"Sweetie? It's Daddy." She stopped rocking.

Joe stretched his hand out to her shoulder. As he touched her cold, clammy skin, she fell backward. He swiftly knelt and caught her before she hit the floor.

Joe gasped at the sight of her. Scarlet blood stained her clothes, and her head flopped loosely. He cradled her head in his hands.

"Sweetie, Daddy's here."

Her little eyes flickered with life.

"Oh Daddy," she said. "You're too late. I told them you'd come. They laughed at me. They said you'd never come, not for me anyway. I told them you would."

He squeezed her to his chest, barely able to breathe. Joe had seen many people die. He knew he wasn't going to save her. The room spun around him, and he felt like he might puke.

He pushed her back. "I did come for you, sweetie, don't die," he said. His voice strained with painful emotion.

Her eyes didn't open, but in a whisper she said, "Why'd you leave me? Now I'm lost." The air exhaled permanently out of her chest.

Awful laughter hidden in darkness echoed through the room. Joe couldn't tell where it came from, and he covered his ears to block it out.

The fading light wobbled and dimmed even more. He jumped up, dropped to his knees, and began feeling the floor for his gun. The laughter moved around him in a circle.

As he spun around, he noticed his daughter's body was gone, and where it had lain stood an evil-looking black dog. The animal bristled thick and muscular with long wolf-like hair. Its eyes red like embers of glowing coal.

Joe readied himself, as the hound growled low, took two steps forward, and then leapt at him with snarling teeth dripping rancid foam.

Joe covered his face with his hands and screamed out in anger.

"No!" The old man jumped awake, screaming into the night. Sweat soaked his white tank undershirt. Confused, he looked around the little room in the muted darkness. Moonlight shone through torn, white curtains and cast an odd light about the bedroom. He swung his feet to the cold floor as he tried to catch his breath realizing it'd been a dream - a terrible dream.

"They're getting worse," he mumbled.

Joe cradled his face in his hands and wept. The image of his daughter covered in blood stuck in his head. Lonely, bitter tears smeared over his wrinkled face. He slowly stood with a stern shift of his jaw. The deep pain of choices long made and consequences still being paid wore heavily on his old shoulders, but determination drove him on.

"Damn dreams," he muttered as he hobbled, bow-legged to the bathroom. "You won't scare me out of it."

He turned on the light and lifted the lid to the toilet. As he urinated, the water filled with blood. He clenched his teeth against the internal pain. He went to the sink and splashed some cold water on his hands and face.

Joe stared into his own eyes in the mirror as water dripped from his chin. He couldn't believe what he saw. The deep wrinkles, the drooping jowls, the age blemishes.

"How'd you get so old?"

His bright eyes appeared even more sharp blue than ever, set within the face of an old man. White hair stuck out from the top of his undershirt. He dried his face with a small towel, still muttering to himself as he ambled out of the bathroom.

"You think you're going to scare me with a dream like that? Well you're not. It just reminds me how strong I was and will be again. Then you'll have hell to pay."

Joe gave up going back to bed and went into the kitchen to make coffee. A faint light grew on the eastern rim of the surrounding mountains. Spring in the Rockies meant the temperatures dipped low at night. His smoky breath reflected the chill inside the poorly insulated house.

Joe whistled a marching tune as he stepped out the front door, his plucky attitude had returned. A fresh layer of frost glistened like crystal in the morning light. He carefully selected two small pieces of wood from the stockpile.

"This old house looks as bad as me," he said. The clapboards had aged and needed new paint, a gutter hung down at one end; the front porch was mostly disconnected from the main structure.

"You're so darn weak," he said to himself. "You can barely carry these two little sticks. Ha! I must still be making somebody nervous with all these dreams coming like they are."

He shuffled into the house and put the two logs in the wood burner.

The coffee pot groaned, spitting out steam and black coffee. After pouring a cup, Joe sat down close to the stove in an attempt to stay warm. He carefully put on his wire-rimmed reading glasses and opened his old Bible to a scripture he knew by memory.

"Luke 16:26, And besides all this, between us and you there is a great gulf fixed: so that they that would pass from hence to you cannot; neither can they pass to us, them that would come from thence," he read out loud.

He closed the Bible and left it lay on his lap, closing his eyes.

"No crossing back and forth. Only one way into either place and no way out." Joe exhaled loudly at the weightiness of the thought. He struggled up from his chair and sat on the arm of the brown-and-tan-speckled couch. The couch was ugly and it had been several decades since it was new, but it still felt good. He thumbed the little black notebook he kept in his shirt pocket.

"Ah there," he said, picking up the harvest gold phone. His big fingers carefully dialed the numbers. The rotary whined as it returned itself and the cord bobbed against his arm.

It rang a long time. He was about to hang up when he heard a sleepy woman's voice answer, "Hello?"

"Hello, Joan?"

"Yes, who's this?" the woman asked.

"It's old Grandpa Joe."

"Grandpa Joe?" she asked, sounding confused.

"Yes, Grandpa Joe, you know, Joe Rellik, Matt's dad."

"Joe. It's been a long time. Is something wrong? Do you know what time it is?" she asked.

He looked at his watch. "It's nigh onto 6:30 here."

"That makes it 5:30 in the morning in California. I was sleeping. We all are sleeping," she said, with a deep sigh into the phone. "Can I help you?"

"I was hoping to get your address and pertinent information on you and the boys, like social security numbers or whatever you got," he suddenly realized he hadn't taken the time difference into account, but since she was up now, she might as well help him. "Sorry to wake you, it won't take but a couple of minutes."

"Joe, you call me after God knows how many years, with no contact with your grandsons at all to ask me that, at 5:30 in the morning?" Her voice held an edge to it, which made her sound a little aggravated and not as sleepy as when she first picked up the phone. "I should tell you where to go."

"You could tell me where to go," Joe chuckled to himself and continued. "And you'd be more right than you know."

"Just out of sheer curiosity, what do you need all of that information for? Dare I ask?"

"Well I'm sure it won't break no hearts, but I'm fixing to kick off. It won't be long before I'll be gone. You see, I've been pretty sick for a while now, and I can tell things have turned, you know, for the worse," his gravelly old voice trailed off.

"I'm sorry, Joe. Have you seen a doctor?" Joan asked.

"What the hell would I do that for? So they can charge me to tell me that I'm an old SOB and gonna die pretty doggone soon? I just told you that for free," Joe said.

"Sometimes doctors tell us what's wrong with us, and then we can fix it," Joan said in a condescending, motherly sort of way.

"There ain't no doc in the world gonna fix me up, as old as I am. Who'd want to?" Joe took a moment to calm down. "Anyway, I'm selling my patch of dirt to some greedy land-sharks. I'm making 'em wait till I'm dead to move in on it, but other than me dying, it's a done deal. You know lawyers and realtors and the like. You should see 'em drive by my place real slow, circling like buzzards, wonderin' if I'm dead yet. Gonna build a strip mall or something." He stopped, but Joan didn't say anything, so he continued. "You see, it's gonna be a pretty fair chunk of change, and I always thought you were a real good woman. You done right by those boys as near as I could tell anyway, and with no help from that fruit-loop son of mine. I was aiming to give you and the boys the money."

"How much money are you talking about?"

Joe chuckled again. "Got you awake now don't I?"

She laughed too. "Yeah, you've got my attention."

"Well it ought to end up around three-hundred-thousand or so," Joe said.

The other end went silent. Joe thought he could hear crying.

"That ain't as much as you think. Just enough for you to buy a car or put a down payment on a house or pay for college for Matt Jr. or Blake, or do whatever you like with it. I don't care. It's yours. I'll be dead anyway."

"You aren't giving any to Matt?" Joan asked in a shaky voice.

"I shouldn't, he'll just blow it on something. It'll be gone like the wind," Joe stated.

Joan chuckled, "You do know your son, after all. Have you spoken to him?" she asked.

"Well, not since he told me he never wanted to speak to me

or see me ever again," he answered. "Even so, I'm planning to give him ten-grand. I have his address, so I don't need to call him. He won't know how much you and the boys got. So it's up to you, if you want to tell him, don't make no difference to me."

"Joe, I want to thank you. That will mean the world to us, to me, to the boys. Really, it changes everything. Things have been hard for us, and I've had to work two jobs. I've really tried…"

"Don't thank me; thank the good Lord. It's all His anyway," Joe said with conviction.

"I wish we'd known each other better. We should've stayed in touch. My boys would've done well to know you."

"You might think so, but I haven't been too good with kids. If you haven't noticed, my son hates me, and my daughter, well, you know."

"Don't be too hard on yourself," Joan said. "I haven't spoken to Matt Jr. in weeks. Blake told me he's living with some potheads in a shack on the beach, and all he does is surf all day."

Joe snorted. "Well the apple didn't fall too far from old Matt's tree there now, did it?"

"No, but he's not like Matt entirely, so maybe he'll come out of it. Let me tell you about apples not falling too far. Blake's sixteen and has his heart set on going to West Point. He wants to be like you, Joe."

"West Point? He wants to be a military man?" Joe asked, excited by the surprising news.

"Yes, he's serious. He's getting straight A's and volunteering in the community, doing everything he can to build his resume. Until now, he was going to need a scholarship, but your money will send him."

"Well, I'll be, I'd no idea," Joe said.

"Of course you didn't; it's been years since we spoke. He was a little boy."

"If he wanted into West Point, all you had to do was ask. The man in charge of admissions served in 'Nam with me. All I have to do is call him," Joe offered.

"Thank you, Joe, but I know Blake would want to earn it."

"Oh he'll earn it. Everybody gets in any way they can. You better ask now 'cause I don't know how much longer I'll be here, like I said." Joe coughed a little.

"Let me ask Blake first," Joan said.

"Straight A's, huh?" Joe said. "That must be from your side. West Point, my grandson? That'd be something. He'd learn things I never did. I learned quick when they put a machine gun in my hand, strapped a parachute on my back, flung open the side door of an airplane and said, *See you on the ground, private!*"

"Joe, I can't thank you enough. Maybe if you went to a doctor you could buy some more time?"

"Nah, no docs. It's finished. No use fighting it. Life's but a vapor, you know," Joe sounded tired. "I have to be going now, Joan."

"Thank you again, Joe."

"Do you have that information? I have to get going."

"Sure." She gave him what he needed and they said their goodbyes.

Joe rubbed his ear after hanging up with her. He stretched out his legs on the couch, and drifted off to sleep.

❦

Joan set down her phone and swung her feet to the floor. The tiny bedroom had cracks spider-webbed across the stucco, but it was clean and all she could afford. The housing prices in San Diego were outrageous. Anyway, with Matt Jr. gone, it was just Blake and her now. She picked up the phone, noticing herself in the dresser mirror.

I look old. When this boy leaves, who will want me?

She dialed the number that had once been her own. It rang and rang, and she bit her lip.

"Hullo?" a sleepy and familiar voice answered.

"Matt, it's Joan."

"Joan, what time is it? What's wrong?"

"Nothing much, your father's dying. Have you spoken to him?" She asked, taking a little pleasure at the obvious dig.

"You know we don't talk. What do you mean dying?" Matt asked.

"He called and told me how sick he was. I need to get a hold of little Matt. Do you know if he has a phone?" She said, upset at having to ask him in the first place.

"Mattie, yeah, he's doing great. We hung out last week at the beach. It was way cool," Matt said with his hippie surfer drawl. "No, he doesn't have a phone. I can give him a message though?"

"I doubt he would get it," Joan said viciously.

"Who is it Matt?" Joan heard a woman say. "Hang up."

Joan's anger flared. "Good Lord, Matt, you aren't alone. Why didn't you tell me?"

"You didn't ask."

"Well, how old is she? Seventeen?" Joan didn't have time for this.

"Sweetie, how old are you?" Matt asked without moving the receiver away from his mouth.

"You're sick!" she yelled into the phone.

"I guess she's twenty-five, but I can't remember her name either," Matt snipped back.

"She's barely older than your son; you were thirty when she was born!"

"It's been nice talking to you, Joan," Matt said in a lazy voice. "I feel much better about divorcing you, thanks for the reminder."

"Your father wouldn't treat his family this way!"

"He knows a thing or two about leaving a family," Matt said sharply. "I don't care if he does die. It means nothing to me."

"You don't care if your father dies? He seems like he's become a very, uh, nice old man," Joan said cautiously.

"Don't buy all of his good-ole-boy bullshit. He abandoned all of us years ago. He can rot in hell for all I care." Joan knew Matt spoke vindictively from years of repressed anger.

"How would you like it if one of your boys said all this about you?" Joan questioned him.

"I may not be perfect, but my boys *know* me, and I'm their friend."

"Oh yeah, I forgot, you're a great dad. I apologize. That's why your oldest son is living in a shack on the beach smoking dope all day, good for nothing. Tell your hussy to roll over! Maybe she should call her mom to let her know where she is!" Joan yelled and angrily hung up before Matt could say anything else. She threw the phone savagely across the room.

She ran her fingers through her hair and measured her breaths, attempting to regain composure. She felt so distraught and emotional, she wanted to cry, but she was too angry to let him have that kind of victory.

"Why on earth did I call him?" she asked herself. "I knew what would happen." Her head snapped up at the sound of the light tap on the bedroom door.

"Mom?"

"Yes, honey. I'll be right out." Her countenance dropped under the weight of life. "Not a good way to start my day," she whispered. She slipped on her robe and opened the door.

The young man before her always took her aback. In a split second she could see him in her mind as just a little boy. Now, here he stood, looking more like a man every day, his dark hair trimmed short in precise military style. Everyone noticed Blake's sky-blue eyes, just like his father's and grandfather's. Despite the color being the same, Joan found it odd that the biggest difference between this boy and his father could be found in the eyes - something just beyond the color. It was the depth. Blake's eyes held a solid assuredness, a steadiness that belied an inner strength. His father's contained only uneasiness and insecurity.

"Who was on the phone?" Blake asked. "I heard it ring."

Joan cracked a brown egg into a sizzling pan. "I was talking to your Dad just then, but when it rang before, believe it or not, it was your Grandpa Joe." Joan stopped a moment to watch Blake's reaction.

The smooth-skinned face of youth lit up with excitement. "What did he want? Did you tell him about me? Why did he call? What did he say?"

"I did tell him about you."

"Really? What'd you say?" Blake's eyes sparkled in anticipation.

"I told him you were an amazing young man, determined to go to West Point," Joan said with a smile filled with pride.

"What did he say to that?" Blake prodded impatiently.

"He said that if you wanted into West Point, all you had to do was ask. He served in Vietnam with the admissions guy, and with a phone call you could be in," Joan said, trying to contain her excitement at the possibilities.

Blake looked away as he absorbed the offer. "I can't believe he offered to do that," he said. "What'd you say?"

"I told him I couldn't speak for you, and we'd let him know if you wanted to accept or not. He said that people got in any way they could and there's no dishonor in accepting his help."

"He said that?" Blake asked.

"Yes."

"What should I do, Mom? Should I accept the offer?"

"If you really want to go to West Point, then I think you should let Grandpa Joe do all he can," Joan said. Her heart soared at the prospects for Blake.

Blake nodded and said nothing, his brow wrinkled in contemplation.

"There's more," Joan continued. "Grandpa Joe said he's very sick."

"Sick like what?" Blake asked.

"Sick like he thinks he'll not be here much longer," Joan said tentatively.

Confusion and loss kicked Blake in the stomach. "Mom, he can't die now."

"Also, he's leaving me, you, and Matt Jr., most of his money, and it's quite a lot," Joan said. She tried to contain her excitement at the idea of someone dying.

"Like how much?" Blake asked.

"Enough to pay for someone to go to West Point." Joan smiled.

Blake remained quiet; all of his young dreams had just been

handed to him on a silver platter. It was a lot for anyone to take in, much less a teenager.

Joan slid the scrambled eggs onto a plate in front of her pensive son. She sat down and watched as he ate in silence.

"What're you thinking?" Joan finally asked. "Are you okay?"

"I'm fine, just confused. Why would he do all that for me?" Blake asked. "He doesn't even know me. We haven't heard from him in years."

"I think he's a loner. There's been a lot of pain in his life, and now I'm guessing he wants to help us as one last act of kindness on this earth."

Blake picked up his backpack, and shouldered it. "I gotta get going to school. Can we talk about it tonight? Don't call him, alright?" Blake asked.

"That's fine, honey. Whatever you want," Joan said.

"Did he call from Colorado?" Blake asked.

"Yes, it was the number I have for him from his place near Salida. I guess some people want to buy his campground and turn it into a strip mall or something, probably because it's right on the highway. That's where the money's coming from. I was there once with your father, a long time ago, before you were born."

Blake leaned over and hugged his mother. "See you tonight." He opened the door.

"What time?" Joan asked.

"Uh, I'll be late. I have practice, and then I'm going over to Collin's house to study. We have a chemistry test coming up and we need to work on it."

"So I'm on my own for supper?" Joan asked.

"Yeah, I'll call you. If it gets really late, I may just crash at Collin's, if it's alright with you," Blake said with a hopeful smile.

"That's fine, just call me?" Joan didn't suspect any subterfuge from this son. Blake had never lied to her before and she didn't suspect it now.

"Yeah, we can talk tomorrow night. See you." Blake flashed a smile that melted his mother's heart.

She watched out the window as he climbed into the red

Pontiac Sunbird that was 'his' car. Her heart swelled with pride. He'd worked all summer for the money to buy it. Most of his friends had nice vehicles their parents bought for them. They didn't have that much extra, so he'd earned the money and bought the car himself. It wasn't much, but it ran good and got him around. He took good care of it too. She turned away as he pulled out of the driveway.

⚜

Blake smiled at his gas gauge. It registered full. He drove past the street that would've taken him to school and turned his car onto I-15, chasing the unknown.

II
THE SUM OF LIFE

Joe blinked his eyes, confused by the darkness, searching for what had awakened him. It had been daylight last he remembered. His mind wandered in fog as he noticed the door to the wood burning stove hung open, brilliant coals of sunset-orange consumed the remaining chunks of wood. Joe shook his head and sat up.

He couldn't have slept all day, could he? Could he have been so careless as to leave the stove door open?

You old fool.

Joe leaned forward, placed his elbows on his knees and rubbed his eyes. The kitchen sink dripped. The sound from the little drop ripped through the thick silence like an explosion and Joe was instantly alert. What was it? He sensed something unseen; he wished he had a weapon in his hand. His head snapped toward a flash of light across the room. Joe gasped loudly, startled by the tiny glow of flame. An ember flashed a ring of lava-light.

"Who's that? Who's there?" he cried out as he struggled to see in the darkened room.

There it was again; the glowing end of a cigarette as someone inhaled. Joe focused his old eyes; he couldn't see as well as he used to.

"Who's there?" he demanded. "What are you doing?"

No answer, only silence.

Joe leaned over and switched on the lamp on the end table. The 60 watt bulb began pulsating as if only at half-power. Joe thought it might go out altogether. He could hear the filament sizzling. He strained to see the man in the corner, smoke from the wood-burner gave the room a surreal, foggy ambiance.

Slowly, Joe's eyes adjusted to the novel lighting, and the two men stared at one another. The man inhaled deeply again and blew a perfect smoke ring in Joe's direction. His ashen-white cheeks were sunk deep into his face and dark skin encircled hollow eyes. The man wore a uniform – an old uniform, but Joe recognized it immediately as that of a World War II Nazi soldier. The room brightened just a shade allowing him to see more clearly. Joe could hear the man exhale.

Joe noticed a crimson stain growing in the middle of the man's chest. Dark drops dripped to the carpet as he sat with one leg crossed casually over the other. He didn't appear to be in pain and seemed to be enjoying his smoke immensely.

"If I'd seen you two seconds earlier. . ." the pallid figure of a man spoke. His voice was raspy, as if he'd smoked too many cigarettes. "I'd be an old man, and you'd be me." The German accent was thick.

"Who're you?" Joe asked. "This is just another damn dream, when I wake up you'll be gone."

"Not this time, you are wide awake, my friend. Hard to tell sometimes which side you're on." The Nazi flicked ash on the floor. "You do not recognize me, do you? I'm disappointed. Look closer." He sneered and stared directly at Joe. The rusty wheels of Joe's memory finally recognized the man.

"Ha! I know you!" Joe smiled, and shook his head. "Yeah, I know you alright; I killed you a long time ago. You're the first man I ever shot, right after I hit the ground on D-Day more than sixty years ago. Come for revenge, have you? You're too late. I'm already dead."

"Soon, soon, you'll be dead, to be sure, but not yet. My name was Karl Albrecht. I just wanted you to know that. I was engaged back then and she was beautiful, blonde hair..." The Nazi coughed horribly into his hand and wiped blackish blood from his lips with his shirt sleeve.

"It was war. Like you said, you would've killed me in a second, and I'd kill you again if I could. What do you want? Tired of haunting libraries?" Joe snapped.

"It won't work, you know," The Nazi said with a thin smile as his eyes darted from side to side. He glanced out the window over Joe's shoulder.

"What won't work?" Joe demanded.

"He won't ever let you have her. You'll never even find her," The Nazi said in a loud whisper. He smiled wickedly, enjoying the taunt.

Joe grimaced and put his hand to his stomach; he felt as if he'd been kicked. He knew exactly what the man meant.

"What are you talking about? How do you know anything?" Joe yelled at the apparition.

"I follow you around some. You're planning a mission. Doing your research; making your strategy. I've seen you and I'll say this for you; you got guts. Wildest idea I ever heard of. It still won't work, though." The Nazi shook his dead-looking head.

"You're dead and you know nothing about me or my plans," Joe stammered.

"First of all," Karl continued. "You can't get in. You're marked already; you're written in the book, to go up. And even if you did get in, which you can't, you'd be imprisoned and enslaved just like all of us."

"I promised her I'd come for her, and I will. I'll get in and I'll get her out," Joe stated with as much confidence as he could muster.

The Nazi laughed. "How're you gonna get in? Once you believe in the realms, and especially once you're forgiven, it's not as easy to get into hell as everyone thinks. Get her out? There's no getting out - ever! You've read the book. Does it say there's any getting out?" Karl Albrecht dragged on his cigarette.

"I'll get in the same way she did. The same hand that killed you will kill me. As for getting her out, well, all things are possible to them…" Joe's eyes sparkled as his voice trailed off. "Why don't you tell me where she is, and when I come for her you can come back too. How about that? We could make a deal," Joe offered.

"A deal? There's no deal. You're an idiot. I'd like to see you kill yourself though; do it right now. That'd make coming to see you worth all the risk," Karl said, a giddy excitement growing in his voice.

"I'll do it when I have everything ready. You wait and see. I'll be coming to hell soon. I promised her and I won't let her down again."

"Stop talking like this. What's done is done. You're an old fool!" The Nazi said loudly. He looked sharply out the window as if he'd heard something.

"When was the last time you saw your fiancé?" Joe asked.

The Nazi mumbled to himself, "She was lovely. They're coming. I can hear them. I must go, or they won't let me out again for a long time. They can't know that we've talked. This was a warning, you won't get another one." He stood and turned his back to Joe.

"Karl!" Joe called out. He stopped at the sound of his name, and looked over his shoulder.

"Karl, if I see you on the other side, think about my offer. Tell me where she is."

"You won't see me or her. You don't understand the darkness. She is utterly lost." Karl Albrecht dissipated and was gone.

Suddenly, a loud ringing tore through the silence. The noise was so loud it startled Joe. The power to the lamp returned and the door of the wood stove was closed and latched. Normal light streamed through the windows illuminating the empty chair in the corner. The phone rang again, loudly.

It was a dream, I guess. It's getting hard to tell.

Joe picked up the phone, "Hello."

"Hello," a perky, female voice said. "This is Mary, from Mr. Heaton's office. You've an appointment today at one. Mr. Heaton just wanted me to remind you."

"Yes, I know; I set it up, didn't I? I'll be there." Joe hung up the phone without waiting for her to respond. He glanced at his watch, 11:45.

"That was a different one, they haven't tried that before," Joe grumbled as he thought of Karl Albrecht. He could barely remember the events of when he'd killed that Nazi; it was so long past, so many killings ago.

He hobbled over to where Karl had sat, and stepped firmly on the worn carpet. A dark stain bubbled up from the nylon. Joe smiled and shook his head.

He was real. I knew it.

Joe rubbed his face and tried to remember what he could. Slowly the memory of that day returned to him. He'd cut his way out of his chute and started forward to the rendezvous point. He came to a country homestead, and as he rounded the corner of an old stone barn, he came face-to-face with a Nazi. It was the first one he'd ever seen and he looked like he was just a kid, barely eighteen. The young Nazi had his hands up to his face, lighting a cigarette. His rifle hung on his shoulder in a sling. In that split second, Joe raised his rifle and fired one round right through the young man's chest. The bullet found its mark and took the third button down with it as it tore through flesh and backbone. The Nazi dropped like a rock. Joe dragged the body into the barn, covered it with straw, and went on with the mission.

He often wondered why that Nazi, this Karl Albrecht, was all alone like that. Now he'd missed his opportunity to ask him.

Joe fixed himself a meal of peanut butter toast and went out front to eat his little lunch. The day was warming up nicely, and the sun made sitting outside quite comfortable.

The stillness of the mountains was marred only by the sound of traffic from Highway 50. The high desert-sage country was beautiful and rugged, but this place was filling up. More people than there used to be. The sound of a semi-truck laying on its *'Jake Brake'* made an awful sound, *rat, tat, tat, tat, tat.*

"I'll get her out," Joe whispered out loud. "I don't care what that dead Nazi says!"

He checked his watch and found it was time for him to head into town to the meeting. Joe frowned as he slipped on his jacket; his body ached all over. He couldn't help but smile as he settled in behind the wheel of his old truck. The old truck was a white, '88 F-150 with a full size box and a regular cab. When it was new, it'd been the nicest truck Joe had ever owned. It still looked new in Joe's mind. In reality, it showed about as much age as Joe; a combination of faded white paint, rust, dents, and scratches. The bumper had been bent up pretty good and the tailgate was entirely gone, but when Joe turned the key, the engine fired right up and then purred loudly with sweet rhythm.

Joe put the truck in drive and gunned it out onto the highway. He followed curves and canyons on a slow descent east, making his way right through Salida toward Canon City. He didn't realize or care that he barely kept the truck between the lines, and the speed limit didn't matter much, as he was a solid ten miles-per-hour under it. A line of cars backed up behind him, but he was oblivious to the honking. Joe's eyes focused on the road, but his mind raced ahead.

The man directly behind Joe had plenty of time to read the bumper stickers. One was for the Buffalos, and the other said, *Keep honking! I'm reloading!* Most people thought the Jesus fish was some kind of joke, but it wasn't to Joe.

The road was winding and traffic remained steady, yet Joe pulled into the parking lot right on time. He slowly made his way up the sidewalk and pulled hard on the heavy glass door lettered in gold.

Heaton and Yankovich, Attorneys at Law. Canon City, Colorado.

A young woman in her early thirties greeted Joe immediately, "Hello, Mr. Rellik." She had blonde hair pulled back for business.

"Come on in, Mr. Rellik," she said to Joe. "We're expecting you." She took his arm to help him, but he abruptly jerked it away.

"I'm not dead yet. I can walk down a hallway without an escort."

"Yes sir, Mr. Rellik, I'm sorry, I'm sure that you can. I didn't mean to offend," Mary said with a slight roll of her eyes.

"On second thought," Joe stuck out his arm. "I don't get too many offers from beautiful, young women."

She smiled at the compliment and helped Joe into the office. "May I get you anything; soda, coffee, water?"

"No, thank you," Joe said.

"Well then, Marty will be right in," Mary said as she left the little office.

Joe scanned about the room while he waited. The name plaque on the desk said, *Marty Heaton*. The wooden desk held the usual; a computer, pictures of Marty with his wife, his kids, and a black Labrador retriever complete with a red-bandana around its neck. Scraps of paper notes were strewn about and thick law books were stacked high along the walls.

Joe waited for only a couple minutes and then Marty entered the office. His worn leather chair creaked under his weight.

"Darn, Joe!" he said. "I haven't seen you in a couple weeks. You look like hell. You feel alright?"

"Only if you're dyin'," Joe teased.

Marty, a jovial man of about fifty, had a short, stocky build and was a little soft from both his age and lack of activity. He'd absolutely no hair left on top of his head, but he kept the sides nicely groomed. Today he wore his usual western business attire – dress jeans, a starched snap-button shirt, and black cowboy boots.

"Well if that's true, we better get this finalized, huh?" Marty joked.

"I've got all the social security numbers and addresses you wanted," Joe said as he slid a sheet of paper across the desk.

Marty skimmed over it quickly. "This looks good. I can fill these people in just like we talked about earlier, and it should all be in order."

"Marty, let me ask you a question."

"Sure, go ahead."

Joe glanced out the open office door and leaned in so only Marty could hear. "What happens to this deal if I don't die of… say…natural causes?"

"What do you mean, Joe? I don't think it matters. There aren't any provisions as to how you die. Rocky Mountain Real Estate Investors Group has agreed to pay you and your heirs no matter how you die, I guess. Do you mean, like say, you get hit by lightning or something?"

"No, I meant more like, uh," Joe paused for a moment, "what

if I killed myself? Any clauses against that?"

"Joe, are you kidding me?" Marty's face went white. "You aren't going to do that, are you?"

"Marty, you're my lawyer. I need to know all my legal truths here," he said with a straight face.

"No, you're fine," Marty said. "They'll pay, even if you die that way, but Joe…don't think like that."

"I didn't say I was doing it. I was just asking," Joe argued.

"No one asks a question like that without thinking about it," Marty said, staring him in the eyes.

The two men sat silently looking at each other for a moment.

"Joe," Marty finally said. "You know I don't normally mix business and religion, but I feel I must. I know you. I know you're a 'saved' man. I know you accepted Jesus many years ago. We've talked about it. As a Christian man myself, I feel that is paramount to anyone's life. You've been forgiven for all you did in your younger days. You'll be with the Lord in Heaven. With that said, if you kill yourself, you'll be sending yourself to hell and eternal separation from the Lord - forever. Why on earth would you do that? Are you depressed or in some pain?"

"Marty, some might debate you on that one point, but I know my Bible, believe me," Joe said.

"Please don't do it, Joe. Whether this money gets properly transacted will be the least of your concerns. I don't mean this badly, but just wait it out. You're near the end, man. Finish the race. Please, Joe?" Marty pleaded.

Joe stood up and stretched his hand over the desk for Marty to shake.

"Thanks for everything. You're a good lawyer and a good man. Anything I need to sign before I go just in case I don't see you again?"

Marty looked around his desk and slid a couple of documents over to Joe. "Just a minute," Marty said. "I want my partner to witness the signing." He yelled out the open door to the office down the hall. "Jim! Can you come in here?"

Joe could hear the heavy steps of a big man coming down

the hallway.

Jim Yankovich filled the doorway when he came through it. He was about the same age as Marty and had a big head on a big body. He wasn't really fat, just big. His face was oval and he had a brown and gray mustache that wrapped his mouth all the way down to his jaw. His back was slightly hunched forward, courtesy of an angry bull back in Jim's rodeo days. His face was plain and honest.

"Here I am, wha'd'ya need?" he asked in a slow Colorado way.

"Just your eyes," Marty told him. "Watch old Joe Rellik here, sign on the dotted-line and make the last deal of his life."

Joe looked at Jim and then at Marty. He took the pen off the desk and signed the documents in all the appropriate places. "Well, that's it then?" Joe said.

"That's it," Marty said quietly. "Think about what I said, Joe, please."

"I will Marty, thanks again," Joe said as he shook both men's hands. "I gotta be getting back, you know, I get tired easy."

Joe ambled out of the office. He wasn't really tired; he just wanted to get on his way. He still had another appointment in Canon City, and it wasn't the Royal Gorge or Buckskin Joe's.

Heaving himself into the old truck, he grunted, and his face strained with some pain as he slid behind the wheel. Driving past the old prison and through town, he could hear the Arkansas River flowing steady not far off. He turned the Ford down a familiar street, his left arm resting on the open window as he drove. The tops of headstones came into view. He pulled in and parked in the same spot he always did, right next to a couple of big junipers. Joe climbed out of the truck. He closed his eyes and inhaled deeply of the pines. How he loved that smell.

Slowly, he made his way through the stone-garden; ordered rows of finely crafted granite. The sound of the river babbled over smooth rocks and a soft breeze blew through the pines.

Joe didn't waver as he walked slowly, but with purpose. He knew exactly where he was going, and could probably navigate the cemetery in the dark. He stopped his march and looked down. He'd read the simple words a hundred times, maybe a thousand times. This would be the last time he'd come to read it. The gray-and-black-speckled granite headstone read:

Joseph David Rellik
July 17, 1924 - _____
Veteran

"To April 6, 2011," he said out loud. "Tomorrow." Joe took two steps to the left.

This stone marked the real reason he'd come back to this place. The marker was almost white with subtle veining like Roman marble; the craftsmanship displayed someone who cared. Joe stared at the words he'd read so many times before.

Kelly Marie Rellik
January 3, 1952 - July 17, 1968
In Our Hearts Forever

Joe dabbed his eyes with a white hankie.

"Kelly, oh my little Kelly," he sobbed. "It's Daddy. I've told you before, but I'll tell you again. I'm sorry I wasn't there... so stupid...I'm...forgive me, please...it wasn't your fault...all my fault...if I had..." Joe stammered as he wiped his eyes with the back of his hand. His lower lip quivered, making his words almost unintelligible. It didn't matter. No one was there to listen as he talked to the lifeless stone, and to the earth that contained the body of his beloved daughter.

"It's almost time, sweetie. I've a plan. Just a little longer and I'll be coming for you, just like I promised. I'm coming, it's almost time. I love you. I'll see you soon."

Joe slowly regained control of his emotions and suddenly felt his age. He shook his head, set his jaw, and turned back toward the truck. The air felt heavy, he had to get home and get everything ready. He didn't want to sleep anymore; no more bad dreams, no more visitors.

Nothing can stop me now. It's time to get on with it. Everything is in order.

Was he stalling? Was he afraid? The thoughts meandered through his brain like water over stones.

Hell & Back

He closed the door to the truck and said goodbye to Canon City on his way home. Joe rounded a familiar corner in the road, and he could see his place up ahead. No need for a blinker, it broke years ago anyway. Much to the relief of the line of cars behind Joe's truck, he slowed down to turn into the driveway.

The aging sign could still be read easily, even though most of the paint had faded. The olive-green color was flaking off of the plywood cutout of a soldier standing at attention, and the red, white, and blue lettering wasn't so bright anymore, but the sign could still be read.

G.I. Joe's Campground. In smaller lettering underneath, it said, *Open April to September*, but a red line had been drawn across that and in newer red letters it said, *Closed.*

No one needed the sign. Just a look and anyone could see it was not a going concern. Brush had grown up in what resembled campsites. Rocks that had ringed fire pits were carelessly strewn about. The door on the small barn hung open, and the corral had more poles down than up. Despite the lack of care, the picturesque site held its natural beauty. Juniper trees, with their pungent-smelling berries, fought with Pinon Pines and their cones for space on the steep hillside that sandwiched the property between Highway 50.

Joe smiled at the memories of a time when the place had been a nice business. He could almost picture the young families camping on the hillside and happy people talking and laughing around a fire. Now the only signs of life that remained were the large stack of firewood and the slight tendril of smoke gently filtering from the chimney.

Just as Joe turned off the highway onto his gravel driveway, the man in the car behind him honked, accelerating past him at breakneck speed.

What's his problem? Jerk!

He left the keys in the ignition and slammed the truck door as hard as he could muster. Joe filled his arms with wood for the fire. He hoped he wouldn't have to do it again in the night.

After depositing the wood into the firebox beside the stove, Joe fixed himself a bowl of Cheerios and sat at the small, metal-edged kitchen table and ate in his usual, comfortable silence. The wood in the burner crackled. Joe decided to have a second bowl. When he finished eating, he went to the sink, washed the bowl and spoon, and set them out to dry. Joe picked up a threaded jar, *"Ball"* embossed into the glass. He dropped in a couple pieces of ice and then filled it half full with Gin. He tightened the lid on the bottle and slid it across the counter. Darkness grew outside the little kitchen window. He put the glass to his lips and took a solid drink, exhaling after he swallowed. "Ah."

Pain racked his body and he nearly dropped the glass. "Dang, that!" He rubbed his left arm, against the tingling prickles that were becoming more common.

Joe went to the bedroom closet and uncovered a shoebox tucked in the corner. He returned to the kitchen and placed it on the table. He cast aside the lid; ribbons and sparkling brass appeared as he carefully arranged the old medals in two neat rows.

"There it is," he said. "All I have to show for my life." He shook his head, so many. Service awards, merit awards, bravery awards, purple hearts, a medal of honor, and virtually any award given to a man who'd spent his life in harm's way.

"Hello, there you are," he said as he withdrew a 40 caliber, semi-automatic handgun. It weighed heavy in his old hands, but even so, it still felt good. He popped out the magazine, fully loaded. He gently eased the action open, and noted a round in the chamber. *Good. It's still there.*

After laying the matte black pistol next to the medals, Joe took his drink with him as he went back to the closet and fingered through the hanging clothes. "I know it's in here somewhere."

Joe slid the hangers containing his one black suit, for weddings and funerals, and two white dress shirts. He paused over several different full dress uniforms, from different decades, and each for different occasions. The uniforms all held their dignity, even as they hung in the closet. None of them felt right. Joe reached up on the shelf and grabbed hold of a set of basic army fatigues. He carried them to the kitchen and placed them on the table, next to the medals and the gun. His fingers flattened out the clothing, while he admired the faded, olive-green cloth and read his name above the left chest pocket.

"Rellik," he read out loud. "Perfect. I wore this most of my life and it'll do well to go out in them. Enough of my friends have." Memories of all the men gone brought tears to his eyes. His body ached and his shoulder hurt a little. Joe knew he didn't have much time.

He sat by the stove and thumbed his old Bible. The worn black leather felt good in his hand, like an old friend. He opened to the second page. The scripted, black letters on the thin white paper said, *Holy Bible. King James Version.*

Joe's icy blue eyes followed the handwritten note scrawled on the page. He couldn't help but smile at the fine penmanship, a delicate cursive. The words were meticulously a woman's writing, both crisp and flowing. She'd used a ballpoint with blue ink. The note began in the top left corner, written in neat, horizontal rows which carefully wrapped around the printed letters as to not touch any of them with the blue ink.

Daddy,
Please forgive me for doing this on your birthday. I'm in a living hell. I can't take it anymore. It has to end and there is no other way. You are gone from me. Mom doesn't care or believe me. With you gone, her men have been scum. I'm scum and I'm ruined. No one loves me. No one will ever love me. I am nothing. God has forgotten me. I remember being happy when I was little and you were around. Why did you leave me? Why didn't you love me? Everything is darkness. I can't go on like this anymore. I'm sorry I was born. I wish I could have seen you one more time, but you will never come for me, as I have so long dreamed that you might. That only happens in fairy tales and there are no happy endings. There will always be another war for you to fight, and I am nothing to you or anyone. I'm sorry about your birthday. Goodbye.
Kelly

Joe closed the book and left it in his lap. He reached for the jar and took another drink. The cold, bitter liquid worked its way down into his joints, but did nothing for his heart. In his mind, he imagined his daughter writing those letters; so precise, so sad. Joe didn't want to sleep, but he closed his eyes and leaned back.

"Only one war left to fight. I'm coming for you, my girl. From the four corners of the four winds, I'm coming."

His body ached all over and the warmth from the fire and the Gin did its work well. Joe quietly dozed off against his own will.

Joe awoke to the sound of rain falling on Detroit tin. He sat behind the wheel of his truck. Looking out the window, he could see the familiar headstones. *What am I doing back here?*

He opened the door and found his feet, his clothes were instantly soaked through from the downpour. Streetlights forced some light through the blackness, while peculiar shadows moved about. He smelled the junipers on his way into the cemetery.

As he reached the familiar stones he cried out, "No!"

Kelly's grave lay open. "Why?" Joe stepped over a fresh pile of dirt with a shovel sticking in it. He looked in the hole and saw the top of the coffin. Without thinking he slid down the steep walls into the grave. Joe grabbed the edge of the coffin and held his breath against what he might see next. He pulled hard expecting resistance, but the lid flew open with ease. Joe fell back, his arm over his face. Slowly, he lowered it, and with a slant eye he peered in. His heart leapt into his throat at the sight before him; absolutely nothing. The beautiful, fine satin cloth was getting wet with rain and mud, but nothing else. No decaying body to be found nothing, but a deep emptiness.

"No!" Joe yelled as he stood up.

He slammed the coffin lid shut and painfully climbed out of the hole. Staggering back toward his truck, a man stepped out from behind one of the large pine trees directly in Joe's path. Instinctively, he swung the shovel that he still held in his hands. The shovel rose high and Joe slipped in the mud. He fell flat on his back, knocking the wind out of him as if he'd been punched. He coughed for air and the man hovering over him came into focus. He recognized the face immediately and suddenly felt like he was eight years old.

"Dad? Is that you?" he asked, his voice unsteady.

"Get up," his father commanded in a familiar, demanding voice Joe hadn't heard in decades. It had the same effect; Joe obeyed.

"Yes, sir," Joe said as he struggled back to his feet. "Dad, where is she? Someone took her."

"You failed her. You fail everyone. I've known it since you were a little boy," his father said, an evil sneer twisted his face. "You were always a cry-baby, afraid of everything. I knew you were weak. I knew you'd fail everyone you loved."

The words cut deep, and a sharp ache enveloped Joe's heart. "But, I became a soldier; I'm tough, I'm afraid of nothing. Isn't that what you wanted?"

"You became a coward. You're a killer maybe, but nothing more," his father jeered.

"I became strong, Dad. Where is she?" Joe pleaded, realizing his voice begged for his father's approval.

"You've failed. You failed her. You failed her mother. You failed your son, and you're nothing - weak. If I were you, I'd kill myself!" The image of his father taunted him.

"Wait a minute," Joe said. Realization brought a smile to his face. "You're not my father! My father wouldn't say that! This is another bad dream. You're some demon from hell!" Joe laughed out loud.

"You won't ever see her again! She's ours!" The face of his father darkened, and the voice was no longer familiar. It sounded low and growling - full of evil. A sound so awful it made Joe shudder.

Wolves snarled from the darkness all around, and he felt a sinking feeling in his stomach. He knew he was in trouble. He was too old and weak to fight, so he turned and started to run as best he could. He could hear the wolves closing in behind him. The truck was still sitting in the light of the parking lot. He knew he had to get there to safety, but something was wrong. With each step it appeared to move further away.

Joe's arms flailed in the air as the searing pain of teeth sinking to the bone caused him to stumble. He fell forward, falling endlessly into a blackness that had no bottom. He just kept descending into the deep darkness until nothingness devoured his scream.

III
Unexpected Visitor

Joe jumped awake with a gasp, spilling the Bible and his drink onto the floor. His breath came in fast gulps as he looked around the room and regained his bearings.

"Damn dreams, can't give me a moments peace." The pain in his shoulder had worsened.

Just then he heard a knock on the door and realized that's what had awoken him. Most of the time he noticed every car drive up to the place, but the intensity of the dream had kept him from hearing anything. He struggled to his feet and shuffled to the door, cracking it just a bit.

"Who's there?" he demanded with a gruff, old growl.

"It's Blake - Matt's boy, your grandson."

He swung the door wide. Before him stood a young man with a precise military haircut that looked sharp, and his eyes were a familiar shade of blue. The quiet strength of this youth was not lost on Joe. The young man stood patiently, allowing his grandfather to size him up.

A thin smile formed on Joe's lips and he nodded. "Your face looks like your dad, but you ain't much like him - that I'll bet. Come on in."

Joe turned his back leaving the door open. He picked up the Bible and the glass jar off the floor. "I fell asleep and you startled me. I wasn't expecting you. Don't get a lot of visitors anymore." Joe set the Bible on the kitchen table with the medals and discreetly pulled the fatigues over the pistol to conceal it from the boy's view. Joe turned to look at him. The boy stood in the open door watching him.

"Shut the door, you're lettin' the cold in, and have a seat if you like. You want a drink?" Joe asked, as he got another jar down and put ice in both of them without waiting for his grandson to answer. He filled them half-full, walked over to where Blake stood, and handed one to the boy.

"Sit down, boy, you're makin' me nervous." Joe flopped into his old recliner near the wood stove and Blake finally took a seat on the couch.

"What's on your mind, son?" Joe asked, watching the boy with an intensity he didn't know he still had. "Your momma didn't mention that you'd be visitin'."

"I'm sorry to have disturbed you, if you were sleeping, sir," Blake stammered. Joe smiled and they sat in silence for a moment.

"I should thank you, for wakin' me up," Joe snorted. "Sleep is no bargain for me anymore. They come after me as soon as the lids touch, almost too dangerous to sleep." Joe took a sip of his drink.

"My mother doesn't know I'm here. I told her I was at a friend's house studying."

Joe leaned forward and didn't say a word for a moment. "Not a complete lie," he said in a slow, deliberate voice. "You could say we're friends. But, from what I know of mothers, which I don't claim as much, you may want to pick up that phone. Let her know where you are, and that you're fine and all that. Tell her you'll start home tomorrow. She'll sleep better with the truth. We all do, no matter how ugly it is."

"Yes, sir." Blake obeyed, and picked up the receiver to the phone.

Surprise grew across his face as he looked at the phone attached to a cord. His fingers tentatively dialed the numbers. Blake laughed out loud as he watched the dial return after every number.

"Where did you find a phone like this?" he asked. "It's cool!"

"I don't know, Sears, I think, had it for years."

Just then Joan answered the call. She spoke loud enough;

Joe could hear her from where he sat across the room. Blake told her the truth, and Joe felt a certain pride in his grandson, something he hadn't felt in a long time. He could tell from Joan's voice that she was upset at first, but then calmed herself down, and told her son to be careful and to call in the morning before he left.

"Goodbye, Mom," Blake said.

"I love you," Joan answered.

Blake's eyes glanced at Joe. "I'll see you tomorrow night, I'll call you when I leave," Blake said and then returned the phone to its cradle.

"You shoulda told her you loved her. She said it to you, I heard her clear over here, and I don't hear that good anymore," Joe said. "I got a few regrets, and that's one of 'em. Tellin' people things like that, before it's too late. You think about it, I ain't your boss. You can make your own mistakes. I made mine already."

"I'm sorry, sir, I just," Blake said.

"You just didn't want me to hear, I get it. I'm just saying it don't hurt to say it, not too many people deserve it and who the hell cares if I laughed at you? Who am I? She's your mom," Joe said with a chuckle. He focused on Blake's features. It was like looking into the past and future all at once, contained in young Blake's blue eyes. He began to wonder if he was still dreaming.

"You look a fair amount like I did at your age, that's amazing," Joe said. "What brings you here, son? What was so pressing that you set out like this, risking the wrath of your mother?"

"Well sir, Mom told me this morning you were very sick and might not have long." The young man looked down at his cap, fingering the visor. "Something inside of me just had to see you. She said she told you I want to go to the Point. My dad and my brother are nothing like me, and I thought you might, might, understand me, if you got to know me. I was afraid I might lose out on the chance to talk to you," Blake spoke in a clear, respectful tone, maintaining very appropriate eye contact and showing a confidence that was in no way mustered.

"Well let me tell this, that feeling is called many things: a gut feeling, the Holy Spirit, conscience, maybe. Call it whatever you like, but you keep following it your whole life, as you have here, because had you waited, even one day, you may never have spoken with me at all, at least not in this life," Joe said in all seriousness.

"Yes sir, I'll try to follow my gut or the spirit, sir," Blake stuttered.

"Thank you for all the sirs. They're very respectful and I admire it, but you can drop it, right there," Joe waved his hand slightly as he spoke. "For all my medals and honors, in a few hours I'll be Private Rellik once again. You're the one who's gonna be an officer soon. I should address you as, 'sir'."

"No sir, don't do that, sir," Blake said. "I'm sorry sir, no more sirs, sir?"

"I can't say that I'm not thankful for the company tonight. I've had my fill of sleep; these damn dreams are killin' me. If you're willing, I'll talk with you awhile, man to man, as soldiers."

"I'd love to speak with you, as, uh, soldiers," Blake said with a smile.

"You don't know it yet, but I do. I look at you and you're already a man. No one's told you yet, have they?" Joe asked and took another sip of his drink.

"No, no one has ever told me that. My dad never--"

"Your dad doesn't know the first thing about being a man," Joe interrupted. "He isn't even one himself, hardly. How'd he know if you're one?"

Blake just stared and shrugged his shoulders.

"I'm not saying that it's not all my own darn fault, but your dad, is as useless as tits on a bull," Joe chuckled. "I wasn't there when he needed me, and his mother, your grandmother, well, she's as crazy as a loon, and did her own share of B.S. All that affected him. It's too late now - short of a miracle from above to change him. If you want to be a man, he certainly won't show you how."

"What happened to Grandma?" Blake asked. "Nobody ever speaks of her." Blake eyed his drink, raising it to his nose for a smell.

"She's down in the Springs in a home, lost her mind to Alzheimer's. It's been ten years ago already. She doesn't know who she is or nothin', very sad." Joe raised an eyebrow.

"I'm sorry. I never knew her," Blake said, compassion on his face.

"Don't be too sorry. She also forgot how much she hated me," Joe said, laughing at his own wry humor. "We grew apart and weren't close, to say the least. Something wrong with your drink?" he asked. Blake hadn't tried it.

"No, nothing." Blake lifted the glass jar to take a sip. He paused just before the ice cold liquid hit his lips. He swallowed and puckered his face as it went down.

Joe laughed at that. "Never had Juniper Juice before, huh?"

"No sir." Blake coughed a little. "Thank you, sir, it's very good."

"Yeah, it looks like you liked it," Joe chuckled. "It's an acquired taste, I guess. You'll do fine, if you don't acquire it. Too late for me though, it reminds me of the high, wild, desert. I love it and it settles my stomach." The old man tipped up the jar and swallowed a hearty swig. Joe stood and put another log in the wood burner. After returning to his chair, he asked, "So why do you want to be a soldier so bad?"

Blake's eyes lit up at the question. "It is all I've ever thought about. I don't know why. I want to serve my country, I guess."

"Don't give me that crap, I ain't a politician. When you think of a battle, what do you *feel* like?" Joe asked in a casual, relaxed manner. He watched out of the corners of his eyes to see the boys face, and to read his body language. That usually meant more than the words.

"When I think of a battle, my blood boils." Young Blake couldn't hide his honesty from Joe. His excitement poured out as his voice quickened and his eyes sparkled with enthusiasm. "I want to be in it, with my gun, firing and fighting. Doing great things and risking it all."

Joe gazed at the fire through the open door on the wood burner. "That's a real fine answer. It's exactly how I've felt all my life. I never outgrew it and I feel it right now. I want to get into the battle too." He looked up at his grandson, whose eyes glistened with hope and promise. "You've the heart of a warrior, and believe me, I know it when I see it. I've seen hundreds of boys like you through the years, and I got so I could pick the good ones out right away. You'll do, boy, you'll do. It may be a curse, but I know exactly how you feel."

Blake leaned forward. "I can't wait to get out of California and go to West Point; it's all I think about."

"It'll be here and gone before you know it. It seems like yesterday I was thinking I was going to puke in a plane over France, and now, here I am, an old man. All the battles behind me -- except one," Joe said sadly, longing for his years to return to him so he could right all wrongs, yet aching for the battle that still lay ahead of him.

"Tell me about your battles, sir. Please," Blake pleaded.

Joe thought back over the long years and all the battles, and he felt tired. He didn't want to go to sleep, though, so he began talking. Time ticked away as he talked for a couple hours or more, telling story after story.

"It all started for me on June 6, 1944. I was twenty-years-old and I jumped the first night with the Parachute Assault Section of the 82nd Airborne. We had the 'Jumping General' with us, James Gavin. Man, he was really something. We'd have followed him into hell, some of us thought we did. We miscalculated and a lot of men died that night from landing in water, drowned. I made it through and some of us ended up taking the town of Sainte-Mere Eglise. I cut my spurs in France, and got it so bad into my blood that I never got it out my whole lifetime."

"The thing you should know about battle; it's sheer random. We all jumped that night, and plenty of the boys who drowned, were just as gung ho as me or you. No way to know whether some stray bullet will clip you in the forehead, and you never saw it coming, sheer randomness. All your training at West Point, and you could die in the first two minutes of your first battle -- or you could live to be eighty. No way to know."

"Anyway, after I got back to the States, I had some normal life between wars and started a family after WW II. I met your grandma and we got married. It was pretty good, but nothing like being in a firefight. We had your dad in 1950."

"Korea was heating up, and I couldn't resist going, so I got myself assigned and away I went. I was in Korea in '52 when your aunt Kelly was born. I got a telegram that said I had a daughter. I was out in the field and didn't find out till a few days after the fact. Her mother never really forgave me for not being there for that."

"I was stateside again when Korea ended, and we opened this place. We'd a house in Canon City, and by '62 I had my twenty years in, and your grandma convinced me to get out of the military and just be a family man. Those were some good years when the kids were little and your grandma and me; we were getting along pretty good."

"Then Vietnam took off and my old blood began to boil again. Without settling it with your grandma, I got back in and got myself assigned to a good unit. In '67 I was 43 years old, but I was as hard and strong as when I was twenty-three, and my heart beat with such a fire. I couldn't wait to get to Vietnam and get into it."

"Your grandma, she'd had it with me, and divorced me as soon as I left the country. She was tired of the military and tired of me. I didn't care. I was tired of her, too. All I could think of was the battle. Once I got to 'Nam they thought I was too old to be on the ground and too valuable, with all my battlefield knowledge, so they promoted me off the battlefield. Does that make any sense to you? I hated it. No matter what I'd seen or done, nothing prepared me for what happened in July of '68."

Joe stopped talking and stood up. He handed the worn Bible to Blake. "Read the note on page two, the title page." He turned his back to Blake and walked into the kitchen. After refilling his glass, he returned to his seat. He sat the bottle on the coffee table between them. The old man watched as his grandson read the sad words of his aunt. When Blake finished, he had a hollow look in his eyes, like he didn't know what to say.

"On your birthday? She. . .?" Blake managed to say in a quiet voice.

"Yep," Joe said without looking up. "On my 44th birthday my little girl wrote that note to me in the Bible that my mother had given her, and then climbed up on a chair and hanged herself." He paused a moment to gain his composure. It'd been a long time since he'd told anyone the story of Kelly.

"I got a call from my CO and he told me to go to the shrink for some news from home. I thought it was something about your crazy grandma. I never thought...she was a beautiful girl. Precocious, sweet, like an angel," Joe stopped talking and Blake did not interrupt the silence. Joe's old eyes welled up and his lip quivered a bit, he shook his head to gain his composure before continuing.

He thought, this kid is a man, and he might as well hear it from me instead of hearing some twisted version from family members who don't know anything about what I've gone through.

"After that, I went kinda crazy. I got a chopper-pilot friend of mine to take me as far as he was willing to fly, into enemy territory. He just barely touched down, and I was out and he took off. I went AWOL, but everyone knew where I was, and nobody filed any paperwork on me. They were my buds and they knew what had happened with Kelly. Everyone just figured it was my way to go out. They didn't want to hurt my record or my reputation."

"I became the night. I was the terror in the shadow -- smoke and mist. I would sneak and hit anyone who looked important. I killed so many that I lost count. The more I killed, the emptier I got, and it didn't bring Kelly back. But I didn't know what else to do, so I just kept killin'."

"I lived off the jungle and traveled by night, picking targets and taking them out. I heard later that news of my escapades had escaped out of the jungle, and people began to wonder if I was a ghost, with every tale they heard of the mysterious American. They heard I was in Cambodia, then Laos, and then in the North. I was in many places, but my legend moved faster than I did."

"I was gone from the world -- living in a shadow world. I don't think I was even human. I felt lost; I felt nothing at all. Killing was all I knew."

"Then I found a small village that had a pretty large quantity of weapons. The leader of the village was my target. I planned to kill him and blow the weapons. I set a trap for him. It was easy;

he wasn't really a soldier, and no one suspected an enemy so deep behind the lines. I slit his throat and blew the weapons in one move – the perfect strike."

"I started slinking away as I always did, when I heard a shriek that curdled my blood. Something in the sound sank deep into me. I looked back and saw a young girl straddling the man that I'd just killed. She wailed and cried and hugged his lifeless body. But then she stopped, and she stood up. She looked into the jungle, directly at me, as if she could see me. I knew she couldn't, because I was well hidden. Her face was covered in tears and blood. She looked about sixteen, just like my girl. She stopped crying and stared directly into my eyes, into my soul. As I stared back at her, I realized I'd just killed her father. She changed me. She'd looked into my heart, and it was black and dark."

Joe shuddered and opened the door to the wood burner.

"I made my way out of the jungle, and back to our side of the war. When I returned, I wouldn't have cared if they'd have locked me up for being AWOL or for insubordination. You name it, murder, or Section Eight. I didn't care. Instead, they gave me another medal, an honorable discharge, and a one way ticket home."

Silence filled the little room and the fire cracked.

"I never knew what actually happened to her. Dad won't talk about it," Blake said.

"Well, that's cause he blames himself for it. He was off smoking dope every day and didn't know what was going on at home. It wasn't his fault. It was my fault. I left her behind, uncovered and unprotected. I never suspected the attack would come there. I was very selfish, it's my fault," Joe said with a heavy sigh. "I haven't told that story to anyone, for many years. I tell you now because I'll be gone soon, and I don't know why, but I felt the need to tell you."

"I'm sorry, Grandpa," Blake said. Joe felt the compassion in his eyes.

"Sorry for what? It's not your fault. Just remember this story, and know that there is a heavy price to be paid. Sometimes the casualties of war aren't always on the battlefield. This life you're choosing, it don't come cheap. If you still want it after that story, then tomorrow I'll call my friend at the Point, and get you your foot in the door. After that, you make your own way. It'll be all up to you."

"I still want in Grandpa," Blake said with a determined look on his young face.

"I knew that you would, Blake. I knew that you would." Old Joe smiled at his grandson and nodded. "Do you see those medals over there on the table?"

Blake looked into the kitchen. "Yes."

"They're yours. Take them with you when you go in the morning. They're the only mementos of deeds long past. You can have them, because you're the only one of my line who understands the price paid for them." Joe rubbed his left forearm as he talked. Then he looked his grandson square in the eyes. "If you aren't too tired, I've one more story to tell you. That is, if you've the courage to listen, and hear with your heart."

"What story is it, Grandpa, tell me?"

Joe and Blake both took a sip of their 'juice', and Joe hesitated, doubting his decision to tell the boy the story.

"This is the story of what was, what is, and what is to come."

Blake looked puzzled, but he nodded in agreement for Joe to continue.

"When you look at me now, you see the shell of what I once was. I look at you and see the foundation of what you will be. I have a worn out old body, and I'm about to remove the shell, like a coat, and enter my last battle."

"Last battle?" Blake asked.

"Yes, the battle for all things. I intend to take the fight to my enemy," Joe said.

"Who is your enemy?" Blake asked, his long forgotten drink still resting in his hands.

"He's everyone's enemy. The great dragon, the old serpent, called the devil and satan," Joe said in a whisper.

"What do you mean the devil?" Blake swallowed hard, and Joe thought he saw the boy shiver.

"I mean, that in the last thirty years, since Kelly's death, I've determined that it was a murder, not a suicide." Blake's face went pale. Joe thought the boy wanted to say something, but he didn't.

"I've found my peace with the Lord, for all of the evil that I've committed under the sun, and though many wouldn't believe it, I know I'm forgiven. My name's written in the Lamb's Book of Life. I'll see Heaven," Joe spoke with complete assurance.

"Well, that's good, Grandpa. You'll go to Heaven." Blake smiled innocently.

"No, that's the problem. I want to go to hell," Joe said in all seriousness.

The boy's mouth dropped open. "What do you mean, Grandpa? No one wants to go to hell."

"I do and I will. That's where she is. . . probably. Most people feel suicides are all in hell because they broke the commandment; *thou shalt not kill*, and didn't have the time to ask for forgiveness due to the finality of killing oneself. Also, the most noteworthy suicide in the Bible was Judas, who betrayed the living God; therefore it's thought to be an especially evil alliance one makes with the enemy by joining the likes of Judas. Others have argued to me that suicide is not the unforgivable sin - that blasphemy of the Holy Spirit is - and that each suicide is judged on an individual basis. Believe what you want but I believe she's in hell, because of me."

Joe sipped his 'juice' and pursed his lips. "The truth is I can't be entirely sure where she is, but wherever it is, I'm going there. I've promised her I'd come for her, and by God, I will. I'll enter hell, if that's where she is, and search and destroy until I find her, and then I'll find a way out with her. I'll save her. She was innocent. I was the one full of darkness and death and murder all around me. She paid the price for my selfishness. It will be my last battle; I will not leave her behind and enter Heaven without her. I won't do it," Joe almost shouted the last part.

"Grandpa, I don't really know anything about Heaven or hell, my parents don't really have any faith. I don't think we even have a Bible?" Blake said, staring into the fire.

"I've searched the scriptures over and over these last decades and would say to you, make your own way. Just because your parents have turned from the Lord, doesn't mean you have to. Seek Him and you'll find Him." Joe felt a fire burning in his heart as he talked about all of this with his grandson, whom he'd come to admire in such a short time.

"How can a soldier have faith and kill?" Blake asked deftly.

"What happens to a soldier with no faith, who is killed?" Joe returned question for question.

Blake didn't answer, and shrugged his shoulders.

"I've seen many people die violent deaths. Many died by my own hands, and many of my friends by the hand of an enemy. I've noticed something, and at first I thought it was weakness." Joe leaned forward and pointed his finger at Blake in order to drive home his point. "The boys with faith in Christ who were dying, and waiting on death for the most part, didn't cry out; while many boys with no faith who waited on death, cried out in fear, begging and wailing, cursing the enemy and carrying on." Joe sat back in his chair.

"What do you mean?" Blake asked.

"I'm saying, the boys who were at peace with their hereafter, died with a dignity and serenity that those boys without that knowledge, didn't have," Joe explained while stirring the fire again.

"How do you plan to get to hell if you're going to Heaven?" Blake asked.

"I'll buy myself a one-way ticket in. Getting out will have to be worked out on the ground."

Joe watched Blake's face as the boy thought for a moment about what he'd said. Then, as the realization of what Joe intended to do sunk in, he watched the expression change, from one of confusion to a mixture of astonishment and exasperation.

"No, Grandpa! You wouldn't!"

"I wouldn't? Why not? I'm willing to risk my eternity for her. It's the least that I owe her. I'll enter the battlefield the one way I know. It's the only sure way to know that I will follow her in, and if I fail, I'll be where I belong anyway," Joe spoke of his own death with calmness, maybe even a little excitement.

"What if I said you were crazy?" Blake asked.

Joe smiled. "I've already heard that."

"From who? I thought I was the only person you've told."

"I get visitors sometimes."

"You told a visitor? Who was it?"

"He wasn't a normal house guest," Joe said, keeping Blake guessing.

"What do you mean by, 'he wasn't a normal guest'?"

"He was from the other side. A Nazi I killed some sixty years ago, sitting here as real as you, havin' a chat about my mission," Joe said as if this were the most natural thing to be talking about.

"Grandpa, I don't know about all of this." Blake squirmed in his seat.

"I didn't ask for your approval, young man. I was just telling you some things I thought you should know, because I wanted someone to know what I was up to. You knocked on my door, didn't you?" Joe asked with a serious edge growing in his voice. "Have I misjudged you? Is this too much for you to handle?"

"No sir, I can handle it." Blake straightened his back a little.

"I knew you could," Joe agreed, nodding his head slightly. "I'm sorry I won't get a chance to serve with you. You're going to make a fine soldier. I'd like to ask you one thing."

Blake waited in silence for Joe to continue. He liked that about the boy – taking his time to think things through before rushing headlong into it like others his age might do.

"If they make you a big shot officer," Joe began. "And by the look of you, they will. Promise me you won't ever get too big to climb down in the mud and blood. Don't forget the guy with his boots on the ground and the gun in his hand. They'll pay the price for your decisions. Don't make them lightly." Joe looked right into Blake's eyes to make sure his point hit home.

"Yes, sir, I won't forget that. I won't ever forget it," Blake spoke with assurance.

Joe labored his way back to his feet. "As much as I'd rather skip it, we better get some shut-eye. You've a long drive home tomorrow, and I've a long trip as well. The couch there is yours. There's a blanket in the hall closet, and you could throw a couple more logs on the fire if you like, wood is outside. It won't be long till morning now anyway."

"Goodnight Grandpa Joe. Thank you."

"Don't thank me," Joe spoke as he waddled toward his little bedroom at the end of the hall. "You're entering a life of hardship and strife. May God give you strength and peace to handle it."

He heard Blake put a couple more logs on the fire before he lay down. Joe sat on his bed and prayed.

"Dear God, bless that boy in his lifetime with strength and peace. Let him feel your presence and guidance all of his days. Lord, please give me a night of peaceful sleep, just a few hours, Lord, with no dreams. I ask for Your protection Lord. Amen." He leaned over and laid his head on his pillow, instantly asleep.

❦

The house remained quiet and dark except for the sounds and smells of the woodstove, which permeated everything. Blake lay awake on the old couch, rethinking every bit of the conversation, every gesture. He wanted to burn it into his memory forever. It would probably be all he'd have to remember Grandpa Joe. These few moments had changed everything. The cool howling of a night wolf pierced the wind and echoed up and down the valley, serving everyone notice of his existence. It was faint at first, but then it grew louder. Blake sat straight up and stared out the window, which overlooked the old campsites and the river flowing by. The full moon illuminated everything in an unnatural, pale blue light. Off to the left he saw a flash of movement. What was it? A wolf?

Blake strained his young eyes, and then caught a glimpse of a couple of wolves darting back into the darkness of the trees. He almost missed them at first because of their blackness, but then he noticed them moving toward the house, very slowly, and deliberately. Blake rubbed his eyes and swallowed the hard pill of fear, doubting his own sight. He looked again; they were still coming. There looked to be several of them, five or six at least, but they were difficult to count.

They appeared to walk upright on two legs like humans.

Their very existence seemed to be made up of blackness. From what he could see of them, they were mostly just dark, black forms, like shadows walking. The edges of their beings were somewhat rough and hazy, making it hard to tell where one creature ended and another began. If the night had been black, there would've been no way to see them at all, but the moonlight provided contrast.

Blake continued to watch in paralyzed fear. As the creatures crept closer, he could see they had orange and red eyes that glowed like fire. Within moments, their numbers grew, and they filled the valley entirely. Blake, frozen, watched in horror as they swarmed around the house.

The only sound was the continued howling of a lone wolf. The demons, or whatever they were, seemed to be unable to enter the house, but only covered the outside. Blake lay back down on the couch, trying to decide if what he saw was real…or if he'd imagined the things…or if he should go get Grandpa Joe. He sat back up and looked out again. Nothing, he saw nothing but old campsites bathed in the moonlight. Sighing in relief, he lay back down, determined he would get some sleep. Had he been imagining things, or was there some explanation for what he thought he saw? No logical answer came, and he finally succumbed to sleep.

Joe's eyes opened, and he found himself sitting in a rocking chair. Everything in the room was in black and white. He could feel the warmth of a little body in his arms. When he looked down, he found himself lost in the eyes of his little girl. It had been a long time, but she looked like his dreams of her, beautiful. She appeared to be about seven-years-old, and her big blue eyes stared up at him in vibrant color. Neither of them said a word. Joe knew he was in a dream, but it was such a sweet dream that he didn't want to do anything to make it end. Little Kelly smiled at him and nestled her head against his chest.

He noticed he wore his fatigues and his black Government Issue boots, which were laced up tight. Joe quickly surveyed the room, recognizing it as Kelly's room from their house in Canon City, before he left for Vietnam. He felt strong and young; his M-16 lay on the floor by his feet.

He looked back down to feast his eyes on the sweet vision of his daughter. She had closed her eyes and slept in his arms. Great flashes of lightning began to burst out the bedroom window, complete with frilly curtains that now bordered violence. The sound accompanying the lightning was wrong, and Joe realized it was not lightning at all.

Mortar fire! The sound of a chopper buzzed overhead. Joe looked back down at his sweet little girl. Just then, an explosion took off the corner of the house. Kelly didn't stir and Joe dared not move. More explosions went off around them, but it felt as if the sound had been turned down on the television, and Joe was only watching it happen. All he heard was the sound of Kelly breathing and a slight humming as he continued to rock his girl. Suddenly the entire room disappeared except for a small patch of floor where he sat in the rocking chair with Kelly. She opened her eyes and climbed down without a word. She looked so lovely. Her heel reached the very edge of the abyss behind her, and Joe implored her to get back up in his arms.

"Sweetie," Joe said softly. "Come back over here with me, please. Don't go any further."

"Daddy, I told them you would come and they laughed at me," Kelly smiled and said in such sweet voice it was like the most melodic sonnet being played on the perfect violin.

"That's right, baby girl," Joe said. "I am coming."

"I hope so, because they're not nice." Kelly's face and her entire countenance darkened. "I have to go now. Goodbye, Daddy." As the last word left her mouth, she turned her back to Joe and stepped off into the darkness and she was gone.

"No!" Joe jumped up out of the chair and reached to grab her, but he grabbed only air. He stood there for a moment and held his head in his hands in sorrow as he sank to his knees.

Joe blinked open his eyes and looked around the bedroom. He realized the dream hadn't awakened him. It had taken place earlier in the night, and he'd remained asleep. This morning he felt more rested than he had in many nights. The thought of his sweet moments with Kelly left a smile on his face.

"Soon, sweetie, soon." He got up and noticed a soft morning light growing out the window. "A new day dawns and my life here sets."

After a painful, bloody trip to the bathroom, Joe walked into the front room and opened the door to the stove. He stirred the coals and added a couple little logs. Blake had refilled the wood-box. They caught immediately and started to crackle.

Blake must've heard the noises, and he sat up immediately, wide awake.

"Good morning, young man," Joe said with a smile. "Want some cereal? It's all I got, so if you say no, there's nothing else."

"Yes, sir, cereal sounds just fine."

They went into the kitchen and Joe fixed two bowls of cereal for them. "So do you have a girlfriend?" Joe asked as they ate.

Blake blushed and smiled. "No, most of them don't understand me. Most of the guys in my school are only interested in getting drunk or sleeping with all the girls they can. They don't know what to think of me, working so hard to be a soldier." Blake took a bite of cereal and chewed a moment before continuing. "Most of them have a lot of money. The girls just want to be fawned over all the time, and they want guys with all the stuff I don't have; a fancy car, a big house, rich parents. Most of them dress like slu… well you know. I just don't fit in there."

"My only female advice is this; if you don't find the right one…the most amazing one…a real partner in life…you're better off without one. Because believe me, the wrong woman, oh my, can make your life a living hell. Let me tell you that from experience."

"I'll keep that in mind," Blake said with a smile.

After they finished their breakfast, Joe walked out to Blake's car with him. An awkward moment passed between them; Joe figured neither of them knew what to say. Just how does one say goodbye, forever?

"I'm real glad you came," Joe said to break the tension. "It was something special to get to talk to you. Blake, you're a fine man. Keep your honor. I'm proud to have a grandson like you. Maybe not everything I did here was for nothing."

Blake stepped closer, leaned in, and gave Joe a shoulder hug. "Grandpa Joe, I'm proud to be your grandson. I'll try to make you proud."

"You already do, boy. You got it where it counts. You don't need an old man like me to tell you that. You know it, don't you?"

"I guess so."

"What do you mean you guess so?" Joe snapped, and Blake stood up straight as if at attention.

"I mean, yes sir, where it counts. Sir."

Old Joe smiled. "And don't you forget it. You're a Rellik, rough and ready."

Blake smiled back at him. Joe could see by his face that the young man tried to hold back his tears. How he wished he could've gotten to know him a little more.

"You better get going. Don't forget to call your mother and let her know you're on your way," Joe said and turned to head back to the house.

"I won't forget. Goodbye, Grandpa Joe."

Joe looked back sort of sideways; he didn't like long goodbyes. "Depending on how it all works out, maybe we can sit by a fire on the other side someday, and you can tell your stories."

"I'll look forward to it," Blake smiled as tears he could no longer hold back slipped down his cheeks. He then climbed into his little car, fired it up, and headed out the driveway and west onto Highway 50.

When his grandson drove out of sight, Joe ambled back into the little house, more determined than ever to complete his mission.

Today's the day.

IV
Knocking Down Death's Door

Joe went straight to the phone. The room was silent other than an occasional crack from the fire and the highway outside. Loneliness had never really affected Joe, but he felt it now, watching that boy drive away. He hadn't expected to feel this way. He leaned forward and coughed violently into his hankie. Once it had passed, he exhaled a deep sigh, wiped his eyes and blew his nose loudly. Joe knew he had it to do. He dialed a number from his little black book.

"West Point Admissions Office. How may I direct your call?" A very professional-sounding woman answered the phone politely.

"I'd like to speak with Tom Walcott, please," Joe said in his most authoritative voice.

"One moment please," the woman said, and with a click was gone.

"Captain Walcott, how may I help you?" the familiar voice said as Joe's old friend came on the phone.

"Are you the oldest captain on the planet?" Joe joked.

"Joe, is that you? Did you ever make captain?" Tom asked.

"I was a captain, twice. Bet you thought I was dead already."

Captain Walcott had been an eighteen-year-old private when Joe Rellik made his amazing reputation in Vietnam. They'd spent some time together and forged a friendship, the kind that lasted through the years. They didn't talk often, but each knew they could count on one another whenever they were needed.

"Well, I'd wondered about it, but who'd take you - Heaven

or hell?" Captain Tom gave it back.

"Wally, you nailed it there, that is the big debate. We'll all know soon enough. I'm not calling just to talk. I've a favor to ask of you, before I die and you retire."

"You name it. What can I do for you?"

"You remember that I had a son, Matt?"

"Yeah, he was some kind of hippie or something, right?"

"Yes, he's still a fruit loop," Joe said with disappointment.

"I'm sorry, Joe," Captain Walcott said.

"That's alright, the truth is the truth, whether we like it or not. Why I'm calling is apparently his boy, got all the backbone that my boy didn't. I got a grandson with his heart set on coming to West Point and becoming a Cadet," Joe said proudly.

"You're kidding me. How old is he?" Tom asked.

"He's a junior in High School this year, so he'll apply next year for admittance the year after that," Joe said.

"How are his grades? What's he like, is he Point material?"

"Straight A's, he's everything you guys want. Plus, I'm asking on his behalf for any help you can give him, because I won't live to see it. I'm real sick you see, and we already talked about his dad, there isn't anybody else," Joe said.

"Joe, I'm sorry to hear that. I'll do everything I can for him. A grandson of yours here at The Point, who would've believed that when you left 'Nam? That's great. I'll keep my eye out for his application. What's his name?"

"His name's Blake Rellik," Joe answered. "Why don't you send him some pamphlets, posters, application, and anything you think he might like. Could you do that for me, Tom?" Joe wanted to do all he could for Blake.

"Anything for you Joe you know it, and I'll look out for him, I promise," Captain Walcott agreed.

"I can't thank you enough for that, Wally, it means a lot to me," Joe said quietly.

"I'll give you back to the secretary. You can give her the address, and I'll take care of it. I've an appointment that's waiting on me; I have to be going, so I'm sorry to cut this short, Joe." Joe knew promptness was paramount in the military.

"No need to apologize, thank you for all your help. I've got an appointment myself. Thanks again. Goodbye, Wally."

"Goodbye Joe. I'll try to give you a call next week so we can really catch up."

"That's just fine," Joe said, knowing that would never happen. Joe was transferred back to the secretary, and he gave her Blake's address.

Joe hung up the phone and went into the kitchen, staring out the window. "Well, that's it then. Good luck, Blake, ol' Wally, he'll look out for you, he's a good man." Joe washed his bowl in the sink and picked up the faded green clothing. The matte black pistol stood in sharp contrast to the white Formica with gold flecks.

"Enough stalling!" He slid his arms in, carefully buttoning all but the top button. Joe's old fingers didn't cooperate and the dressing took some time. He was surprised that it still fit, only now a little loosely. Saggy, wrinkled skin had replaced the muscles that once filled this shirt. Joe picked up the pistol and placed it to his temple.

He hesitated a moment to build up his nerve. His trigger finger twitched slightly, but he didn't pull it.

"Damn!" He had to go the bathroom badly, so he set the pistol down and walked down the hall to the bathroom. As he walked, he mumbled to himself.

"You're stalling. You're all talk, old man. It's time to walk the walk. It ain't gonna hurt; you won't even feel it. You'd better be ready to hit the ground running on the other side."

The pain of urinating was excruciating. After he finished, Joe turned to walk back to the kitchen, resolved to pull the trigger. Sweat beads covered his forehead, so he paused and splashed some water on his face, one last look in the mirror. His eyes settled on the reflection and the Army shirt he wore with his name printed on the tag on his left breast.

"Killer," he whispered as he read his name backwards in the mirror. "Time to pay the price."

Joe reached up to pull the string and turn off the bulb that hung loosely in the center of the tiny bathroom. A sharp pain ripped through his chest like a dagger from an unseen attacker. Joe hung onto the string as he fell forward, snapping it off the chain and turning off the light as he hit the floor with a shoulder. Joe rolled onto his back. The light bulb swung back and forth above him, the pain raging deep within his chest. It felt as if a great weight had pinned him to the floor and was pressing the air out of him.

"Kelly...." The hand that clutched his chest relaxed and fell to his side, and it was over. A few moments, and Joe's heart stopped beating. His eyes glossed over to a matte stare as he slowly exhaled one last breath.

※

Marty Heaton called Joe, but there wasn't any answer. Concerned about Joe's state of mind after their conversation, he allowed the phone to keep on ringing. He finally hung up and decided he'd stop by his old friend's house after lunch.

Marty drove up to the old campground that afternoon. The rusty truck was parked in the driveway. He knocked on the door, but Joe didn't answer. He tried the knob. It wasn't locked and he cautiously entered, "Hello, Joe? Joe, you in here?"

He noticed the pistol on the table and then Joe lying on the floor in the bathroom doorway.

"Oh my, Joe." Marty went to him and could see immediately that he was gone. "Rest in peace, my friend." Marty smiled to himself as he thought of Joe in Heaven.

PART II

THE KINGDOM OF HEAVEN
Repent: for the Kingdom of Heaven is at hand. Matthew 4:17

S.C. Sherman

V
Eyes to See

A great light shone like the sun; more than just bright, it permeated everything. Joe shielded his eyes against it and discovered himself walking up a stone staircase, the source of the white light coming from somewhere ahead. He felt drawn ever upward toward it. Joe climbed higher and higher, realizing it was much farther to the top than he'd originally thought, but he never tired or thought of turning back.

White clothing, smooth as silk and hemmed with gold ornamentation, flowed around him. His legs felt strong and muscular, and his hands were youthful once again with a firm grip and tight skin. All pain within his body was gone and he walked upright with ease. His bare feet gingerly touched the soft marble treads as he continued to ascend. The white marble contained strong, swirling lines that changed color, as if veined with opal. The stones themselves were unusually warm to the touch of his bare feet. Joe couldn't take his eyes from the light streaming past what appeared to be a closed door at the top of the stairway. It invited him to come and enter in.

A familiar ringing sounded from behind him, forcing him to turn his head and look. Joe frowned as he saw an open door at the bottom of the beautiful stairway. Framed in the doorway darkness reigned, but he could see an old man lying on his back dressed in olive green. The obnoxious phone continued as Joe recognized himself as the old man lying dead.

That's peculiar, I'm not dead. Maybe just the old part of me is dead.

    Joe's attention was drawn back to the amazing streams of white light and he continued on. It felt as if his entire body gained rejuvenating strength and warmth with every step he took. He never looked back again.

    He noticed others walking upward with him. He didn't know who they were, but they smiled greatly, as if they were long lost friends. They proceeded up together as the width of the stairway grew to accommodate the growing crowd. Joe continued on realizing the aches and pains were gone from his body. No worries or concerns pressed upon him in any way, he felt complete contentment in his being.

    With no warning the door was suddenly directly in front of them, and just as they reached it, it made a great heaving sound in the process of opening. A sliver of vertical light appeared, and what Joe thought to be one door, was actually two, and they were opening apart from each other. The light grew larger as the two doors swung wide, which now looked more like ancient gates to some kind of a castle. Sweet music and pleasant aromas poured into the stairway from the other side. The people of the stairway stepped up to go through, but as they reached the door, everything narrowed again. The narrowness of the gate forced them to enter one at a time. Joe waited patiently for his turn; he felt like he could wait all day.

    The woman behind him carried two little, fluffy dogs, and they looked as happy as she was; it seemed like the dogs were actually smiling. Joe had never liked dogs, he'd even eaten a few, but he felt a love for these and reached out to pat one of them on its fluffy head. It pushed back against his hand to aid in the patting.

    "Nice little dogs," Joe heard himself speaking, but it sounded muffled and somehow strange.

    The woman smiled and said, "Thank you. I love them. They've been waiting patiently for me in the stairway all these years."

    Suddenly, it was his turn. He faced forward and stepped through the open door without any hesitation. As he crossed the threshold, all light and perception changed. Joe felt his foot land on firm ground, which turned out to be green grass. His eyes went entirely blind at the moment of crossing, then once through the gate, he could see more clearly than ever before.

He could see for miles, so crisp and clear that the detail was almost bewildering. Joe stood in a great forest with lush plants all around. Some looked familiar like oak and pine, while some were like jungle ferns and wide leafed plants. Still much of the foliage was the likes of which he'd never seen before, and definitely not living in the same type of climate. A swift brook babbled over rocks. He tried to scan it all, but it was too much to take in. There were others who looked as bewildered as he felt. Animals meandered through the trees and munched on the grass. They looked like mule deer, but had antlers like elk, and were only roughly the size of a Labrador retriever.

"Amazing," Joe whispered.

Joe eased along an obvious path with the others. A creature that looked like a horse crossed the path in front of Joe. He stretched out his hand to touch the animal; it was the most beautiful horse he'd ever seen, so dazzling, in fact, that he doubted it was a horse at all. The creature's white coat glistened, as if the tips of the hairs had been dipped in silver. Its hooves were coal black and its mane and tail flowed in the light breeze. The animal saw his outstretched hand and bent one of its front legs and knelt with a bowed head. Joe stared in wonder as the horse moved off.

"Wow, that horse bowed," a man said as he passed Joe.

The path wasn't made of marble like the stairway, but rather great chunks of slate laid perfectly one piece next to another. The slate contained magnificent colors that ranged the spectrum. Joe noticed colors that have no name, because no eye on earth has ever seen them.

Joe saw small game - rabbits and squirrels and such - but there were more bizarre creatures too. A leathery looking monster, obviously some type of dinosaur, stood by the stream chewing grass, and many African game animals bounded across the intermittent fields in small herds. There were all types of flying, running, and crawling beasts; some Joe knew, some not. None of them seemed at all interested in eating one another, as if some strange harmony existed between them. They were beautiful in their ferocity and diversity. Several of the animals seemed familiar, yet something was slightly different about them. It felt as if these creatures were real, and the ones Joe had known before had been poor copies.

Joe noticed the others on the path were as young and strong as he felt, as if everyone here were at their peak or in their prime. Each individual retained their earthly differences in appearance, except their garb was identical and perfectly fitted to each being. The proportions of height and weight, strength and weakness, were all uniquely different, yet all looked perfect. For the first time ever, Joe felt no lack within himself, either mental or physical, or the judgment of anyone else's.

Joe and his group crested a little knoll, and what they saw made them all catch their breath. An incredibly larger valley expanded itself below them. Many roads and rivers could be seen winding their way across the wide-open plain, which was a patchwork in varying colors of green.

A myriad of people and creatures trekked toward the center of everything; all roads led to it. It shimmered like a star, and Joe somehow knew it was the White City of God. It stood many miles off, but with Joe's new eyes, he could see every vivid detail of it. In his heart, he suddenly knew that he was within the Kingdom of Heaven, and that the very City of God stood before him. All plans and cares of his old life melted away.

At the sight of the magnificent city, Joe and the others knelt and worshipped the Lord with songs, in many voices and languages, as tears of joy flowed from their eyes.

The Lord be praised! Lord, Almighty be praised!

All the creatures of the land were praising as well, the sound consisted of much more than voices. It contained instruments of unknown and unseen origin, birds singing, and the wind lolling. The sound was the essence of pure joy.

Slowly, one by one, they lifted themselves from their knees, and returned to the path leading them home. Every turn contained some new wonder, some new creature, a new smell, or a new sight, full of colors and textures never seen before.

A cougar crossed directly in front of Joe. He had no fear of the cat, which should have been strange, but it wasn't. Then as the tawny animal passed, it paused and rolled its back to rub against Joe's legs, as if it were a purring housecat in need of affection. Without hesitation Joe ran his fingers along its beautiful back, and then it continued on its way. He looked over at the man next to him who'd been watching the cougar as well, and the man just smiled at Joe. They both shrugged their shoulders in disbelief.

Dazzling birds floated lazily in a sky that sparkled blue. From horizon to horizon it was full of a depth and richness unseen on earth. White, fluffy clouds only added to the beauty of the Kingdom in which they hiked. Off in the distance majestic mountains hid in a haze; their snowy caps ruggedly beautiful, calling out to be explored. Joe longed to go and trek those massive peaks, and seek out their hidden treasures. He sensed secrets awaited there. The mountains would wait, as his first desire was to enter in the shining city ahead.

One moment the White City was far off, like a beckoning star, and then suddenly it stood abruptly before them. Joe looked left and right to discover his little group had been joined by other groups. Now it contained a multitude, a mass of people all staring in awe at the city before them.

Joe looked on in wonder and amazement as he attempted to take it all in. A continuous wall surrounded the giant city that rose to great heights. From his vantage point he could see the city was formed in a twelve-sided shape, upon twelve foundations. The ground level began with shining white marble boulders, and trees separating the various foundations and gates. Even with the natural objects separating the structures, they all appeared as one continuous entity. The architecture was unlike any seen upon the earth. A giant, two-part gate stood upon each of the immense foundations. The gates were hinged on the outer marble walls and swung apart outwardly in the center.

From where Joe approached, he could only see three of the gates clearly, and each was unique. One appeared to be a burgundy color, wine-wood hinged in a metal that sparkled as if it contained tiny stars. Above that gate, the rampart was lined with jewels, not like jewels from a ring or necklace, but rather they were like boulders several feet across and were smoothed, polished, and honed. Above the wine-wood door, the jewels were rectangular and looked like giant, solid boxes of emerald. The brilliant, deep green stone was mesmerizing.

Then in the center, directly above the gate, was what appeared to be a giant pearl. Perfect in both roundness and texture, its creamy surface looked like solid milk, and it had sheen to it that only a perfect pearl could boast.

Also above the gate, etched into a granite slab, and written in a language that was both familiar yet foreign, was a name. The lettering was lined with black jewels sparkling in the light. Joe somehow knew that the name was one of the names of the twelve tribes, but he had not yet the wisdom to know which was which. He found himself being drawn away from the wine-wood gate to the next gate to his right.

He hurried in anticipation of something wonderful, and it couldn't happen soon enough. As he approached the next foundation, he looked back and realized, he'd traveled several miles from the first foundation and gate. The size and breadth of this place began slowly penetrating his thoughts.

Joe looked on the new foundation before him with a feeling of love and kinship. Again, a name was written on the masonry, as well as above the gate. He didn't know why, but somehow he knew this was 'his' gate.

Just then, as if Joe had asked out loud, a man walking by spoke. "The one down there says *Paul*," he said without Joe asking or commenting. This man was dressed in different clothes than all of the rest of the people in Joe's group. He appeared to be the only person who seemed to be going away from the gate. .

"Thank you," Joe's voice sounded more normal. The other man kept on about his business and was gone.

Joe paused, analyzing the foundation for a moment. The majestic gate stood open as if it never had any need to shut, and many people and creatures flowed freely in and out. The gates themselves were of a metallic substance that shone with brightness like polished aluminum, yet had the beauty of antique steel at the same time. The jewels above this gate were a deep, dark-blue, and they sparkled as if they contained water. They were as large as basketballs, and again, in the center was lodged a great and mighty pearl.

    Each gate had its pride and was filled with both strength and beauty. A vast array of tiny stones lined the edges of the base. These crystallite gems were grouted right into the surface of the structure, and each piece fit with the precision of intense craftsmanship. Precious stones filled the mix as gravel in concrete. They were the size of baseballs of jasper, sapphire, chalcedony, emerald, sardonyx, sardius, chrysolite, beryl, topaz, chrysoprasus, jacinth, and amethyst. Each gate boasted its own giant pearl and its own name.

    Joe and everyone else in the white flowing garments stopped before the entrance - not really in fear of going in, but rather out of reverence and a knowing that entering in would change everything, forever.

    Suddenly, from within the center of the crowd there appeared a fierce creature. The main flow of people who were heading into the city, parted around the creature as it marched straight toward the bewildered group. The creature's height elevated it at least a foot or more above the tallest of the humans. It wasn't just the height that impressed Joe; this thing was both ferocious and beautiful at the same time. Its head was round and where a person would have hair, it had a type of feathery hairs. These hair-feathers were a golden, blonde radiance, accenting a face similar to a human face, yet hawkish. The eyes looked like human eyes, but that's where the similarities to a human face ended. The creature had a larger nose that was almost like a beak, which covered a mouth containing teeth like a lion's. The feathery hair flowed behind like a mane concealing any ears.

    The mysterious animal wore tight-fitting clothes - definitely built for battle. The shoulders, chest, and stomach armor appeared to be crafted of a combination of leather and braided steel. He walked upright on two feet like a man, but both the hands and the feet contained retractable claws like a cat, that appeared with each step. The areas that weren't covered with battle armor showed that the creature's entire body was covered with the feather-like hair. His face wore the expression of seriousness. Not really angry, just serious and most certainly marching straight toward them. Joe noticed several nervous glances as the creature approached. No one ran, but it would've been a logical thing to do in a normal situation.

The creature stopped a short distance from the group and looked them over; he cocked his head to the side as a bird does when it looks at something.

"Welcome, to you all," the creature said in a strong, clear voice. "Welcome to the Kingdom of Heaven. You're the redeemed humanity. The Lord be praised and the Blood of the Lamb honored. I'm the keeper of this gate. My name is Barakiel. I am an angel, a war-bird, a gatekeeper, and your humble servant." The angel Barakiel bowed his head and flexed his bicep as he placed his right fist to his chest. He raised his head and continued, "I will show you in. You are expected, and the Lord has prepared a place for you. There are many who await your arrival, but first your questions must be answered. Once inside the gate you will each find another of my class, a guardian who will walk with you and talk with you for an appointed time. Then you'll be ready to enter the Throne Room and see the Almighty God. Follow me."

Barakiel turned abruptly and started back toward the gate. Joe followed without question or hesitation. He knew someone in command when he saw it.

Many talked and laughed while they followed the angel, as if this was the most exciting place to be. Some people held hands, others walked slowly, some marched briskly; all entered in. Joe shuffled on in silent awe of the entire experience.

As he passed through the gate, he looked up and realized it was much higher than he'd first guessed, which also meant the blue stones were even larger than he'd originally calculated. He began to realize that most things here were bigger, deeper, wider, or longer than they initially seemed. Most everything held more dimension than Joe could see with his eyes, and only after some careful observation and pondering could it possibly be comprehended.

After passing through the gate, he found himself in a market. The angel Barakiel disappeared amongst the crowd, and his group mixed into the array of people. The place was alive with sounds and activity, people, creatures, and a plethora of shops and cafes.

Joe sat beside a fantastic little water fountain. He watched the waterfall splash from one stone container into another, finally ending in a large basin. That pool contained fish colored like some salt-water fish, only these were shaped like a trout. One of them swam up to the top and rolled to its side. Joe smiled as he saw the playful fish. He reached out his hand to touch it, and to his surprise the fish softly purred as he rubbed it.

"Hello Joe, I've waited for this moment for quite some time," Joe heard a voice behind him as a wonderful aroma filled the air unlike any he'd ever smelled.

Joe turned to find another creature like Barakiel standing beside him. "You were the old man, Joe Rellik."

Joe wasn't sure whether it was a question or a statement. "Yes, I was," he said.

This creature was virtually identical in shape and size to Barakiel, but there were some differences. His hair-feathers were a silvery-gray, like gun metal. This one wore the same type of battle armor as the gate-keeper, but Joe noticed a deep gouge on the breastplate. He stared at the wounded armor as this was the first thing he'd seen in this place that was in any way marred.

"I'm the angel, Karial, a guardian," the angel continued. Joe could see his razor sharp teeth as he spoke. "I've been your guardian in the unseen realms all these years. Now I'm very pleased to walk with you, and serve you. Shall we continue on?" the angel Karial motioned with his hand and cocked his head.

Joe stood. "Yes, walking here is grand."

"Much smoother walking on redeemed flesh, yes?" Karial said with a smile, that looked like a snarl.

"Yes, I feel as strong as ever, even better than I ever did in my life. How long does this last?"

Karial led them along the cobbled streets, which reminded Joe of some old village in Europe. The cobblestones sparkled like gold, but not like polished gold from a ring or a coin. They were more like chunks of gold that were cast away to be used as street goods and paved together to be trod upon. Joe purposefully scuffed one, and it shined as bright as any pure gold he'd ever seen.

"This body will last for all lifetimes," Karial said. "Lifetimes as you knew them are past. You're in eternity. It'll take a pilgrimage or two to the mountains for you to comprehend that."

"What do you mean?" Joe asked.

"Flesh here is not what flesh was there. It does not die, break down, or deteriorate. No one here cares about his or her flesh. It's always at its peak. Redeemed humans are in the image of the Lord, and that makes them all wonderful, not like before when people would say 'everyone is beautiful' but not mean it. Here everyone is at peace with their appearance, and that of all the others too. There exists no jealousy, envy, or judgment for anything. Those things belong to the World of Flesh. A person's spirit attracts us one to another, not their appearances. When you find another of a like spirit, you're drawn to that person or creature," Karial walked slowly as his voice soothed Joe's unasked questions.

"Do people love and marry and uh. . .?" Joe asked, unsure if he should continue his line of thinking.

Karial looked sideways at Joe, "Things you knew a lot about before?"

"No, not really. I wasn't good at being married, or at loving," Joe said pensively.

"There's deep love here, deep intimacy, and there are some who find their spirit-mate, but families are different here, you will see. We are all a family." Karial looked up and watched several speeding birdlike objects flying in a formation like a squadron.

Joe reached over and touched Karial's arm. The angel stopped walking, and Joe leaned closer to him, "Can I ask you something?"

"Of course, that's what I'm here for," Karial said.

"Do you, or more importantly, does the Lord know what I was planning right before I came here?" Joe whispered.

"Yes, Joe," Karial said as he looked him in the eye and smiled with a nod. "I know because I was assigned to you, and He knows everything. He knows the end and the beginning."

"I'm not sure what to think anymore about anything. So much has changed," Joe said.

"It's good to be patient. The old world is still fresh with you, and you're on the lowest of the levels here. It's most confusing for the new arrivals. In time, a deeper understanding will come, but the Lord will grant you peace, right where you are. Tomorrow, he'll give you your new name, and you will know Him. It will change everything for you."

"Tomorrow?" Joe asked.

"Well, not tomorrow like you think. It's more like *soon*. Darkness never falls here, and your body never tires. It doesn't need sleep, but it does need quiet. If you don't quiet yourself and be still, it's difficult to walk in all the fruits of this place. It has a feeling similar to tired, but it's more like run-down. Understand?" Karial asked.

"Not exactly," Joe looked over at Karial and said, "You know what?"

"No?" Karial cocked his head.

"Even though I asked the Lord for forgiveness for what I'd done, and I truly believed I'd asked genuinely, I wondered if God could really forgive me. I mean, what I did was pretty bad." Joe hung his head.

"What is pretty bad? All sin is bad, and believe me, I've seen it all!" Karial said with a smile.

Joe pointed to the scarred leather on the armor. "How did you do that?"

"In the war." Karial looked straight ahead.

"War? Which one? I was in a few," Joe said, looking for a common bond.

"Not one of your wars," Karial looked saddened. "Our war."

"Oh, that war. I am sor--" Joe said.

"He was so beautiful; he was an Archangel like Michael," Karial's voice drifted off a moment. "After you see the Lord we can talk about it. I'll tell you all about it, maybe on the way to the mountains."

"We get to go to the mountains?" Joe asked.

"Yes. I'm sure of it. It's not for angels, but we occasionally get to go there. It's for the redeemed. Not everyone goes, but most people who come through Paul's gate go. They're generally those who committed great violence - not unlike Saul - and then underwent great conversions. The violence committed against others, innocent or not, deeply wounds the spirit, and even here it's common to go to the mountains to seek healing and knowledge. The knowledge will heal the spirit and allow you to be closer to the Lord. I'm sure you'll get to go," Karial laughed. "Remember, I saw your life."

"You saw it all? Everything?" Joe winced.

"Everything," Karial smiled, "But don't worry about it, I'm not a judge; only a witness and a guardian. I do what the Lord commands. I also will do whatever one of the redeemed commands, as long as it doesn't conflict with any command of the Father."

"I see no children or old people," Joe said after realizing everyone appeared to be within ten years of age from each other.

"Everyone is at their perfect state. Regardless of what state you were in at your death, old, young, sick or healthy, once redeemed, all is right. Children and parents come together on a spirit level, much more intimate than the relationship they knew before. I have noticed many family groupings that have found great bonds here. The relationships before were but shadows of the ones here," Karial talked with skill and patience as if he'd done this a thousand times, but also like he enjoyed the banter.

Joe hesitated a moment, then decided to ask a question that had been on his mind ever since he got there. "What about someone in your family, someone you loved, who for one reason or another is not here?"

Karial stopped walking and looked at Joe, "They're lost, and are over the great chasm. You'll have to ask that of the Lord Himself."

"But-"

Karial put up his hand. "I'm here to answer questions that pertain to your transition and to prepare you to engage the Lord. Those types of questions, the why's and what for's, are for the Lord, not an angel. A question like that will only be settled between you and the Lord; I'm but His servant."

Joe nodded. He didn't feel like pushing the issue, for it wasn't as consuming as it once had been. Something about this place soothed the pain of the old world like salve in a wound.

Joe and Karial paused in front of a café. People were talking with one another and enjoying themselves, seated both inside and out. Bright candles flickered with a green flame on the center of each table.

"I see these cafés and shops," Joe said. "It looks like a market. Do people run businesses and work here?"

"Yes, but not exactly. People do work, but out of pure joy and for the love of it. This place is ever changing, and all people are encouraged to create and make things as they wish. The cafés are lovely places for fellowship and enjoyment of company. Eating and drinking is only for the pleasure of the redeemed, because of the Lord's great favor upon you. Your body does not need food for survival like it did before. Eating and drinking is more like a form of love or worship or communing with someone as a shared experience. This body is perfect," Karial said, gesturing to Joe's body. "There's no waste created from eating; all food is dispersed throughout your body, and it is merely absorbed, for lack of a better word, or evaporated. No harm comes from it and it doesn't provide energy; however there's no gluttony either. Everything is in perfect harmony for the pleasure of the Lord and the redeemed. There are no addictions as you once knew them to alcohol or any other thing. All is right."

Joe nodded his acknowledgement. "How about the different languages? I can hear strange languages, but it seems that I understand them all."

"Yes, all languages that existed in your former realm are here, as well as some you've never heard. Even some of the higher animals have languages, but not the beasts. People usually speak the language they have an affinity for, or the one they spoke before. It doesn't matter what language I speak," Karial changed his language to something that sounded Russian. "You can understand me, can you not?"

"Yes, I can understand you," Joe responded in English. Excitement welled up inside Joe and he smiled. "Try another one!"

Karial smiled and said in a language that sounded like Chinese, "As you wish, I am at your service."

"I can understand you!"

"Of course you can. Language is not a cumbersome barrier here. It's also a thing of beauty. I'm speaking English because it's your chosen language, at this point anyway, and I'm here to serve you. Therefore, I'll speak any language you find comfortable. We, the angels, even have our own language and many of us can communicate without words at all," Karial said with a smile.

"You can read each other's thoughts?" Joe raised an eyebrow.

"Yes, something like that. It's really closer to speaking through body language," Karial answered.

"Why are there no cars, computers, or technology?" Joe asked.

"There's no need for those types of burdens. They were created by the minds of men, who were imitators of God, but not God. You'll see. You won't miss any of it. There's so much to see and experience here, it would take twenty lifetimes, as you knew them, to touch it. It won't be long, and those memories of before will seem foolish to you," Karial said with a knowing smile.

"Are my parents here somewhere? They were Lutherans," Joe asked, but the question sounded silly to him after he asked it.

"They're here, but not because they were Lutherans or anything named of men." Karial smiled a little. "People who find the light in the darkness of what was before are the elect, the redeemed. You'll see them soon, as well as many other generations of yours who came before you. You'll experience family bonds in a new way. We're all His children here."

"Do we get to watch those that are still living?" Joe asked.

"For what purpose?" Karial's tone sounded more serious than before.

"I don't know? To see how they are doing, I guess."

"They're in God's hands. You only get the opportunity to

affect them while you're there. Only angels and the Spirit travel to the other realms. The redeemed don't leave the Kingdom. There are certain windows to the other realms, but I know of none in use anymore. You've only just arrived. The time for hurrying is over. Rest and all will come to pass," Karial's easy manner reassured Joe as he struggled to grasp the secrets of the Kingdom. "Of course, the Lord has personally gone to the world. He created all the entrances like the stairway you came up, when He invaded the world with His Son, the Christ. He creates everywhere He goes. Ever since that time, there's been a steady stream of redeemed coming into the Kingdom. Now He usually sends the Spirit or one of us, into the darkness, answering prayers for protection and so forth."

"I had many dreams and visits from odd characters," Joe stated, wondering if Karial knew about them.

"If they were not me or from the Spirit of the Lord, they were from the other place," Karial explained.

"The other place?"

"The other Kingdom, named Abaddon and Hell. The details of that realm will be explained by the Lord, again, not from an angel. Our enemy assaults the World of Flesh, especially the redeemed. He is merciless; that's all I will say for now," Karial bared his teeth and it wasn't a smile.

It made Joe think that he wouldn't like to see an angel with his anger up.

"What about all the different creatures? They weren't all present before?" Joe asked.

"The Lord is the Creator; some things were created just for here. Some for both places, some with different versions for here or there. Some days I see creatures I've never seen before. The Lord continues to create new things all the time. It's part of who He is and who you are."

The street they walked suddenly opened up with a view of a large body of water. A pillared railing wrapped the stone-walk jutting out over the edge of a sheer drop. The cliff fell upon jagged rocks below and a sparkling sea crashed fiercely against them. The sea stretched out as far as Joe could see, until on the misty horizon, he could see more mountains or a coastline of some kind. The breaking crests produced a gold froth, and as Joe leaned on the rail a warm sweet breeze hit him in the face.

"Wow, that's beautiful!" Joe said.

Karial looked out as well and smiled, revealing his teeth. "You should see it from the air."

"The air? You have airplanes?"

"Not exactly," Karial smiled and winked an eye. Without another word Karial climbed up on the rail and jumped off into the sea.

Joe jumped instinctively to pull him back from crashing to his death, but he realized the angel hadn't fallen at all. Instead, Karial laughed wholeheartedly, and Joe discovered a secret; angels love to laugh.

"I'm sorry. I love that part. I do it to all the new people. You should've seen your face." Karial tried to contain his laughter.

"What do you mean all the new people?"

Karial chuckled, "You're not the only human that I've guarded. A life of flesh is but vapor and mist, surely you know that?"

"Well yes, I know that, I guess. What are you doing? Flying?" Joe asked realizing that Karial had not exactly returned to his place on the ground.

"Flying? No, not exactly. The truth is this is a *Kingdom*, not a planet. It doesn't have gravity as you knew it. It only takes reaching a certain level to access the ability placed within you already," Karial's explanation thrilled Joe.

"I can do that? It's not just for angels?"

"Of course you can. Angels have very few gifts that the redeemed don't have access to."

"Will I get that in the mountains?" Joe asked.

"Some do," Karial answered. "But not usually on the first few trips." Karial hopped over the rail with ease and landed back on his feet in a flash.

Joe shook his head in a mixture of disbelief and excitement.

"There's such blessing and abundance here, most redeemed are only limited by themselves," Karial said, smiling again. "It's truly as you all say down there…paradise."

"What keeps us on the ground then, if there's no gravity?" Joe asked.

"We stay on the ground because that's how the Lord designed it. He willed it this way."

"When do I get to see Him?" Joe asked.

"How about, right now?"

S.C. SHERMAN

VI
The Throne Room

Joe scanned the large courtyard spread out flat as a table. Stone walkways systemically dissected lush green grass leading to the center of all things. The ancient paths came together at the foot of a course of great steps that lead into a massive Romanesque structure girded with fluted columns. At the base of the steps, a river sprang forth, as if it emanated from within the building. Where the stone paths culminated, several bridges spanned the water to allow access to the steps. The crystal clear water flowed through the courtyard and exactly in the center of it, stood a tree. Not just any tree, but *the* tree. The river flowed and holy water surrounded the base of the tree, like a moat would protect a castle. The canopy of the tree was wide and green, birthing many different fruits. One section had large, red apples dangling from its branches, while another was full of magnificent oranges. Upon closer examination, fruits of all kinds were born of the tree creating a kaleidoscope of color amongst the green leaves.

"The Tree of Life," Karial whispered as if knowing what Joe's next question would be.

Karial led them on a path and across one of the bridges. Together, they climbed up the marble steps leading into the building. Joe noted twelve stone columns, reaching many stories in height. The base of each column appeared to be formed of the twelve-named precious stones. Royal plum colored banners trimmed in gold tassels flittered in a gentle breeze.

"Are you ready?" Karial asked. Joe didn't answer. He just kept staring, his mouth hung open.

"Let us proceed to the Throne Room of God," Karial said as he gestured toward the grand hall. Karial continued on and Joe followed like a child.

Seven angels evenly spaced themselves on the steps. The angels stood three on either side and one in the center of the top step. They were virtually identical to the angels Joe had encountered in both size and dress. Each an individual in appearance due mostly to the hair feather coloration, as well as facial shape. The colors of the angels varied as much as the color spectrum; one was a rust color, one brownish, another golden, another iridescent green, one steely gray, another black, and finally the one in the center; a startling opalescent white.

"Absolutely breathtaking," Joe whispered.

"Aren't they wonderful?" Karial said.

"Yes, they're amazing," Joe answered, continuing to stare.

"They're the Vial Keepers," Karial said with reverence and respect in his voice.

They passed near enough that Joe could see each of the seven wore a golden chain around their neck, holding a golden vial. The intricate vials were glass encased in gold, and the top was shaped as a lion's head. Inside the glass, smoke and many colors swirled around as if it contained a gas of some sort.

"What are the vials for?" Joe asked.

"They contain the wrath of God," Karial said matter of fact.

"Wrath?" Joe wasn't sure he wanted to hear this part.

"Yes, wrath. The seven await their appointed time to unleash wrath as prophesied, when the Lord announces the time is at hand and wills it. Until then, they faithfully wait and guard the throne."

The crowd in the courtyard grew with people and angels who appeared to all be walking in pairs.

"Who are all these?" Joe asked.

"They're like you, new arrivals, coming to meet their Lord and receive their inheritance and citizenship in the Kingdom."

Joe marveled at the size of the crowd. "We all meet the

Lord?"

"Yes, everyone and one-on-one. Take as long as you like; ask every question you have ever had," Karial said with a smile.

Due to the huge host of people filing in, Joe was skeptical that all that could be accomplished and began shaking his head in unbelief.

"You're still thinking with your old precepts, your old senses of reality. Those are no longer fact. Sight, sound, touch, taste, smell; all exist here yes, but they're no longer bounds," Karial explained. "Do not worry about the size of the crowd. He'll see you and hear your individual questions. You forget; He can see all of you at once. You'll also be given your new name."

"New name?" Joe asked.

"Of course, you don't want to go around with a name of dead flesh, do you?"

"No, I suppose not."

Karial placed a hand on Joe's chest and faced toward him looking over his appearance. He straightened out Joe's clothing, making sure he looked presentable, like a mother would do to her son.

Suddenly, Joe felt a queasy feeling in his stomach.

"Are you nervous?" Karial asked him.

"Yes. It's rather formidable to think of coming face-to-face with the Almighty Creator of all things, Knower of all things, High King of the Kingdom of Heaven! I have a few butterflies in the belly."

Without any warning, Karial swung his fist and hit Joe hard, right in the stomach. Joe doubled over, gasping for air.

"That always takes away my butterflies," Karial said, laughing. "Pain is easier to manage than nerves. Don't you think?"

Joe recovered and stood up straight, giving his guardian angel a frown. "I didn't think there was supposed to be any pain here."

"Oh no, who told you that? We have pain just no death, nothing wrong with a little pain now and then. Are you still nervous?"

"No, I'm just right. No butterflies. No need for any more . .

. uh . . . help."

Karial laughed again, "Just let me know if you need another adjustment. I'm here to serve you." He half-smiled with the side of his mouth again and showed some teeth. The angel stopped in the shadows of the entrance, and Joe stumbled into his backside.

"This is as far as I go. You'll be fine; go on now. Everyone must go in alone. I'll be here when you get out."

Joe nodded at Karial's encouragement, took a deep breath, and turned away from the angel. He proceeded through the columns amongst a great crowd toward an open door. One by one, the people disappeared inside.

Upon passing through the doorway, Joe found the crowd gone as he stood alone in a formal foyer. Ahead of him were shiny, emerald doors with glass handles. Four stone faced angels stood at the four corners of the room. A strong wind blew, despite the fact that all of the doors were shut.

The angel, who was yet another color Joe hadn't seen before, an opaque orange, stood at the left front and spoke to him. "Come and enter in." The angel proceeded to the door centered perfectly on the wall, and struggled to slowly wrest it open.

As it opened, glorious music filled not only Joe's ears, but all of his senses also. It was as if he could taste, smell, and feel the music at the same time. A sweet calm entered Joe's spirit as he entered. He heard the door clang shut behind him, but he didn't turn to look. His attention was full ahead. It took all of Joe's newfound faculties to begin to comprehend what he saw.

A great room existed before him. It was wide and long and filled with light and music. Arching masonry raised the roof and lined the back and sides of the ordered and majestic room.

The focal point centered towards a rock that was the very throne of God. It appeared to be a large boulder of white marble with pure gold veining that glittered continuously as light rained down from high. Hewn into the surface was a smooth seat for the King while the edges of the rock remained jagged and natural. Stretching from the Lord's judgment seat were twenty-four more perfectly and equally-spaced smaller thrones. Four were large seats of gold, crafted in an ancient style and with wonderful detailing fit for a king of any world. Two were on one side of the Lord's seat and two were on the other. Then each side of the Throne Room had ten more thrones, glinting with silver and only slightly smaller than the gold thrones, but no less detailed in their craftsmanship. Each of these silver thrones was unique to themselves, other than one large, circular pearl embedded into the top center of the metal. The pearls themselves were clutched within the silver claws of an eagle.

Suddenly, a rumbling sound like thunder filled the air, and Joe felt the floor actually shake slightly as a door opened on each side of the room. Men briskly marched into the hall, while the sound of trumpets announced the entrance of kings. The twenty-four kings were robed in flowing, white raiment, and topped with crowns of gold. They walked in a single line until each stood facing Joe with a throne behind them. Joe scanned their faces and did not recognize any of them. They were mighty and beautiful, all in the peak of their appearances and strengths. In each face Joe recognized an undeniable strength that permeated their presence, as well as an underlying compassion.

As the four higher kings sat, lightning zigzagged its way across the ceiling and the floor; thunder echoed through the hall once again. Joe jumped and slightly raised an arm to protect himself, but it soon became evident the lightning would not harm him; he put his arm down and stood straight. The entire floor reaching from where he stood to the throne of God was a clear, shining sea of glass-like crystal.

Then, with more heraldry and horn blowing, a great angel entered from behind Joe and walked right past him without giving him a look or a word; his footfalls strong and true. He immediately realized this one was different than the angels that he'd seen up to this point. This angel was markedly different; he stood taller and heftier in both muscle and heraldry. His hair-feathers were a magnificent, deep green that almost looked black. His face bespoke strength and somberness, much like most of the generals Joe had known. His uniform differed from the others, but was obviously battle ready, which gave him an appearance both royal and deadly.

their Creator for their very existence poured forth in song, harp, flute, and all manner of joyous sounds, smells, and all senses. Joe could no longer tell time and had no way to know how long this all continued, but he knew he didn't want it to stop. Everything was right within him, and he felt a pure love that is entirely unknown to all who dwell in the darkness of the other world. It was a love with no motive, agenda, thought, or gain; a truly pure love felt from one to another in all directions. The King sat upon the seat of judgment, and all present quieted to hear. Every eye watched as the great angel carried a scroll, and with head low, he approached the King.

"Who is worthy to break the seals and open the scroll?" the mighty angel cried out in a thundering voice.

Silence filled the room as no one present could answer 'yes'.

Then the crisp, clicking sound of little hooves echoed from the back, and everyone turned to see a snow-white Lamb walking down the center amidst all the four animals and the twenty-four elders. The Lamb looked like no lamb Joe had ever seen. On its head were seven tiny horns, and at the base of each horn there was a little eye. Joe ached with pain deep in his chest and nearly wept at the sight. He could see the little Lamb had been slain. The brilliant white wool along the neck of the Lamb dripped with fresh red blood as if the knife had just run deep only a moment before. Joe stared as he wondered how the tiny creature managed to continue walking at all. He expected it to fall over dead any second. The Lamb approached the Throne of God and looked up at the King who held the scroll in His right hand. All other creatures, the kings, and the elders, held their breath in submission. The little Lamb stood alone before God. Joe did not know what to expect and kept watching in complete rapture.

The King stood, and it surprised Joe that He looked like a distinguished, middle-aged man. His hair was a deep, warm brown, slightly graying, and His facial features were strong and striking. He wore a full, but neat beard. The crown upon His head contained twelve points, each adorned with a different jewel. He wore kingly robes of rich colors, and as the robes swayed, he saw the armor underneath and a sword upon His hip. His authority was complete, and it was alive and flowing amongst all present.

The King knelt and put His arm around the little Lamb. As He did so, the Lamb disappeared, or rather it was absorbed into the King, and as the King stood, another also stood beside Him, who was His Son. The Father gave the scroll to the Son and returned to sit upon His throne. The Son, whose appearance resembled that of His Father's in most every way, looked at Joe with such love on His face that Joe physically felt His touch deep in his innermost heart of hearts. Tears of joy began to stream down Joe's face.

Suddenly, from inside the hall, as well as outside, a great voice of many angels cried out, "Worthy is the Lamb, who is slain; with your blood you purchased men for God, to receive power and wealth and wisdom and strength and honor and glory and praise!"

The singing continued a little while, and the strong angel declared, "To Him who sits on the throne and to the Lamb be praise and honor and glory forever and ever!"

With lightning and thunder as a backdrop, the Son took the scroll and broke open each of the seven seals. Once the seals were broken, He unrolled the ancient parchment and looked upon it as if to read it. The Son looked up and directly into Joe's eyes. Joe could not be sure if he heard the voice inside his head or if it actually rang out through the hall, but it was a beautiful sound in every way.

The clear, assuring voice of the Lord spoke to him, saying, "As it is written here, in the Lamb's Book of Life, the man Joseph David Rellik is found. I see the redeemed has entered the Kingdom and stands before the throne of the Lord in all authority, and ransom paid, I offer the redeemed citizenship in Heaven for all eternity. If you accept, come forward."

Joe stepped forward without fear or hesitation as a sheep goes to the voice of its shepherd. He stopped directly before the Son.

"Kneel, to receive your inheritance," The Son commanded in a soothing voice. "You are now a citizen of the Kingdom of Heaven, subject to the realm of the Lord God, King of Kings."

Joe knelt as commanded. The Son stepped to the side, and the great King himself stood from His seat. The steel of His sword made a clean, crisp sound as it came from its scabbard. Afraid to look up Joe stared at the King's feet protected in armor, as He stood over Joe with sword in hand.

The King placed the sword first on one shoulder, then the other shoulder of His subject, saying in a loud voice, thunderous and clear, "The man, Joseph David Rellik, is dead. By the Lamb, I accept you, the redeemed spirit, Elion, into the Kingdom of Heaven. Arise."

Elion stood to the ovation of the entire Kingdom. Sounds and feelings of acceptance and love filled the air with sweet delights. The kings, elders, and the creatures in the hall all cheered loudly and clapped with joy that actually filled Joe's heart with warmth as if he'd swallowed a hot drink. Joe turned slightly to look upon the acceptance that poured forth from every inch of the Kingdom.

The voice of the Lord spoke softly from behind him and it felt like a dream, a fantastic dream. "Elion, walk with me."

Joe answered to his new name as if it had been sewn into the very fiber of his being. It felt as if it had always been his name, and the name Joe Rellik had been a poor façade to hide who he really was, Elion. He took a step and felt the hand of God touch his shoulder. Immediately, they were no longer in the Throne Room.

※

Elion blinked wildly and looked about, discovering a lush, green meadow of grass and flowers, backed up to a small bluff. Cool, clear water fell over round rocks, creating a swirl of mist, and a lovely, soothing sound. Thick, hardwood trees encircled the meadow in majestic poses of pride and virtue.

"It is good to walk with you, my son," a voice close behind said.

Elion turned to face the Lord, who had already taken a seat on a kingly looking blanket that lay over a boulder. Another blanket lay on the ground with a basket of fruits and several plates of foods that smelled and looked delicious. A feast had been prepared.

"My Lord, I wondered what you would look like and now I know," Elion said after finally finding his voice. It sounded the same to his ears as Joe's voice, but it felt entirely different in every other respect. A giddy smile spread ear to ear, as he stared at the Lord.

"Elion, my son," The Lord spoke with respect, but slowly, as if speaking to a child. "All that you currently know is that you are now a citizen in the Kingdom of Heaven. Be careful to presume any knowledge beyond that." Immediately after the Lord spoke those words His entire appearance melted away, and then solidified again as an old woman.

She cackled an old laugh, and then she disappeared. In her place appeared a young, Asian girl who giggled, and then vanished. Then appeared a middle-aged black man who laughed heartily, and then he too disappeared. The first image of the great King reappeared, and He chuckled slightly.

"My dear, Elion, all people are created in my image. I appear to you as you would most like me to appear. I do that out of my love for you. To know what I look like would be to know my heart."

"I'm sorry Lord. I meant no disrespect." Elion bowed his head humbly.

"I know that, my son. Most newcomers from the World of Flesh think all learning ends when they enter the Kingdom, but in reality learning has only just begun."

"Thank you, Lord, for allowing me to come here and for forgiving me of many, many, grievous sins. I honor you and I am your servant," Elion spoke with deep passion.

"Elion, you are my son, in whom I am well pleased. You are a citizen of Heaven. Henceforth, you may explore and discover all that you will. As you start your journey here, you will begin to forget the world that was; I know the questions that are in your heart, the questions that you have carried from there to here."

"Yes, my Lord," Elion said with all humility.

"I will answer many of the questions now." The Lord paused for a brief moment.

Within that brief moment every question that Joe had ever had for God, or held against Him, were simultaneously answered. These were the questions of life - the old life - the kind of questions that people carry their whole lives.

Hell & Back

When I get to Heaven, I will ask God why? What for? And why not? How could you allow this? These questions that were used to tempt the old spirit into believing falsehoods about the King were now answered in full.

Elion smiled as the sweet answers found their way home and healed wounds and pains buried deep within his former self. His love for the Father enlarged at that quintessential moment as the blockages of old were removed.

The Lord looked up and watched an eagle soaring overhead. Elion looked up as well and was amazed by what he saw. He was still getting used to being able to see the eagle well enough to count his feathers so far away. The Lord spoke, and although He may not have used His mouth, Elion did hear.

"Some questions, I have only quieted and left unanswered. I have hidden the answers for you in the mountains. Take your guardian and go there on a quest for knowledge. Forgotten things will be remembered, and wisdom will take root. The wounds of battles fought in other realms will be healed there with a salve that leaves no scar behind. Our Kingdom is rich with what must be learned, and you will find that her secrets are often earned through perseverance and strong will, but they bear a fruit of sweet abundance."

"When you have found that for which I send you, you will come back to the White City. From the moment flesh conceived you and I breathed life upon you, this mission has awaited your arrival. Go now, my son, and begin your journey, and know that I am with you always. In Heaven, we are never separated."

As the Lord stood and prepared to go, Elion stood too, and the great King stepped forward, wrapped His arms around Elion, like a masculine bear hug. Elion heard no words, but the Spirit of God flowed between them, and they knew one another.

After the Lord released Elion from His embrace, His visual presence was gone. However, the feeling inside Elion remained. He opened his eyes, and found he sat in a garden overlooking the great river. The river flowed directly through the White City, and Elion assumed it was the same river from the courtyard. Many people walked by, going about their business. No one seemed to notice as he leaned his elbows upon a wooden table. Elion's thoughts lingered with the King and all that He'd spoken and left unspoken.

"My lord, Elion, shall we go?" the now familiar voice of Karial said from behind him.

Elion turned and smiled at his friend and nodded. "He told you my name? Ha! Yes, let's go. Where are we going?" Elion asked.

Karial smiled, "It's always been your real name. Come on, I'm taking you home."

"Home?"

"To the place the Lord has prepared for you. It's the place for those of your line. There are several redeemed who knew you in the flesh and anxiously await your arrival. There are also many whom you never knew, who wait upon you as well," Karial said as they walked.

"They're waiting for me?" The news stunned him.

"Yes, there's a great feast planned to honor the Lord and your arrival in the White City, and we must not tarry," Karial said as he tried to speed Elion along.

They wound their way through a maze of gold-stoned streets lined with people and sounds and smells that were all invitingly pleasant. Paved walkways led to higher levels of the city only to discover many higher levels appeared above them. After walking for some distance Karial stopped and nodded at the building ahead. Elion smiled as he knew it was his home.

"This is the entrance to the mansion which belongs to your line. Ready to go in?" Karial said in a whisper.

"Yes, indeed," Elion said.

Elion longed to enter, as he felt like he'd been here before. It felt comfortable - like home.

The façade was the color of desert sand and castle amongst a maze of castles. Ramparts and parapets, spires and tops, all running together. Busy people went freely about their business as gates were open and bridges spanned small motes. Karial led Elion toward his entrance marked by a dark, wooden gate tied open with heavy ropes. Royal standards on poles wobbled slightly in the gentle breeze. In the center was a tapestry hanging from its two corners displaying the image easily. The edges of the standard were a chestnut brown with little tassels. The center of the fabric held a crest that was a shield of blazing goldenrod and upon the shield was the black shape of a warrior lion. Three deep green leaves gently adorned the outer shape of the shield.

They passed through the gates, and he knew he was finally home. Elion suddenly felt weak and strange, as if he was tired, but different.

"Karial, I think I'm tired like you said," Elion said.

They entered a grand hall with a winding staircase that spiraled upward to a second floor and beyond. The room was quiet as they stood alone.

"I'll take you to your room, and you'll have peace and rest for a moment. Quiet yourself, and the strength of Lord will fill you up once again."

"That sounds just right. I can't thank you enough, Karial," Elion said.

"I am here to serve you, my lord. I'm glad you're pleased," Karial said as they stopped before a door. A long hallway full of doors continued on, but this one was arched and worn with a black metal handle. Elion's name had been burned into the surface of the ancient door.

Karial opened the door and stepped out of the way. "Here you are, my lord, the place that has been prepared."

"Thank you. Why do you call me 'my lord'? I'm quite obviously not a lord."

"You're a redeemed life, created in the image of the Lord. Therefore, by lineage you are His son, and a king, and my lord, sort of like a prince."

Elion nodded his understanding as he stepped past the angel and entered his room.

"I will come for you when it is time."

"Thank you." Elion smiled. With a nod Karial pulled the door shut, leaving Elion to his room.

Fantastic furniture and intricate rugs on a hardwood floor accented by an inlaid fireplace presented a chalet type of atmosphere.

"My compliments to the decorator. Just as I would've dreamed it," Elion laughed.

A fire crackled as Elion followed the living space out onto a balcony overlooking the White City below and beyond the golden froth sea. Light fabric hung across the opening to the balcony and gently swayed in the warm breeze as fresh as the sea. Waves methodically maintained their never-ending rhythm. Elion searched the room and discovered several passages and doors. Within one of the rooms, a four-posted bed covered in silk pillows and sheer cloth draped from above beckoned him. The other doors would have to wait. He pushed back the delicate fabric and lay down on his back amongst the pillows, his eyes wide open. Thoughts raced about his mind like the lightning of the Throne Room. Elion rubbed his hands on his face and quieted his thoughts. He rested for a few moments remembering his time with the Lord. He thought of little else.

A tap sounded on the door, and he sat up. "Yes, come in," Elion said walking into the living quarters.

Karial stepped in. "They're ready for you. Are you ready, my lord?"

"Yes, I feel much better."

"You may change your dress as you will. You're no longer a *new arrival*. What you're wearing is for the new ones. Look in there." He motioned to the bedroom. "There should be several things exactly your size and just your style."

"What is my style?" Elion laughed.

He was learning to trust everything Karial said as truth. The closet was filled with a variety of clothing in many different colors and styles. Elion selected a shirt and pants that were comfortable and fit him perfectly, as if they'd been custom tailored and he'd owned them for years.

Elion presented himself to Karial, "Now then, shall we?"

Karial nodded and opened the door. Elion followed Karial down a long hallway, alcoves containing busts sculpted of both man and angel stood on marble displays, while murals lined the walls.

Subtly the echoes of the sea mixed with sounds of the castle and created a fine ambience. Music lightly danced upon air, as they entered a room, warmly lit by oil lamps attached to the ancient walls. A fire blazed in a tiled fireplace capped with a rough-hewn wood mantle that reminded Elion of a railroad tie. A long, rectangular table filled the center of the room, and steam arose from an array of foods. The aroma of freshly cooked meat instantly tantalized the brain and invited the stomach. The banquet room was a buzz of people talking, laughing, eating, drinking, and enjoying themselves.

Karial and Elion paused in the doorway for a moment, watching the event as outsiders. Someone noticed them standing there and let out a cry, which caused the conversations to halt. At the sight of the angel and Elion, clapping and cheering erupted. Elion glanced at Karial, to find he smiled and clapped as well.

The ovation lengthened until Elion noticed a young woman, crying, tears streaking down her pretty face. Fair skin and amber hair fit nicely around her crystal blue eyes. She smiled as she wept with joy, her hands together, resting her chin upon her knuckles. Elion couldn't take his eyes off of her, and suddenly the memory of her returned. She was his mother when he was Joe. He almost hadn't recognized her. She was so young and beautiful, not at all as he remembered her. She died in that awful hospital with cancer raking her body; he remembered dark blotches covering her skin. She stole a glance at the man next to her, and they shared a smile.

Elion realized that it was his father beside her. He was young and strong with an apparent love for Elion in his eyes. Nothing at all like his memory, either. His father hadn't approved of the military life Joe had chosen. Elion looked him in the eyes, and he returned the stare and did not look away. His father smiled proudly. Elion felt a feeling of love and respect, accepted as never before. There were many others in the room, but he walked toward his mother; she ran to him and embraced him, burying her face against his chest and weeping for joy. Elion felt the strong arms of his dad encircle them, and then everyone in the room closed in around them. Many people wept and smiled their welcome.

"It's good to see you so well," Elion said to his mother. "I missed you when you left." Elion wiped a tear of his own.

"We're so glad to see you, oh yes," the man who was his

earthly father said. "Welcome to the White City. It's everything and more. We're so pleased you've made it. Just as Joe is gone for you, Frank and Doris are dead from us. Our names in the Spirit of the Lord are Elberon and Lovilia. We love you as our son and as our brother. We're all children of the Lord here."

Many more people stepped up and introduced themselves. They told him who they were on earth, and then who they were here in the Kingdom. Elion met many redeemed that had lived long before his time. A grandfather, two great grandfathers, two grandmothers and on and on until the last one he met was a woman who had lived five hundred years before his time. She hugged him as if she loved him as her very own son.

"My lord, if you do not need me," Karial interrupted the introductions. "I will take my leave."

"Yes, go. Thank you again."

"I'll return after a time, my lord, and we shall leave for the mountains. Until then," Karial said as he bowed slightly, and then left the room.

Lovilia motioned for them to sit in the leather-and-wood-frame dining chairs. "Let us eat and celebrate another of ours coming home." She was all smiles.

"We give thanks to the Lord our King and His Lamb," a man who had introduced himself as Boone prayed. He'd told Elion that he'd been in his line eleven generations back. "We partake of these blessings and enjoy the fellowship of our kindred redeemed, Elion. Thank you, Almighty!" He picked up an earthenware chalice and toasted Elion.

Elion picked up the cup in front of him. It looked to be full of a burgundy wine and smelled like roses.

"To our dear Elion; welcome to the Kingdom!"

Everyone drank their toast and passed food, resuming the talking and laughing without reserve.

Elion caught people stealing looks at him every now and then, with sweet smiles on their faces. They'd nod their head a little and smile a welcome smile, and then go back to their conversations. Popular discussions ranged from the King, to the mountains, the sea, the mansion, what some other member of the house was doing, to rumors heard about people not yet arrived. Elion listened and imagined them talking about the first half of his life.

None of them could have hoped I would be here. I was so far gone. His mother held his hand as she talked with someone to the other side of her. Lovilia did not turn to look at Elion.

"I've always had hope for you, my love," Lovilia whispered in his head.

Elion smiled in shock. "You heard me think that?" He said out loud. She turned her gaze his way with a smile. She gently squeezed his hand.

"You will learn it too. I have to be touching you for it to work." Again he heard her thoughts without her lips moving.

"I love you," he thought to himself.

"I love you too, my son, Elion." A tear slipped from the eyes of a pleased mother.

Hours passed and the feasting continued. Here and there, people said their goodbyes and filtered out of the room while still others wandered in. Elion joined a group in a large room with comfortable couches, chairs, and rugs around another fireplace. Everyone relaxed and drank wine and continued talking as if they would never tire. After a time, Elberon and Lovilia rose and said their farewells. They both hugged Elion as they departed.

Elion stayed and continued talking with ancient relatives about things long done in the old world. It was exhilarating to hear and see the depth and breadth of the stories of his ancient kin.

Elion felt as if he could feel the Lord speaking to him.

Do you see that it is so much more than one lifetime?

After a time, Elion went back to his room and sat on the balcony listening to the sea. He'd never felt such a peace and warmth, like a deep, solid belonging. There were no pressures to do this or that, he felt complete peace, only a desire to become more a part of this place and to learn all that could be learned. He closed his eyes with visions of the mountains dancing in his head.

S.C. SHERMAN

VII
To The Mountains

"Aahh! That's sweet," Elion whispered to himself. He swirled the wine in a circular motion under his nose inhaling deeply.

He took a sip, and returned to his book as a sea breeze filled the veranda with salted air. White birds flew lazy circles overhead. A library next to the bedroom offered many books, all of which Elion had never seen nor heard. The texts were of all sorts; poetry, novels, historical stories, he even found a comedy. Each book written in a different language, all of which Elion could fully read and understand. Old Joe had never been much of a reader. However, since everything had changed so, Elion was thoroughly enjoying a little prose. He'd just laid his head back, book open on his chest, when a knock sounded at the door.

"Come in," Elion said from his seat, rubbing his eyes and straightening up.

Karial entered with a toothy grin on his face. "I trust you've met some fine friends and ancient kin?"

Elion motioned the angel to have a seat, but Karial jumped up and sat on the railing with his back to the sea. "Are you ready for an adventure?"

"Absolutely! I've read enough books, what adventure?"

"Shall we leave for the mountains? We've got it to do."

"I'm ready when you are."

"Let's take some of your things and go, no reason to wait," Karial said. In a moment they left the castle behind and tramped down the winding cobbled streets.

A twilight sky meant the lively cafés glowed with amber candlelight.

"Maybe we should set out in the morning, it will be dark soon," Elion commented on the dwindling light.

"Not to worry, it never gets dark in the White City," Karial answered. "The Throne Room is here and the presence of the King is rooted here. The farther you get away from the White City, the more we'll see darkness. We'll experience some darkness in the mountains."

"Are we going to walk all the way? How far is it?" Elion asked.

"Distance isn't measured that way here. It's *all* the way, and we may not walk it all, but we could." Karial smiled and slapped his friend on the shoulder. "Maybe we'll hitch a ride from a friend." Karial evidently enjoyed being mysterious.

"You're my guide, and I have no choice but to trust you explicitly," Elion joked.

"Trust should be earned, not granted, especially with an angel," Karial looked a little dejected, betraying a serious side.

"What does that mean -*especially with an angel*?" Elion asked. "Will you tell me about The Great War on this journey?"

"Yes, I'll tell you about it. Soon, very soon - in the mountains, agreed?"

"Agreed," Elion noticed they were passing through another of the city gates. The adornment was intricately impressive and entirely different from the other entrances. He could see the great pearl shining above the open doors. An angel stood guard, who appeared to be the guardian class. He was obviously a gatekeeper, and his hair-feathers were a brilliant red like young flames. Karial kept walking, and Elion maintained pace with the angel as best he could.

It didn't take long and they tread upon a vast plain with the White City behind them. The worn, earthen path led over a hill and out of sight, leaving only a promise of firm, smooth clay with a rich, wonderful smell. Green grass littered with wildflowers of dazzling colors blanketed the rolling fields. Elion realized as he stared at certain flowers, he could actually taste them. The red ones especially tasted refreshing like a burst of fruit-juice or candy. The two travelers didn't talk much, and both seemed comfortable with the arrangement. Elion and the angel occasionally paused to absorb especially unique sights or creatures that were new to Elion.

They saw several more species of dinosaur-type animals. One of them had a very long neck and was about as large as a Rhinoceros. The other was covered in a type of scale like an Armadillo, but was the size of a Saint Bernard. There were also some zebras, buffalo, and a variety of other more *normal* animals. Most creatures paid them no mind and continued munching on the succulent grass found in abundance. The mountains could be seen from the path, but they were far off and shrouded slightly in clouds.

Karial paused as they crested a hill overlooking a small valley with a river that fell from a bluff and created a mist filled pool. Sparse trees sprinkled the hillsides, and the beautiful valley teemed with wildlife; a virtual Eden. A small herd of horses grazed across the plain, their white coats glistening in the morning light.

Karial smiled at the sight of them and hit Elion on the shoulder. "Come on!" The angel ran down the hill, laughing and carrying on as he went.

Elion waited a moment, but then felt the indescribable feeling a child must feel when he sees a pile of raked leaves. Something inside of Elion wanted to be free and to just run and yell for no reason at all, other than they could and should do it.

Elion ran slowly at first, and then he sped up to a sprint, hollering and waving his arms the whole way. He jumped into the air, did a spin, and since he was going downhill, he lost his footing upon landing. When he fell, he rolled into a ball as he tumbled downward. He rolled back onto his feet with graceful agility and never missed a step. He felt alive and lost only in that moment. No past or future. Karial acted in the same carefree way as Elion. When they reached the bottom, they both collapsed in a heap. Laughing, they found themselves sitting on the ground with the group of horses staring at them. The horses cautiously approached, nostrils flared.

"Those horses are amazing. The only thing I ever saw remotely close to one of them was the Lipizzaner horses. They were white like these, and could do all sorts of tricks. I saw them in a circus once," Elion said.

"Don't say that again," Karial said out the side of his mouth, The brilliant white steeds stopped directly in front of them.

"Don't say what, circus?" Elion whispered a little too loudly.

"Circus!" the lead horse shouted, much to the delight of Elion. "We are no circus horses. We're not even horses at all as you know them! We're Vandilons. I'm Cass, leader of this band. All praise to the King. We choose who, if anyone rides us, and we don't do tricks!"

Karial leaned over to Elion and whispered, "I told you not to say that."

"I can hear you angel," Cass, the Vandilon, snapped. "What are you two doing out here anyway?" The Vandilon was obviously in no way intimidated by the angel's ferocious appearance and claws.

"We are on a trip to the mountains," Karial answered. "My lord here was sent by the King himself. He's new to the Kingdom, and the Lord has sent him on a King's errand to the mountains for knowledge."

"How far are you planning to go today?" Cass asked.

"I'd hoped we'd stay at the last outpost, Fort LaForest," Karial answered.

All of the Vandilons laughed at that, and Cass asked, "You planning on flying?"

"No, we're not to fly unless ordered, and I have had no such order."

"Of course, no angel would break an order," Cass said with some arrogance in his tone. "We'll take you the rest of the way to Fort LaForest, if only to get you out of our valley."

He gestured to two Vandilons in the group and made some horsey noises. "Take them and come back, nothing more."

The younger Vandilons nodded their agreement and said, "Yes, sir." The two creatures trotted up to Karial and Elion, bending one knee to aid in the mounting. They climbed aboard, and the young

Vandilons immediately broke into a run. Both Elion and Karial were forced to grab handfuls of mane to keep aboard as the shiny black hooves pounded forward.

They passed through woods, streams, plains, descrt, and even some hill country and traveled for what seemed like a long distance, but Elion could not be sure anymore. Then both the Vandilons abruptly halted, and bent down for the two riders to dismount.

Once the rider's feet were on ground, the Vandilons raced off without a word at a dead run, heading back the way they'd come, both of them kicking up their heels and frolicking over the hills.

Elion turned a full circle. "I don't see an outpost," he said.

"It's just up ahead in the edge of the woods," Karial explained.

"Those Vandilons sure were full of pride and arrogance. How can the Lord let that exist here?" Elion asked.

"The Lord put that in the Vandilons. They're simple creatures and they have a part to play, to be sure. I'm thankful the Lord didn't create very many of them, but they served us well. We've covered a great distance."

The twilight seemed to be getting darker, closer to dusk or what it's like when the sun goes down but there's a full moon casting an eerie light all around.

Karial started forward and said, "Let's go on in."

They disappeared into the tree line to find a small, hidden outpost. Many cottages with smoke filtering up from stone chimneys spread out through the forest around the main part of the encampment. The center structure looked like an old, wooden military fort, complete with watchtowers on the corners and a two part gate made of felled logs. The gate stood open and they walked right in. People milled about inside, talking to one another. At the sight of them, they all stopped talking and stared at Karial.

A rough-looking young man with a brushy, black-beard, and woodsman-style clothing approached them. "Welcome to Fort LaForest. I'm the mayor of the outpost. My name is Elbee. May I help you?"

"We just need a bath and a room," Karial said. "And possibly get everyone to stop staring. Never seen an angel before?"

"Never seen an angel? Ha!" the mayor said. "I love angels, we just don't see too many out here. They stay away from this place, bad memories I guess, from the war."

"Yes, I heard about it," Karial said with a growl.

"We've seen more lately. You're the second one that's been through."

"Who was it?" Karial asked.

"Kept to themselves, they did, but he was a guardian like you and with a redeemed man, like you."

"Where is the room?" Elion changed the subject to help out his friend, who he could see was less-than-comfortable with the discussion.

The mayor turned and pointed to the back of the square compound. "Right in there we have some very nice rooms available. We do have a bathhouse out at the hot springs and you're welcome to it. Staying long?"

"Just tonight, thank you," Elion answered, and walked toward the rooms.

"We've a feast planned; you're invited to join us!" Elbee called out to them in his rough loud voice.

They stowed their small bags under their beds, which turned out to be single cots in one wide open room.

"If this is 'very nice', then the mayor should visit the White City," Elion said.

"This is not the kind of trip to be pampered. Is that what you want, *warrior*, babied?" Karial answered with a hint of sarcasm.

"This will do just fine. If you can stand everyone looking at you, that is," Elion replied, adding his own touch of sarcasm.

"I'm used to that. Let's go to the hot springs."

"Sounds like a plan to me."

They went in search of the bathhouse, which was easy to find with steam pouring up out of the great pools of water. The pools were very blue and slightly glowed with an unseen light as the water bubbled hot from the stone.

The two friends soaked for a while, letting the wonderful water soothe them with its gentle bubbles and sweet fragrances. As they soaked, complete darkness fell. Instead of twinkling stars, an amazing display of swirling colors and flowing movement flashed across the darkened sky.

"I saw the Northern Lights in the old life a few times, but this better!" Elion stared at the show. "Dark out…must be getting far enough away from the White City."

"Yes, but it won't be dark for long. Where we're going it will be dark for longer than this place," Karial answered quietly so only Elion could hear.

Elion pointed to the display in the sky. "That's dazzling."

"It definitely is wonderful. The best part of going to where there is night, in my opinion," Karial added as he looked up at the light show.

They were returning to their room when they noticed the people of Fort LaForest having their feast. Long tables full of food and drink of every kind lined up in perfect rows. Lively music being skillfully played on various instruments filled the night air with joy and levity. Many people danced and it was difficult not to smile at the scene.

The mayor saw them and waved them over to his table. Elion and Karial nodded as they each found a seat. The mayor poured them a glass of ale that fit the occasion perfectly.

"I'm sorry for all the staring earlier today," Elbee said to Karial.

Karial waved his hand, "No need to apologize, my lord."

"Yes, there is. We used to see so many angels here. Angels built this fort in the beginning, but after the war most of them were gone, and the rest of you stayed close to the White City. Quite understandably, of course, but I must say, I miss the angels being around," Elbee said looking at Karial.

"Thank you, sir," Karial said.

Elbee nodded in acceptance. "Where are you two bound for?"

Karial looked at Elion and smiled. "We don't know for sure. The Lord told my friend Elion, here, that forgotten things will be remembered and wisdom will come to him and something about his mission awaiting him. Isn't that right?"

Karial evidently wanted Elion's agreement. "Yes, that's right," Elion said with a nod.

"We'll go to The Forgotten City of Angels," Karial continued. "And deeper if need be. The King will lead us."

"I am glad you're here, maybe more of the brave angels like yourself will visit us." Elbee said wistfully. "It's a magnificent place. I'm sure when Michael and Gabriel and Lu-" Elbee cut himself short and then continued. "All the Archangels were here. It was really something."

Elion noticed that gray light was spreading across the dark sky after a very short night.

Karial stood and said, "Thank you for the soak. We're going to rest for a moment and then be on our way."

"If you leave before I see you again, remember you're always welcome here. Blessed be all in the Kingdom of Heaven." Elbee also stood and bid a good rest.

"Yes, yes, and thank you," Karial said. They lay on their cots for a short time. Neither Karial nor Elion slept, but they both gained strength and were soon ready to continue the journey.

As they walked, the brightness grew to full daylight. "The Forgotten City? Sounds interesting," Elion asked.

"Oh it is." Karial snarled his teeth. Elion looked over his shoulder as Fort LaForest disappeared behind them.

They continued on and on as Elion began to get the feeling there would be no end to this Kingdom. As if the boundaries would continue to recede into the distance as they moved forward so that one could never reach the edge. The beauty and ruggedness of the scenery was profound. The plant life contained a varied mixture of known and unknown things and was full of great trees, both hardwoods and cedars, as well as several that were new to Elion's eyes. Creatures were in abundance, both small game and large forest creatures. The creatures had no fear of the man and the angel walking through the woods. They merely raised their heads from whatever they were doing and then went back to it. Elion thought that one, little black squirrel actually smiled at him.

Karial slowed his pace and then sat down on a fallen log. Elion joined him, glancing about the forest as they caught their breath. The trees here had dropped a fine carpet of needles that made it virtually silent as they walked. Birds chirped in the trees, and Elion snapped his head as he heard the distinctive call of a pheasant.

"Is there hunting here? I used to hunt pheasants."

"Yes and no. We've hunting-type sports, but we don't hunt quite like you're referring to in the question. I've heard in the far outer reaches there are animals created for hunting, but they also hunt you, to make it sporting." Karial cocked his head in the angel way. "Do you see the lake down there?" he said as he pointed through the pines.

"Yes, it's glittering."

"We should go set up a camp down by the lake. It will be dark soon, and we've made good progress. We'll reach The Forgotten City tomorrow."

"That is if you haven't *forgotten* your way." Elion laughed at his own good humor; Karial did not join in the laughter.

Karial stood and started walking down to the lake. "I could never forget that place." He'd half-said it to himself, but Elion overheard. Elion raised his eyebrows with a sideways glance, and followed along.

They set up a nice camp and lay their blankets on the ground by the fire. Elion scooped some ice-cold, fresh water into his mouth with his hand. It tasted like life, and the cold liquid penetrated down deep into him. There were fish swimming about in the lake and jumping at flies as they lit on the surface of the water. Moss covered pines surrounded the lake and firelight shimmered on the glassy pond.

Elion lay down by the fire, and Karial came out of the woods and lay down on his blanket as well. They stared at the fire and took in its warmth. There was something soothing about the sound and smell of the dancing flames. The display of lights in the sky slowly warmed up with an occasional burst of color here or there.

"How long will it stay dark?" Elion asked.

"Longer than the other night; we're farther into the

mountains, farther from the White City. Do you feel farther from the Lord?" Karial asked.

Elion thought for a moment. "No. He feels like He's sitting right here with us."

"He is. That is the most difficult part of my assignments into the darkness of the fleshly realm. Once you're outside of the Kingdom, the presence is so much more elusive. It feels like a hole in my being."

"What is The Forgotten City and why is it forgotten?" Elion asked, looking across the fire at the angel.

"The Forgotten City was once a great city, with a name," Karial exhaled a heavy sigh. "It was beautiful in every way, stone cathedrals and palaces and much of the intricacies that you find in the White City. It was our city, our special place the King had created for the angels. The Archangels, the Warriors, the Gatekeepers, the Guardians, and the others, all wanted to come here. The King would come here often and teach us about the Kingdom and all we could do, and what we were created for. It was such a sweet time of innocence."

"And then?" Elion asked.

"And then everything began to change. Lucifer was an Archangel. He was every bit as wonderful as Michael. His ferocious beauty was something to behold even by angelic standards. His flowing hair-feathers were golden and amber, and his sheer size and strength was the envy of many of our kind. Oh, and the music, such music as I've never heard before or since; it was his true glory. Then he started spending more time here in The Forgotten City, well it wasn't forgotten then. I mean it had a name, all are forbidden to utter it, so it is now, forgotten."

"Anyway, he spent more time here with his angels than he did in the White City or going on missions for the King as most of us do regularly. I was not in any of the meetings, but I heard about them. Lucifer began to think of himself as king of The Forgotten City and not as the servant of our King. He used his charisma and status and deceived a company of my brothers into believing his lies that the Lord, our true King, was not good, and that he was holding out on us or even using us. Lucifer's venom filled their heads until it poured forth. He'd swayed many into worshiping him, and they began to kill animals to sacrifice to Lucifer and make idols of his image."

Elion listened intently and nodded occasionally as Karial continued.

"The evil in his heart must've been in there from before. Our King cannot create evil, it's a mystery even to us angels. I heard once that Michael knew, but the guardians don't. Somehow, the evil waited elusive and veiled. Once it began, it spread like a cancer. Even now, the same evil consumes the World of Flesh; all of us are forced to fight it. We will fight evil until it is stamped out. In many ways The Great War has not really ever ended."

"The Great War, yes," Elion said as the fire crackled.

"It began here in The Forgotten City. Michael discovered what had been going on. He found a third of our kind worshiping Lucifer and blaspheming the name of the Lord. Unforgivable."

"Michael called on all of the faithful and we answered his call to arms. He led us, and we entered the city. Lucifer sat upon a throne in the amphitheatre, surrounded by his followers. Michael's voice called out, and all attention was upon him as the entire Kingdom held its breath. *Lucifer, come down off that throne and pledge your allegiance to our Creator, your Lord and King, and beg for His mercy to be upon you!*"

"Lucifer stared with contempt, bared his teeth, and mocked Michael. *You fall to your knees and worship me! I am the new king of this place! Worship me or die as the pawn that you are!* His voice had lost all beauty, it came as a snarling growl."

"*You shall submit, or by the power and order of the Almighty King you will be banished from the Kingdom of Heaven!* Michael spoke with the authority that was innately bestowed upon him from our Creator."

"Lucifer said no more, and with a roar like thunder, he burst forth from his pagan throne into the air. Michael let loose a deafening call to battle, and he flew at Lucifer. Both had teeth bared, claws out, ready for action. They met with full force in the air, and their shoulders collided with a thud as they turned into a swirling, biting, clawing swarm of battle. When the two leaders hit, both forces now fully opposed rose up, and there was war in Heaven. Claws and teeth gnashing, screaming and death bloodied this place, fowling the very ground that had been our gift. We fought until the city lay in ruin, and then we fought in the air all across the Kingdom, reaching almost to the gates of the White City."

"Blood and death and the sounds of civil war rained out of the sky over Heaven as the Lord wept in the Throne Room. We had the rebels outnumbered almost two to one. Victory was assured for us, but the price was heavy. In our victory the ominous sound of silence covered the Kingdom. The ground was littered with the dead. We'd killed all of the rebellious ones, and half of our own were dead. The King himself walked amongst the fallen, and attended to each of our dead, healing them right on the ground where they lay with the slightest touch."

Karial pointed to the gouge on his protective chest piece. "I was killed in the battle; the King raised me back to life. Then He found Michael amidst the horror. His face buried in his hands with tears smeared across his bloodied face. The mutilated body of Lucifer lay on the ground before Michael. He fell to his knees as the King came near. 'Forgive us, Lord. We've brought death into Heaven.' Michael begged for us."

"The Lord walked up to Michael and embraced him as he knelt. Then the Lord spoke saying, 'The Kingdom of Heaven suffers violence, and the violent take it by force.' Then He gave us the order. He said, 'Take the body of Lucifer out of the Kingdom. Take all of the unfaithful dead, and fly across the great chasm to the south. Fly until the sky gets rough and full of lightning and thunder. There you will find a Lake of Fire; cast their evil bodies into it, and they will be consumed by it.'

"We did exactly as told," Karial continued. "Over one third of the angels fell that day and we carried them all and dumped them into the Lake of Fire. Their bodies sank into the dark, burning sea. It changed everything. We've been at war ever since."

"But didn't you kill the entire enemy?" Elion asked.

"Yes, but they rose from death, in their dark penitentiary, in hell. And when they rose, they were different; hardly angels anymore, they had become demons and devils. Transformed and mangled by the Lake of Fire. They are now blinded by their rages and worship their false king. He has many names, satan, the great dragon, the old serpent, the fallen star and others. He's utterly given over to evil. They're but shadows of what they once were. They are desperate as the dragon knows the prophecy well. He conducts war in the only place left to him. The world that is neither here nor there. The place the King created for living flesh."

Elion stared into the fire, "Battlefield Eden."

"Yes, satan believes he lost the battle because his numbers were too small," Karial continued. "And not because the King cannot be beaten by a creature that He created or that good is stronger than evil. Oh no, satan has one goal – to bolster his forces, raise his numbers, and to return to Heaven and take over. He hates all humanity merely because the sight of human flesh reminds him of the King. You were created in His image. Satan also hates humanity because he knows the King loves you above all else, and that angels are to serve you. He tries to steal, kill, and destroy as many of you as possible, not just out of pure malice. Oh no, many people think so, but he really cares nothing for humans at all. His one desire is to overthrow the King, and there is only way to increase his numbers. When he captures a human soul and takes them away to his realm, that person's guardian goes into hell with the lost human."

"Once in hell, guardians like me are turned into demons in Legion's army. It's his only means of recruitment. He also knows the prophecy that a day will come when all will be judged, and all will rise and he will be no more. That drives him mad. He is desperate to beat the prophecy, and overthrow our King."

Elion hung on every word.

"As a guardian, I've been fighting demons ever since the war. I wish I could tell you we always prevail, but we do not. When we're outside of Heaven's realm, the battle is difficult to control. The spoils of the fight are the everlasting souls of all humanity. Those who make it here are the redeemed humanity set right by the Lamb. The Lamb was the fatal blow. Satan didn't expect that, and it was a deathblow; he just doesn't believe it yet. The Lamb took the very keys to hell and death. No one has to go to the place of torment. All they must do is believe in the Lamb. Those who're rebellious become the lost, tormented and enslaved in the realm of darkness. They are ruled over by the evil lord, the devil, and abused by his awful legion of demons; forever separated from this place and their Creator. Satan doesn't think that humanity is the threat. He thinks angels were made for war and that humanity is weak. His contempt for you makes him disregard your power. Most of humanity disregards their own power as well, and many go to the darkness willingly." Karial paused as he noticed Elion staring into the fire.

"Not everyone who is there should be there, and some here deserve to be there," Elion said, firelight dancing in his eyes.

Karial cocked his head. "Tread lightly, my friend. Do not question your King, especially in this place."

"I do not question Him. I have regrets that in the flesh I let someone down. Someone too young and fragile to endure what she had to endure…"

"Your daughter, Kelly, is who you speak of?"

"Yes. She made a choice out of her intense pain. If I'd been there she would be here," Elion said with a sense of great sadness.

"That may be true, but there is a design that even now you do not see. Don't forget that the Lord's will is at work, in all things. Both in the reason why the events in flesh happen, and the reason why the Lord veils it from your knowledge," Karial said as he added a log to the fire. "All of this is very unusual, the King sending you to the mountains right away - most unusual."

"Unusual, why?" Elion asked.

"Most people don't desire to leave the White City for a very long time - or ever, no matter what their fleshly life was like. You were ready, even excited to go, right away. And even fewer redeemed get ordered to go by the King to seek out a mission. In fact, I don't remember it ever, these are strange times," Karial said with some excitement in his voice.

"Strange? How?" Elion prodded.

"Just strange. I don't know the King's design either, but tomorrow we'll go to The Forgotten City and see what is remembered. I'd like to forget this place entirely," Karial said.

Elion looked up at the sky. "I remember some things. I remember Kelly. I can still remember when I left for Vietnam. I had no idea I'd never see her alive again. She prayed for me before I left. She had a faith in the Lord," Elion said with sadness in his voice.

"I knew her guardian well. He was my friend. He fought valiantly, but there are certain times that the evil comes in a rush, and he was knocked back for just a moment, and in that moment the enemy came to her."

Suddenly Elion heard a noise off in the darkness, and the conversation stopped for a few seconds as they listened. After a time there were no more sounds.

"You don't think like any redeemed I ever knew." Karial looked up at the sky, watching the show of light.

"What do you mean?" Elion asked.

"I never met one until you that remembered anything with sadness or a sense of loss until they were here for many ages and had gained many levels. Usually, there is a sense of pure joy that overshadows all feelings of loss and pain from the last place. Like a period of grace. You have that joy, but you also have angst. I wonder what the King is up to with you and apparently me as well." Karial shook his head and lay back.

Elion folded his hands on his chest. "I think I will be quiet for a time."

"As you wish, my lord," Karial said.

Slowly, the darkness began to fade and the brightness of the Kingdom ignited the beauty of the forest. Karial stamped out the fire and they continued on. They traveled for a long distance without tiring, up great slopes and slipping though sweet valleys with springs running free and clear. Elion could feel it, he knew something was about to happen.

S.C. SHERMAN

VIII
FORGOTTEN CITY

Karial held up his hand and brought himself to an abrupt halt. His penetrating eyes examined every shadow as the silence lengthened.

Elion saw nothing but the mountains. The woods dropped off steeply to a wide valley floor. Ruins remained stalwart amongst the fauna. It felt like hallowed ground that mourned in silence terrible deeds done.

"There it is. The Forgotten City," Karial said with a blank stare on his face.

Elion could see great spires of ancient structures rising up in the center of the valley.

"There's the amphitheatre," Karial said. Seating descended in an oval shape and even though major portions of the building lay in rubble, the former greatness of architecture persevered. Twelve pillars of pink-colored granite still stood resolute, amidst many other buildings in various stages of decay. The forest itself appeared to be doing its best to consume the evidence of the crime scene. Growing brush and creeping vines covered entire buildings with new, green growth. The valley floor contained most of the impressive structures, while amongst the trees and right up the steep slopes there were telltale signs of smaller buildings.

Karial was right; this must have been a glorious place when it was alive.

Elion's eyes continued on past the ruins, and he noticed a

mountain stream fed into a bowl-shaped lake sparkling like a jewel at the boxed end of the valley. Rock slopes closed in around the lake, and the reflections of the peaks shimmered on the water - ominous reminders that He who created this place was the Lord and worthy to be praised.

Karial interrupted Elion's thoughts. "There's another guardian over there on the top of the far slope, do you see him?"

"Yeah, what's he doing?"

"He's been sent, just like us. No angel would come here without orders from the King."

"Let's go down, I feel drawn down there," Elion said.

"I won't be going down with you," Karial said with a serious look on his face. "This is as far as I'll go. Angels are forbidden to enter The Forgotten City. The place was a seductress to my kind, and I'll not tempt her. I'll walk around and speak to the other guardian. His name is Jaxim, I know him. When you're done, you'll find us back over the last hill. We'll set up a camp and wait. Stay as long as needed, but don't be surprised to find another of humanity amongst the ruins. Jaxim wouldn't be here without a redeemed human." Karial walked away toward the other angel.

Elion made his way down the slope past several buildings covered by forestation. The forgotten abodes stood with open doors and no evidence of what they once were used for. Some had small statues and water fountains full of old algae-filled water. Elion discovered he was walking on a path as his foot scuffed the stone and it shined a brilliant, silvery color.

Elion reached the valley floor, and even in ruin the greatness of the city awed him. He passed many large buildings, crumbling and returning to the forest; a large courtyard remained surrounded by the half-standing columns of the amphitheatre. Elion paused and imagined what the building would've looked like in its glory.

Sadness suddenly enveloped Elion and he looked up the hillside wishing he could leave. He knew he couldn't go back without finding it, the purpose he'd been sent for. He didn't know whether 'it' was actually a thing or whether it was just a revelation within the senses. Elion continued to press on exploring the inner regions of the amphitheatre.

He struggled up piles of rubble as rocks rolled away underfoot. Elion felt uneasy and repeatedly looked over his shoulder. He saw nothing, no sign of anyone else, and he was glad to have found a way into the seating area. Elion stepped from the rubble onto the portion of the old coliseum that remained unbroken. He paused and took a seat. The seating ascended from the floor in stairway fashion with a couple feet between each riser. Soft grass grew up on the seating areas and tiny flowers dotted the green with bits of color and a promise of life.

At the one end of the oval-shaped coliseum lay the broken rubble of the throne built by the hands of evil. Elion closed his eyes and envisioned the two archangels as they impacted in the air above igniting the war.

Elion put his tongue to his lips, and tasted the bittersweet of juniper, a pistol lying on a table. The memory startled him with emotion and he jumped up wide-eyed. He was still in the amphitheatre.

"Forgotten things will be remembered," he said aloud.

He worked his way down the steps and meandered through the fragments of granite that now stood as boulders with lush green grass flourishing around them. Devoid of any sounds of birds or wind or water, the quiet was deafening. Each step came loudly even in the soft grass. Elion held his breath and he felt a familiar wariness. He suddenly had the desire to have a weapon.

He heard the Lord in his spirit. *You need no weapon, my son, within the Kingdom.*

A peace replaced his growing fear. The broken throne lay at his feet. The sensation of fear felt like something foreign, altogether wrong.

"It must be this place. The throne of death," Elion said aloud to himself.

He noticed an empty darkness behind a tightly knit hanging vine along the back wall. Elion spread the vine apart and felt the prick of pain as he discovered the thorns. The pain startled him; it was the first pain he'd experienced in the Kingdom, other than when Karial had alleviated his belly of butterflies. He smiled at the memory as he wiped the blood from his fingertip. He smiled as the wound immediately healed and was gone.

"Thank you Lord," he whispered.

With a little more care not to get pricked again Elion spread the vines and discovered an old doorway, long hidden and unused. Once he cleared a way through, he squeezed into the doorway. His eyes quickly became accustomed to the lack of light, and he saw stairs winding down and around a corner.

The dank air smelled musty as he descended. The stairs leveled out into a flat floor with just enough light to see that he'd entered a cavern-like room. A column stood alone in the center of the room topped with a round ball. Elion cautiously inched forward stretching his fingers to touch it.

The tips of his fingers slid over the curve easily. It was smooth like glass, and as his palm settled onto the ball, he heard a bang and then a whirring noise. The ball erupted with bursts of lightning, glowing blue. Elion jumped back, unsure what he'd done.

The entire room lit up with a rectangular panel, first glowing blue like the ball, then swirling many colors. The panel, recessed into the carved wall, appeared to be positioned for viewing from chairs. Light bounced from the arched cavernous ceiling illuminating the entire room in a soft glow. The foggy nature of the panel focused into a crisp image.

A young man in uniform stood at a podium in front of a great sea of men and women, also in uniform. His mouth moved like watching a movie with no sound. Slowly, sound accompanied the image.

"I would also like to thank my mother for all of her support through the years," the young soldier paused and smiled at a woman on the front row. She smiled through proud tears.

"Also, I would be remiss not to thank the Lord Almighty for His guiding hand upon my life, and I would like to thank one old man who helped bring me here. My grandfather was a soldier. He was a soldier's soldier. He never graduated from West Point or gave a speech to the future warriors and leaders of this great country. He spent his life in the mud and the blood. He fought in every conflict from World War II to Vietnam. All didn't love him, and he wasn't a success in every area of his life, but he believed in me, when few others did, and without that, I know I wouldn't be here. Thanks Grandpa Joe. I won't forget what you told me," the young soldier, paused as he held back his tears in front of the crowd. Slowly, the crowd began to clap in a show of support.

Elion froze. He couldn't believe what he was seeing. Was it the future or the past? How could he see into the other world? What was this place?

The soldier faded as the image disappeared and the panel grew foggy. Muted by distance he could hear the soulful howl of a wolf. Elion intently focused on the panel, but could see nothing.

Whimpering and then a shape appeared. Not clear like the soldier, but it was unmistakable. He knew it was *her*. She was clothed in dirty rags, her hair and face were matted with filth. She looked deathly thin and pale, lying in a muddy hole. She looked up, and her face filled the panel as she cried. Her crystal blue eyes hit Elion deep in the core of his spirit, and he knew this was why the King had sent him here.

"Kelly, I remember…I'm coming like I promised…" he whispered out loud.

A door opened behind Kelly, and a dark figure approached her. Elion jumped in shock. The jailor jerked hard on the chain attached to a steel link around Kelly's neck. She screamed as she flew backwards lost in the darkness. The panel faded back to static foggy blue as Elion collapsed to his knees holding his head in his hands. He wept from the depths of his pain only now entering his redeemed spirit.

"Kelly, my little Kelly…"

The sound of a foot scuffing on the stone startled Elion. He jumped up and turned around to see what or who had snuck in behind him.

A strong-looking, handsome, black man stood before him. Elion felt no fear, but rather sensed a bond of spirit and an instant trust.

"My name's Belak," the man said. "The King sent me to find one that would be my brother, and I've found you."

"My name's Elion. The King sent me to remember things forgotten."

"What is this place?" Belak asked.

"I don't know exactly, but I gather that evil has corrupted this chamber and this place," Elion said as he glanced back to the panel.

"Who was that girl? Did you know her?" Belak had a low, masculine voice.

Elion looked away. "She's my daughter; she's lost."

"That thing can see the lost? How did you do it?" Belak's face lit up.

"I just put my hand on the round glass there." He pointed to the ball on top of the short column.

Belak jumped toward it and put his hand on the ball. The screen immediately brightened slightly and turned a foggy yellow. The sound of metal clanking on metal could be heard as an image appeared. Black metal bars surrounded a square box-cage, hanging on a chain. Many cages hung close together and clanged against each other. They hung randomly from huge limbs on lifeless trees in the middle of a vast wasteland. Heat danced in the distance of the desolate landscape.

Long, thin fingers with scuffed and bloodied knuckles grasped the bars. Brown skin covered the boney arm, as the figure inside the cage slowly sat up. A woman's face appeared with hollow eyes, circled by swollen, dark rings. Elion could see the young, black woman clearly now, and he noticed Belak stood perfectly still. His lower lip quivered as his eyes filled with tears. Suddenly, a giant bird, much like a crow, landed on the cage next to the woman with a loud, '*kawh*'. It rudely stuck its head through the bars and the woman frantically slapped her hands at it as the panel returned to fog.

Belak's cheeks were smeared with tears. "What are you doing here? Why did the King send me to find you? Who are you? What is this place?"

"More importantly, who is she?" Elion asked, nodding his head toward the panel.

"She's my wife!" Belak screamed. "And she shouldn't be there!"

Elion smiled, "Exactly! I know how you feel, this is why we've met, my brother," Elion said as he walked over to Belak and gave him a sturdy embrace. "Let's get out of here and go somewhere so we can talk." The panel went black and returned the room to darkness.

The two men climbed up the stairway and into the light of the amphitheatre. They didn't speak as they walked through the ancient ruins. The air was thick and difficult to breathe, adding to the somber mood, bordering on despair.

"I can't wait to get out of this place," Elion finally said. "Nothing lives here, other than bad memories."

"She didn't look well," Belak muttered to himself. "I wonder how long she's been in that cage."

"More importantly, how much longer will she be in that cage?"

"What are you talking about?" Belak asked with a frown on his face.

They reached the crest of the valley and turned for one last look. Nothing could be said. The beautiful, ancient ruins stood as white bones on a forgotten prairie, displaying death past and warning of death to come.

Belak finally turned away from the valley and said, "Let's go."

Elion followed him down the path. They could see a thin tendril of smoke backed up against a huge rock face. They hiked toward the smoke, assuming it was the guardians' camp.

※

The camp came into view, revealing the two angels sitting side by side on a rock ledge. The angels waved them over.

Elion and Belak stumbled into camp, weary from the

experience.

"Are you alright?" Karial asked. "You look like you've been on a mission."

The two angels looked at each other with knowing smiles, because only angels went on missions, and they shared the common knowledge of how tiring they were.

The angel with Karial stood and bowed slightly to Elion. "My lord, I am the angel Jaxim, and I am guardian to Belak. I am very pleased to meet you." Karial followed suit with a bow of his own to Belak.

"Yes, my lord, I am the angel Karial, guardian to Elion. I trust that your journeys into The Forgotten City were fruitful?"

"Is that coffee?" Elion pointed to the pot by the fire.

"Not like you've ever had," Karial answered. "But yes, it tastes very much like coffee; it contains the life of Heaven rather than caffeine. Would you like some, my lord?"

"Yes, please."

"And you as well, my lord Belak?"

"Yes, thank you."

Karial produced two silver cups and filled them each with the amber, coffee-like fluid.

"Tell us of your adventure into The Forgotten City," Jaxim coaxed. "We're honored to have been a part of this journey to the mountains. We were talking, and neither of us can remember the King sending any other redeemed here. You two might be the first since the battle."

The two men paused for a moment and glanced uneasily at one another.

"If you would rather not share," Karial said, looking somewhat dejected. "We understand; we're angels and you may not want to-"

"No, it's not that," Elion said. "I trust you explicitly, Karial."

"Thank you, sir." Karial smiled.

"You were right when you said it was beautiful. It has beauty even in destruction. There's a room, a hidden room, under the amphitheatre," Elion spoke slowly while occasionally sipping his drink and gazing at the roaring fire.

The angels looked nervously at one another in anticipation.

"It was an old cavern with a panel of sorts and seats about, and a round stone that glowed to the touch. Images would appear; images of things present, and past, maybe things future, but definitely things from realms outside of Heaven. One image was of the world before, and two were of the other place, I think."

"It's a window room," Jaxim said as he looked at Karial.

Karial nodded in agreement. "Did you see a door? It would've been a big black door of onyx? There should've been a door as well?"

Elion looked at Belak, and Belak shook his head 'no'.

"No we didn't see any doors. What do you mean when you say it's a window room?" Elion asked.

"Have you ever heard of the 'Windows of Heaven'?" Jaxim began to explain, his sharp teeth showing with certain words.

"I've heard of them," Belak said. "But I thought they were all closed since the war."

"They are closed," Jaxim said. "This one just got forgotten, along with the entire city. The King knew you'd find it and each other."

"What are the windows for?" Belak asked.

"They were used for seeing into the other realms. Only the King and the Archangels were ever allowed to see them. No guardian ever saw one," Karial said as he glanced over at Jaxim. "I heard talk that they were closed now because the enemy could tell when they were being used, or maybe he could even see into Heaven with them. What did you see?"

"I do not wish to talk about what I saw." Belak stood and looked away from the fire.

"I saw my grandson of the flesh," Elion said as he looked across the fire at his guardian. "He was older than when I left, and it was a scene that I'll hold dear in my heart. I wish that was what the Lord had for me to remember, but it's not. It all came back to me. I remembered my plan."

"What plan?" Belak snapped his attention back to the group.

The hair stood up on the back of Elion's neck as he thought of it. He first looked left and then right and moved a little closer to the fire. Noises from night creatures could be heard in the forest. The two angels and Belak sat waiting for Elion to go on as if they somehow knew that what he would say would change everything, forever.

"I had a crazy plan before I left the World of Flesh."

Karial nodded his agreement because he knew of old Joe's plans.

"The King sent me here for two reasons: for forgotten things to be remembered and to find the mission appointed to me. Well, I remember and I know my mission." Elion stopped and took a sip of his Heavenly coffee.

"That is good coffee! What do you call it?" Elion said, stalling.

"It's Karaka, new guy, now go on!" Jaxim said with urgency in his voice.

Elion exhaled and shook his head from side to side in disbelief as to what he was about to share publicly.

"I know my daughter of the flesh is in hell because of me. She killed herself because of my failure as a father. I was the strongest warrior that there could be, but I left her unprotected. My ex-wife had men around and things happened to her, things that left her lost, hopeless, and with no way out. None of it should've happened. She went to hell because of me. She left me her suicide note written in her Bible. Her death brought me here, because I read the Bible and believed it after that. I'm here because of what she did. I should be in hell for the death and destruction I paid out on every form of humanity, but the Lord forgave me of my sin. I know He would forgive her of hers, but she never got the chance to ask for forgiveness."

Belak sat staring incredulously as Elion told his story.

"The plan the King wanted me to remember was this, her death was not just so that I could be brought to this place of most amazing wonders. There's more. I promised Kelly I'd come for her, and I will. I don't know how, but I know that I'm going to hell and getting her out. I'll not find peace in the Kingdom with her in that place. If I'm lost in the attempt, the Lord's will be done, but I'm going to hell, and I'm going to find her, I promise you that," Elion's voice grew in volume and confidence as he spoke.

"I'm going with you," Belak said as he stood.

The guardians stared at Belak in disbelief. If Elion's plan was not crazy enough, the fact that Belak would make a decision to go along left the angels puzzled.

"That's why I'm here, my brother," Belak said as he looked Elion directly in the eyes. "This is why the King sent me to the mountains, to find you. The woman you saw in the panel was my wife. We lived just before the American Civil War, slaves on a plantation. Our master was a good and decent man, compared to most of the slave owners that I knew of. McCabe was his name, and his wife got each slave cabin a Bible. Weren't too many of us could read, but we got enough of it to know about the Lord. That little faith was all we had. I was married - as married as a slave can be anyway. We'd jumped the broom, my wife was Marie. Our master grew old, and his son was filled with malice. He viewed us slaves as livestock, and he did as he willed. The old man looked the other way, even when it became obvious what was going on. He began to visit our cabin at night. He'd make me wait outside, and when he was done he'd smile at me as he left. We cried out to God to take us out of that place, but it became too much for Marie. She began to have thoughts of suicide. She told me she'd rather be dead than to birth a baby from that evil son. I begged her not to talk like that, but it was of no use. Finally, it became too much. Marie slit her wrists and bled to death in our cabin.

"I hated everyone," Belak continued. "Even God and Marie, and I took it out on young McCabe. I waited for him that night, and when he came into our cabin I shut the door and beat him to death. I ran that night, and got away. I made it North and found some good people who took me in. They were Christians, and over a couple years they loved me enough that the anger went away, and I forgave and received my forgiveness. Then the Civil War broke out and I joined a black regiment. I took a ball right through the forehead in the first battle. I've been here ever since. My Marie haunts me; she should be here as much as me. If I'd been the one being raped, I might've done the same as her and be lost. I've been dreaming of her while I'm awake, she's calling my name - my old name, John."

No one said a word. Stories from the last world were taken very seriously amongst the angels.

"The King said I'd find my brother here," Belak continued. "It's obvious that our Father orders these steps. Our stories are too similar. I'll follow you into hell, and whatever end that finds us. I've found the brother that the King promised, and I've found my Captain. I'm at your service."

Neither of the angels said anything. Both stared at the two men as if they were talking the only language they did not know.

"First of all," Jaxim said as he finally broke the silence. "You can't just decide, 'Oh, I'm going to go to hell' and then go there. You'll have to get the King's approval, and this sort of thing has never even been heard or thought of. Even if you could go, we cannot go there with you. Hell is full of fallen angels every bit as strong as us." He waved his hand between himself and Karial. "Only they are wholly evil. No human, redeemed or not, could fight one alone, and like I said, you'd leave your guardians behind. If we passed into that world, we'd be lost to evil and become a servant to death, a soldier in the fallen army against the King."

"We mean no disrespect, my lord," Karial said softly. "But that's never been done. I don't know if it can or should be done. I don't know what would happen to a redeemed human who entered hell. How do you plan to get in? It's heavily guarded, not to mention the chasm. There's a prophecy that at the end of the age all will be raised and judged by their deeds. Most angels and redeemed humanity in the Kingdom are waiting for that day to be reunited with those lost whom they loved. You will wait, too."

"That may be true, but I know the King will grant this mission, I know it." Elion had never been more certain of his plan than at that moment. "He has ordered the steps to ignite the mission within me. I trust in His wisdom. I'm blessed that my desires will fill some aim of His."

"Do you have any idea how guarded and dangerous that place is?" Jaxim asked, his voice becoming louder.

"I'm sure it's guarded." Elion smiled a wry, mischievous smile. "Guards have never stopped me before. I'm going. Wisdom or not, the King has planted this in me on purpose; this isn't just my crazy idea, its part of the plan of the King. I'll speak with Him when we return to the White City. I submit to His authority in all ways. If this is His will, then He will aid our preparations." Elion looked around the fire and nodded a smile of kinship to Belak.

"Anything I can do to help you to prepare for the battle, I'm your servant," Karial said with a shake of his head.

"My friend Karial is right; I'm yours my lord, Belak," Jaxim spoke in a begrudging manner.

Elion lay down on his blanket and looked up at the light show. "At first light, we leave for the White City." He spoke in a whisper, excitement mounting inside him.

༄

When the light rolled back the dark, the two angels and the two men marched toward the White City. They started out at a quick pace, and Elion pushed so hard that even the angels marveled at his stamina. With his new vision, he'd found an inner strength that drove him onward. After traveling a great distance, plains of rolling hills mixed with gentle woods surrounded the trail that led to the White City. They paused and caught their breath on a small bluff that overlooked a fantastic valley. The valley below them was alive with life and abundance, and a sparkling diamond of light twinkled on the horizon promising to be the White City of the King. The valley looked like every vision of paradise any human ever had.

"Are you so anxious to leave this place?" Jaxim broke the awe-inspired silence.

"If I could will it," Elion said. "I'd be where she is now, if it meant she could take my place right here with you."

Jaxim smiled and stared at Elion in admiration.

"I've been thinking of many things," Karial said. "One thing

I remember from long ago, as I prepared to go on a mission, I ran into two guardians getting ready to go in as well, they were talking about their humans. One guardian, I think his name was Stepel, explained to me he was really going to be in for a fight. His human was hearing the death lies, and was getting close to suicide. He said he'd heard that the lost humanity who followed that path all ended up in one place."

"Of course, hell," Belak said, practically spitting out the vile word.

"No - well yes - of course hell, but there are certain ones that were written in the Lamb's book, souls claimed by the King, but somehow coerced by evil into killing themselves and turning away."

"What are you saying?" Elion asked.

"Stepel said they were lost, but their name didn't disappear from the book, like it does for the others who reject the King outright. Also, the enemy keeps them stored in a special place, as dear treasures, all of them that should be here. They are stolen from their rightful place here, which makes them different from the others who commit the unforgivable sin or are evildoers. The dragon buries all these precious ones together deep inside his borders because they are a prize to him. He believes that in taking those who should be here, he has claimed a victory."

"It would be a fine thing, indeed, if that were true," Elion said, as his mission became more of a reality with each breath he took. "Storing them together like that will make it easier for us to find our ladies; they may be together."

"He said that they were together, but *especially* deep within the evil realm," Jaxim added with a snarly smile.

"If they're together it'll help us," Belak smiled. "No matter where they are."

Elion stood up, focusing his keen eyes on a herd of animals moving as one fluid object across the valley below. "It's a herd of the Vandilons. Look! We must hurry!" He leapt down the dirt path with a shout. The angels and Belak followed closely behind.

The Vandilons moved quickly, pausing to drink from a sweet-water pond, surrounded by willow trees swaying in the wind.

Elion entered the stand of willows, his eyes scanning about for the Vandilons. At first, nothing, but then he saw their sleek bodies standing, heads down in drink.

"Vandilons! Vandilons! I'm Elion!"

Their heads snapped to attention as if in one coerced motion. The most striking animal approached Elion and lowered his head to bow.

The magnificent creature raised his head. "Yes, my lord, how may I serve you? I am the Vandilon, Tarsus."

"Great Vandilon Tarsus, are you of a different line than Cass?"

"No, Cass is my brother. He leads the Eastern bands and I lead the Western. You know him?" Tarsus queried.

"Yes, and he's a different sort than you," Elion said.

Tarsus and his followers laughed like horses by whinnying and shaking their heads. "Cass is somewhat gruff. We've spoken to him about it, but he's set in his ways. I apologize if he offended you, my lord."

"No, no offense, nothing like that."

"What may I do for you, sir?" Tarsus continued.

Elion gestured at his friends and said, "We must get to the White City as soon as possible. Dare we ask for your speed to carry us?"

Tarsus snorted his nostrils. "We were not headed that direction. Walking, you'll be there soon enough."

"My sir, Tarsus," Karial said. "These two redeemed have been in The Forgotten City and discovered an active window. We must inform the King. We must get to the White City immediately."

All of the Vandilons pricked their ears up. "You saw a window in The Forgotten City?" Tarsus asked.

Both Elion and Belak nodded yes.

"Climb aboard and hang on with your knees!" Tarsus cried. "To the White City!" Four Vandilons stepped forward and knelt to be boarded.

"No one rides Tarsus or Cass, other than the King, they have a special purpose," Karial explained.

Once everyone was aboard, the entire group of Vandilons exploded off their haunches, and ran like the wind. The great steeds with no riders burst out in front and kicked up their heels for the sheer pleasure of it. The landscape seemed to slip by like rain, and it thrilled Elion. His laughter echoed off the mountains as they passed trees, animals, streams, birds, rivers, hills, ponds; nothing slowed the Vandilons. The heat from the creatures' bodies was hot on the riders as their mighty muscles flexed beneath taut skin, their gait as smooth as air gliding over wings.

With every step they drew nearer to the sparkling gem, the White City. The fragrances of the landscape became more scented and pleasing. The air itself tasted sweet, and life flowed from every breath. Music from an unknown source filled the air with sweet melody.

Many people and creatures bustled in and out of the gates. The Vandilons approached a different gate than any Elion had seen before and its majesty didn't disappoint. Redeemed and angel alike stood in disbelief at the sight of the mighty Vandilons being ridden. Tarsus stopped just short of the city entrance, and the gatekeeper approached from his post. The angel placed his fist on his chest and Tarsus dropped his head a little to bestow respect. The gatekeeper nodded, giving an unspoken authorization for them to enter. They walked under a mosaic of precious stones with the pearl in the center. Hooves clicked on cobbled streets as they passed under the named gate.

The Vandilons wound their way through the city and took their passengers directly to the home of Elion, kneeling to aid in the dismount.

"I'll see you soon," Elion said as he grasped Belak's hand. "Enjoy your loved ones for a time, because we'll be going to a place where memories of love will be precious."

"I'll enjoy them, Cap'n, and I'll go with you before the King?"

Elion smiled and looked Belak in the eye. "Yes, you shall accompany me before our King, my brother, and He'll bless our mission, as it is His."

Belak smiled back without saying anything else. Elion then turned to the spectacular Vandilons.

"Thank you for carrying us, Tarsus," Elion said.

"Thank you, my lord, it has been a pleasure," Tarsus said, bowing to Elion. The Vandilons followed Tarsus back the way they'd come, shiny, black hooves clicking on the golden cobblestone.

"Jaxim and I will go to Michael," Karial said.

"Rest," Jaxim added. "We'll come for you when it's time to see the King."

Everyone went their separate ways and Elion walked into his home. Many people greeted him with genuine salutations and love. Elion waited on his veranda, sipping a glass of red wine, the sea pounding the shore. Elion had never enjoyed wine when he was Joe, but now it was soothing and rejuvenating to his spirit. He fell into the big lounge chair, and closed his eyes feeling closeness to the King.

There came a knock on the door. Elion opened it to find his mother, Lovilia. "Mother, come in. Come and sit with me. I'll tell you of the mountains."

She smiled, reached around his neck, and hugged him with a sweet smile. Elion told her about his trip to the mountains, of The Forgotten City and the window, the remembering, and the mission that now lay before him.

Lovilia looked out to the sea. "This mission, you're not serious about it, are you? You're really going to go to the King with it?"

"I'm absolutely serious. This mission has been appointed to me. The King will allow it. I'm quite sure He has willed it. I'll find her, and I'll bring her here." Amber waves caressed the shore, as a salted drop landed on Lovilia's cheek.

"You remind me of your stubbornness, there was no talking you out of joining in the wars. It was what you lived for; it's not the same here."

"That is why she's not here. Fighting in foolish wars for what? Leaving the true enemy an open door to my daughter, he stole her from the Kingdom. She paid the price for me and it's my turn to pay her back. I promised her I'd come."

"My son, I'll pray for your safe return, but my prayers will not reach the place you go. You've been here such a short time. There's much more you could've learned if you waited, before this mission. Maybe you should wait? Knowledge will be your friend. The wars you were in before, yes, but this will be like nothing you've ever seen."

"Exactly, this is like nothing anyone has ever seen. No redeemed has gone into hell willingly with intent. The evil one will be caught unaware; he'll not see it coming."

"No one will see it at all! No one goes where you're going and comes back!" Lovilia all but screamed.

"Some will see; fallen angels, demons, and devils; I'll be the last thing they ever see!" Elion said.

"Such bravado is pride and arrogance. You're not ready for a mission like this." Lovilia looked at her son and then back out at the beauty of the White City.

Elion held his tongue. He remained thoughtful of Lovilia's words.

"She was the most beautiful baby I ever saw. What a sweet little girl." Elion knew she was talking about her granddaughter, baby Kelly.

Elion frowned. "I was in Korea when she was born. I was always somewhere else. Never where I should have been."

"Now you're exactly where you're meant to be." Lovilia smiled and put her hand on his arm,

"Do you remember the Bible you gave her?" he asked.

"Yes." Lovilia answered.

"She wrote me her suicide note in it," Elion informed her.

Lovilia turned a shade whiter.

Suddenly, there was a loud knock on the door. It opened and the angel, Karial, walked in as if he lived there. "Elion, where are you?"

"We're out here."

Karial stepped out on the veranda, and when he saw Lovilia he said, "My lady, it's good to see you again. I didn't know you were here."

"I was just leaving, as it seems everyone around here is," Lovilia said as she stood and gave Elion a kiss on the forehead as she passed.

After she left, Karial snarled his teeth and looked squarely at Elion. "We spoke with Michael. Are you ready to meet with the King, right now?"

"Yes, I'm ready." Elion jumped to attention.

S.C. Sherman

IX
Plan of Attack

    Karial led the way, ducking into narrow alleys and switching back. The ancient beauty of the place was timeless as they weaved through passages and tunnels lined with doors and flowered window ledges. Belak and Jaxim fell in stride without missing a step. Belak smiled at Elion and hit him on the shoulder. "We go to the King."
    "Yes, and hell," Elion said, smiling with crazy eyes.
    The two angels kept a steady pace, too fast for conversation. Their path began ascending until suddenly they emerged on a veranda overlooking the grand courtyard before the Throne Room. Each one stared and held their breath for a moment. The sight of the courtyard was as breathtaking as the very first time. A throng of people dressed in the flowing white garb of new arrivals, followed alongside angels, dazed looks upon their faces.
    "The King will meet you in the garden under the tree," Karial said, turning his eyes to the giant tree in the center of the crystal-clear flowing river.
    "Just us or are you coming too?" Elion asked.
    "Just you," the angel answered. "We'll do what the Lord King asks of us in service to you. He'll speak with the two of you, go now."
    "Thank you, we'll see you after," Elion said. Belak and Elion traversed down a stone walk that angled toward the tree.
    "Do you know what you'll say to Him?" Belak asked.
    "No, I don't know the words exactly. I'm a little nerv…"

Elion instinctively put his hand over his stomach to protect himself and stopped speaking mid-sentence.

"What?" Belak asked a look of confusion on his face.

"When I was new, I was nervous and Karial, well, he has an interesting way of dealing with nerves."

"Angels are interesting in many ways." Belak shrugged as they continued on.

Elion couldn't help but smile and noticed Belak did too. Something about this place just made him smile. The aromas and sights, the love and joy, produced an almost intoxicating experience.

The men reached the edge of the stream flowing swiftly around the base of the Tree of Life. The crystalline water magnified the colors of the streambed, which appeared to be gravel of precious stones sparkling with a rainbow of color. Colors so vivid, that memory of color from the old world, paled in comparison.

"Dazzling, is it not?" a warm voice permeated their very souls.

They turned in unison to discover the Lord of Lords standing before them. Both men instinctively fell to their knees and averted their eyes downward out of fear and respect.

"Yes, my Lord, dazzling indeed," Elion answered.

"Dust compared to you," The Lord said. "Mankind is my finest creation. That is why my enemy hates you so. You may rise. Let us walk in the garden."

Belak and Elion both stood and followed as commanded; one on either side of the King. They found they were in a distinct garden somehow isolated from the goings on of the courtyard. Golden pavers sparkled with peat moss and grass grown up between them. Hanging vines and plants arrayed the walls around them with flowers galore, enhancing the air with sweet nectar.

"Your journeys to the mountains were fruitful?" The King spoke slowly.

"Yes my Lord, as for me, many things forgotten were remembered, and my mission was reborn within me," Elion answered the King, knowing in some way the King already knew the answers and what had happened, but He rather enjoyed the exercise of communicating with them about it.

"Yes, indeed, continue," The Lord said and nodded.

"My Lord, beneath the amphitheatre of The Forgotten City there was a room with a window to the other worlds. I saw my grandson and my daughter. As you know, my plans in the fleshly realm were to find a way to free her from the clutches of the enemy. I now realize the foolishness of that plan without coming here first; I would be lost in hell, just as she is. In your mercy, I was brought here, and for that I thank you Lord. You sent me to the mountains to remember my plan and it now burns within my heart like fire. I come to ask for your blessing and direction on the mission you've put in my heart. I want to invade hell, as the redeemed everlasting being that I now understand us to be."

"And you, my son Belak, what do you say?"

"My Lord, you sent me to find my brother, and I found Elion. We are kindred spirits from our loss in the previous life. I'm humbly before you, fully united with Elion in my desire to invade hell and search for the one that was lost. This desire has been in my heart for a time, and I thank you for bringing this to pass."

No one spoke for a moment.

"Do you not have questions of your Lord regarding the place you seek to go and this mission before you?" He asked the men.

"My Lord, I thank you for the opportunity." Elion looked sideways at Belak.

The Lord smiled at Elion. "You know of the prophecy that all the dead from the place of darkness will be raised and judged according to their works? And that hell will be no more?"

"Yes, we know of it," Elion said.

"That knowledge does not sway you in your desire to seek entrance to the grounds of the enemy. Why do you not merely wait, and all will be returned to you when the new order is established?"

"My Lord, I know that I'll not find peace in this place knowing she is there. My failure put her there. I will go now with your permission and your will," Elion said.

"Your failure, ah, I see, not her free will choice to do what she did? You have been forgiven of all sin. Do you not forgive yourself?"

"Yes, my Lord, I've been forgiven, and I do forgive myself, but something in my heart aches for her. My failure to cover her allowed open doors to evil and great abuses and misery were upon her, clouding her judgment. I know in my heart that she loved you, Lord, and she was stolen from us by the enemy. She asked for forgiveness in her note," Elion pleaded.

"Do you think it wrong that she was not brought here?"

"Lord, I do not question you in anything, and I do not claim to understand the workings that you know. I do not fully comprehend how this evil will be eliminated. What I do understand is that evil exists in all the places not within the Kingdom of Heaven. My own hands committed great evil, but in your mercy you forgave me, and I know that you'd forgive her if she'd only get the chance to ask for your forgiveness. I know that by her hand she threw her life into the hands of the enemy. I also know that you love her still as I do. I intend to give her that chance to ask for your mercy. I will bring her before you."

"Very well, my son," The King said. "Why do you think I would allow your mission?"

"My Lord," Belak spoke up. "I don't claim to know your mind. I can only surmise you would allow it because you love all creation who loves you, as a husband loves his bride. Despite the fact the enemy has made captives of them, you love them still. You love to see the captives set free."

"Yes, my son," The Lord said. "What if I told you within the dark world where the false lord reigns, you will not feel my presence, and I will not be with you? Your guardians and the Spirit as well cannot enter that place, you will be utterly alone. What if I told you I could not guarantee the outcome of your mission, and if you are lost, you will stay forever lost until the prophecy is fulfilled?"

"Lord, I know there are great evils in that place, and that is exactly why I must go. Even a chance to get her out is enough for me to risk it all - even my place here," Elion answered from his heart.

"You know I am the Alpha and the Omega, I know the beginning and the end. Do you not question why I would allow you to go if I know you are to be lost? Or why I withhold that knowledge from you?"

"My Lord, you know my life was filled with wars in the other world. I was involved in many missions where we sent men into enemy territory with full knowledge that they had little chance of success, and probable chances of death. We did so anyway, knowing that there was an outside chance of success, and either success or failure would serve the same end to the war as a whole. We wanted the enemy to know we were willing to take the fight to them, to show them they didn't intimidate us and that they wouldn't keep us from our goal. Also, it was designed to strike fear into their hearts. If I'm to be lost on this mission, then it is your will. I trust that loss will serve some end, greater than my daughter and me," Elion said.

The Lord turned to Belak. "And you, Belak, do you believe as your brother?"

"Yes, my Lord," Belak answered. "I was a slave most of my life on earth and I've known the freedom of this place. My wife was stolen from us as well by the evil works of the enemy. If I can present her to you, she will beg for mercy and forgiveness and pledge her love and loyalty to you. If you grant us this, I know there is no guarantee, and I freely say yes, Lord, I will go. I will pay whatever ransom must be paid for her."

The great King gently wept as a tear slipped from his eye. He raised his head and said, "It is well with you, my sons. The heart of the warrior beats within you, and that is what the enemy doesn't understand about human-kind. He fears other angels as he once was, but he doesn't know the power within the creation of mankind. I weep for your lost loves, as they are lost loves to me as well. You are both correct in that they were stolen from us. Their names are still contained within the Lamb's book waiting upon their arrival here. I will grant you your mission, as I knew this day would come. Your party will be numbered seven, as five more will join you at the Hall of the Angels. Go with your guardians to Michael, and he will prepare you as best he can for battle in the realm of darkness. He has both loved and lost the great dragon. After you are ready, we will feast in honor of your great valor, and prepare the way for you."

"Thank you, Lord," Elion and Belak said in unison.

There was an opening in the hedge before them, and they stepped forward to discover the banks of the stream. They stood just under the Tree of Life, as if they hadn't walked at all. The Lord was gone from them.

"Well, Cap'n," Belak said. "We will go to hell."

"Hell and back?" Elion raised an eyebrow.

"Yes, Cap'n, to hell and back again."

※

The guardians sat on a veranda above the courtyard, waiting patiently and at the sight of the men they stood, "What did the King say?" Karial asked.

"He said to take us to Michael and have him prepare us for battle," Elion replied with a smile. Karial's eyes lit up as did Jaxim's, and they clacked their teeth at each other with hawkish hoots.

"Yes, my lord, prepare for battle. That is why *we* were created!" Karial spoke loudly drawing some nervous looks from newcomers.

Jaxim immediately led off, striding out at a brisk clip. It was not far and they found themselves before another architectural wonder. The columns were hewn as giant swords that held open the sharpened beak of a marble eagle. In order to enter the building they stepped through the open mouth of the eagle. Jaxim and Karial marched directly on into a great hall.

At the entrance stood two angels, each holding a shiny, black lance that looked like razor tipped glass. They stood on either side of the door guarding its entrance. Jaxim let out what sounded like the cry of a hawk. Both of the guards answered with a cry of their own, as if the cry had actually been a word.

Once inside the building, they entered a magnificent hall topped with a glass dome with an open air hole in the center of it, allowing both the sweet light and smells of Heaven to rain down. The room descended downward shaped as the dome above, only inverted like a mirror image, or a bowl. The bowl stair stepped much like the amphitheatre of The Forgotten City. Many angels lounged about as if this were a social club full of friends, laughing and relaxing together.

"Welcome to the Hall of Angels," Karial said.

"Michael will be in the War Room. Shall we? He is expecting you." Jaxim motioned for them to continue on.

The angels sidled along the circular walkway that wrapped itself around the sunken bowl and the glass dome. Many dark hallways led off to unknown locations. Each entrance was accented with carvings of eagles in flight, their claws displayed.

The two guardians led the men into a short, well-lit hallway and then into a large room with a chocolate-colored marble table in the center. The room and the table were round and lit from above. Along the wall stood large carvings, busts of angels and unknown creatures as well as several birds of prey. Each figure sat directly under a skylight, illuminating the artistic beauty. Seated around the table were three obviously larger angels. When they noticed that the four had entered, the large angels stood. Both Jaxim and Karial immediately stopped and bowed their heads slightly in honor.

"Come guardians, bring the redeemed men," the largest of the three angels said, his voice strong and commanding. He was huge in both size and breadth, and Elion knew he must be important. "We've been expecting you."

"Yes commander," Karial said. "We are here with the redeemed elect."

The one Karial referred to as commander had hair-feathers black as night, and they sparkled as if laced with diamonds. His face was hawkish, and his piercing eyes were a hollow blue - like that of an Alaskan Husky dog. The other two angels were brown in color and looked like great lions next to their dark leader.

"I am Michael," the dark one finally said. "I am an archangel of the Lord Almighty. These others are archangels as well, Gabriel and Tanael. We're at your service, my lords. The King has instructed that we prepare you for battle against the one who has fallen."

Karial and Jaxim stood without saying a word.

The angel Tanael, who stood to the right of Michael, motioned to the seats around the table and said, "Please sit. The others will be joining us soon."

"We are honored to be serving you," the angel Gabriel on the left of Michael said. "As you may well know, we look with hope to the destruction of our enemy who has brought reproach to all angels."

"However, we're less than hopeful that you'll find success on this mission; it may be a harbinger of the things to come," Michael added gravely. "The dragon will be destroyed only when the prophecy is fulfilled."

"Why less than hopeful?" Elion asked.

Michael looked directly into Elion's eyes for a moment. Elion did not look away. Slowly Michael extended razor sharp claws from the tips of his fingers on his right hand like a great feline. He slowly rolled the claws from little finger to thumb allowing only the sharp tips to touch the surface of the table. With each finger there came a distinct clicking sound. Most of Michael's hair seemed to bristle as well, and his lips pulled back exposing a mouthful of deadly teeth.

"Look at me," he snapped. "Do you think you could defeat me in battle?"

"I'm sure there is a way to defeat you," Elion said boldly.

Michael laughed out loud and smiled at Elion. "The Lord King be praised. He has sent me the young lions that see the possible!"

Just then five guardian class angels entered the room from the back. The five angels accompanied five redeemed humanity. The five guardians bowed their heads in honor of Michael as they entered.

"This is our squad, Cap'n," Belak whispered to Elion. They looked them over as the newcomers walked toward the table.

"Guardians come," Michael spoke out strongly. "Bring the redeemed and let us plan an attack."

The angels and men came forward, and Michael introduced himself again, and then invited all to sit. There were ten chairs around the table. The seven redeemed and the three archangels sat while the seven guardians stood behind their respective assignment.

"As I'd begun to explain to your Captain, my lord Elion, the mission before you is nothing short of daunting, with little chance of success," Michael spoke with a smile that showed glistening white teeth. "The Lord has ordered me to prepare you for battle, and I will do just that. The outcome of the battle is in your hands. I know you don't know one another as of yet, but let me assure you, you're now brothers. I'd like to see introductions and the story of why the Lord has brought you to this moment. Captain Elion, you shall begin, followed by your second, lord Belak."

Elion nodded and stood. "I am Elion. I've been brought to this place because the Lord willed it. In the world we left behind, I was a warrior, a killer even. I was good at it, but nothing more. My absence and failure in my life in every other area left my daughter unprotected and abused. Her pain was severe, and she was misled by our enemy to kill herself, which she did. I've promised her I'd come for her, wherever she may be.

"She's held captive in the realm of darkness. The Lord has seen fit to use my promise to fulfill His purpose and has granted me the leave to mount an invasion of hell. Our objective will be to secretly, if possible, locate and remove several specific lost souls. One being my daughter; her name was Kelly. I make no promises to you about what will happen from the moment we cross over, but I promise this. We will enter hell with the strength of the Lord in our hearts and attempt the greatest rescue mission ever conceived by the mind of a mortal man! The King of Kings is glorified by whatever happens thereafter!"

Elion sat down and Belak stood.

"I was a slave in the old world. A slave to other men, I knew great abuse and evil. My master's son was an enemy of the Lord. He abused my wife, who was also a slave, repeatedly. She lost hope and turned to the shadows, and she sought death. She killed herself. Out of her pain she sought to flee the dark world, only to be enslaved in a worse place. I've found freedom here in the Kingdom, and I'll do what I can to bring her here. She will know the peace that is our free gift. I intend to go with my brother, Cap'n Elion, and take back what the enemy has stolen from me and from the Lord!"

Belak sat and turned to the man to his left. He was thin and wiry looking with a soft face and a pleasant demeanor. He stood and spoke slowly with a proper, old English accent. "My name is Haydn. In the former world I lived in the late 1500's in England. Life was simple and we worked hard. My name then was Samuel Ward. I'd a grand wife, Mary, and two children we loved very much. A sickness spread throughout the countryside. It came to us, and both of our children were stricken with it. Within a week they both died."

"The ensuing melancholy that engulfed my wife was dark indeed, I'd no comfort for her as I cried out to God myself. She became increasingly distant while I found peace from the Lord and the promise that I'd see the children again in Heaven. I loved her very much and did my capital best to comfort her, but to no avail. She ended her own life and left me behind in loneliness and loss. I cried out to God and felt blessed when the sickness came on me. My will to live was gone, and I died shortly thereafter."

"I yearned to enter the Kingdom of Heaven. Every minute of time that has passed here in the Kingdom with my children of the flesh has been bittersweet water without Mary here. My guardian, Tirzal, came to me with this offer from the King, and I knew immediately that it was my duty and honor to go after her. I'm ready to join this group and seek the one that I've lost, and return her to her rightful place here in the Kingdom."

Everyone listened patiently to the stories of pain and loss, each similar yet different.

The next to the left was a fireplug of a man. He was not tall, but looked muscular like a wrestler. His brown hair flowed back from a steep forehead and his face was rugged and strong. His neatly trimmed mustache concealed his top lip, and his eyes danced under his wrinkled brow as he spoke.

"I am Terel. I was once the man named Gene Yoder. My guardian, Cypress, informed me of this meeting as well. I immediately knew I would join you. The King has known of the desire of my heart even better than I. In my time in the world, I owned several businesses, a restaurant, a construction company, and a few other things. I'd no real earthly father; well, he was of no good to me anyway. I became my own man and was always getting into fights to prove myself. I drank a lot, did a lot of drugs and worked constantly. I was as tough as they come."

"Then my wife's father took me under his wing, so to speak. He showed me a father's love. This was the only man that I ever looked up to, the only man that I ever loved. He owned a real estate company and was very successful. Then he became involved in something he shouldn't have. I never knew all the details, but it appeared that he was going to lose everything and maybe go bankrupt. He hung himself in his office, leaving a note declaring his love for his daughters and his sons-in-law, asking God to have mercy on his soul."

"I didn't see it coming and I was thrown, to say the least. Through the shock of it, the Lord entered my life immediately and I was different. Practically overnight I quit all the drugs and violence and changed radically who I was. Later, we heard rumors that organized crime was involved in my father-in-law's death. He may have been threatened that if he didn't take care of himself, the rest of the family would suffer. Perhaps it was not even a suicide at all. He may have done it to protect the rest of us. I don't know for sure. I've yearned to see him again and been haunted by the lack of his presence here in the Kingdom as I know he loved the Lord. His name was Mac Abraham. We called him Abe. I go willingly into the unknown with you to find him and bring him here. May the King bless our mission!" He pounded his fist on the table as he finished speaking. Terel sat down with fire in his eyes. Elion could feel his strength and was glad to have him aboard.

Questions filled Elion's mind as his eyes fell upon the next person to the left.

She was small. Her long, fine, black hair was beautiful and shiny against her milky white Asian skin. She stood and began to speak in Chinese. "During my life in China, daughters were of little consequence. My mother had a daughter. She was told to kill it or get rid of it. She'd been secretly involved in the underground movement and had changed her life, a servant of the Lamb. She knew she could not kill her baby, nor could she keep it, so she wrapped her baby in a red blanket and left her in a basket on the steps of an orphanage. She quietly sneaked away and thought she saw someone go to the basket. She went by the next morning on her way to work in the fields only to discover to her horror the basket still sitting where she'd left it. She approached it and looked inside; her baby was dead from the exposure. It got very cool at night in the village. In her hysteria she put a knife into her belly and was lost to the darkness. I am Bethalia. I was her daughter in the basket. I will go with you and bring her to the Kingdom." After she finished and sat down, the room remained silent.

"I don't mean to question," Belak said. "You apparently have a strong spirit, but we may need more than that where we are heading. You're very small and-"

"You don't know anything!" Bethalia jumped to her feet and spoke sharply in Chinese, glaring at Belak and pointing her finger at him. "I'm stronger than you. I've been here in the Kingdom longer than you. I know things you do not! I will go-"

"Enough!" Michael interrupted her with his hand raised and a stern voice.

Bethalia looked angry, crossing her arms as she sat back down continuing to glare at Belak.

"I guarantee the strongest of you, will not be strong enough to defeat the fallen one or any of his demons by sheer brute. Do you doubt the wisdom of the King? Did He not select you as His chosen? Do you doubt the King?" Michael asked.

No one answered.

"Do you?" Michael bellowed.

"No!" everyone shouted in unison.

The great angel relaxed his countenance. "The King has appointed you to this mission for His reasoning. Are there not millions of redeemed humanity here in the Kingdom, all who have lost loved ones on the other side? Your stories are noteworthy, but are they more noteworthy than any other? If you doubt each other, you doubt the King, and that will not be suffered by me! I know the fruit of that design all too well," Michael snapped.

"Forgive me, Bethalia," Belak said. He nodded his head

to her and continued, "Michael is right. I don't doubt the King's decision for you to come and you have my allegiance. If we find your mother, we'll bring her home to the Kingdom."

"My brother, Belak," Bethalia said. "You can count on me to help you find your wife."

"Let us continue and hear the other two," Michael said.

The next man stood. He was tall and clean-cut with a sharp face and sandy hair. "My name is Tarkio. In the other world I was Jeffrey Collins." He half turned toward his guardian. "This is my friend, Madrigal. In the other world, as you may have guessed, I too, had a wife who committed suicide. It seems to be our common denominator. She grew up a Christian, and for many years I mocked her. I was an airline pilot and was away a lot. Many women came to me and I had many affairs. After years of this behavior, my wife, brokenhearted and rejected, took her life. I became an alcoholic, lost my job and eventually most everything."

"Our daughter never gave up on me, though. She prayed for me every day for many years. Finally, those prayers were answered, and in utter loss I turned to the Lord for help. It changed me. Shortly after that I had a sudden heart attack and died. Even in my forgiveness in this Kingdom of splendor, I can still see my wife's lovely face, so sad, so defeated, and lost. Her name was Michele. She was weak and lost because of me, alone. She deserved so much more than me. Everyone else from her family is here. I will accompany you if you'll have me, and I pray I find her and bring her to the White City, where I'll beg her forgiveness."

The last man stood. "My name is Jubal. When I was a man on earth I was James Randolph Kensington. I lived through the turn of the twentieth century in New York. My family had great wealth. My sister's name was Laura and we were very close. My father forced her to marry a man whom she did not love. He was full of malice and she paid dearly for it. She became pregnant, and was so excited at the new life that God had given her amidst the bad situation. Then near the time of delivery, her drunken husband beat her to a pulp one night. The baby died within her, and she was forced to deliver its lifeless body. The son she never knew is here. Her depression and grief overwhelmed her to the point of no return. She ended her life, as you may have guessed."

"Surprisingly, less than two months later, I was dead as well, even though I'd been very healthy. I'd recently purchased one of the new horseless carriages. I got it up to top speed and then stopped it right into a tree. I've been here ever since. I've told no one, but I've secretly dreamed of an attack like this. I'll go with you as well. The King's will be done. I'll do what I can to set my sister free."

Michael looked around the table at the would-be warriors before him.

"I've trained a legion of angels for battle, but never any humanity - redeemed or otherwise. The King has sent you to me to prepare you as best we can for the unknown you'll face. First, we'll fit you all with the armor of God. We will then tell you all that we've learned about the realm of darkness. In some ways we know a great deal, and in other ways we know nothing. Any questions, right now?" He paused for a moment and after no one said anything he continued. "First things first, you must know I'll be leading the mission to the drop off point. Your guardians will carry you to that point, and then we'll leave you and return to the Kingdom. You'll enter hell alone. We'll station lookouts that will never leave their posts until you've come back through."

Tarkio raised his hand slightly and Michael nodded for him to speak.

"What do you mean by 'carry us to the drop off point'?"

"It's a long journey from here to there - as far as you can get from the Kingdom. We'll cross the great chasm, and we will be flying."

Tarkio smiled. He seemed very excited at the prospect of flying again.

"Be assured if you make it out we'll be there waiting, to pick you up and return you home," Michael continued. "However, while you're within the realm of darkness, you'll be alone. Alone like never before. Not even alone like you may have felt on earth; really alone - no angels, no Spirit of the Lord, no Lamb, no presence of the King, only pure evil. No angel can enter hell without being transformed into a demon in the army of darkness. The legions of that realm are twisted angels, our lost brothers. The fallen star cannot create anything, he can only twist, manipulate, and degrade things that were once something else, something wonderful. Now that you know that you're going utterly alone, you may want to rethink your decision. If you thought going was a good idea because your guardian would be along to protect you, you were wrong. Now is the time to walk out. The King will replace you. There will be no judgment in it. Anyone? Do it now."

Elion looked around the table at the others, but no one got up to leave. Slowly, smiles and nods spread from face to face as they realized everyone else was committing. Committing their all, the bond between the members of the squad was already growing.

"Just a little more, and then we'll go to the armory. No humanity has ever entered hell other than those who have fallen from the World of Flesh. We've speculated that a redeemed human wouldn't be transformed by the Lake of Fire into anything else, due to the fact that you've already been received here and sealed into the Lamb's book. Therefore, it is promised that you'll not see the second death, since you've already been born flesh, died, and been reborn as redeemed humanity here in the Kingdom. You're an everlasting, spiritual being as are we all; however, redeemed humanity is different from everything else. Those differences are what we think will protect you from transforming into a demon or a devil upon entrance into the dark realm. That's probably the best news." Michael smiled, baring his mouthful of teeth while looking over at Gabriel.

"The worst news is this. We know the realm of the fallen is much closer to the World of Flesh than we are here in the Kingdom. That may make many things more 'flesh-like' than they are here. Some of us believe that you'll be vulnerable to injury and not healed, and that if you're killed there…well, uh. . . you'll probably rise again, but into a bondage that you'll never escape. If killed there, you'll never return to the Kingdom of Heaven." Michael paused and the silence was as sickening as the looks on the faces of the seven.

"Never?" Elion asked.

"We don't know for sure," Michael answered. "You probably would return when the prophecy is fulfilled, and all the dead rise to be judged by their works, but you've already been judged. Would you come again? We don't know, perhaps if someone else came after you. But if this mission fails, I would not hold out much of a hope of that."

Elion exhaled loudly. "The sickness in my stomach at the thought of never being reunited with the King is overwhelming," Elion said. "But it is how my Kelly has lived every day since she died. I will go after her, I will turn away from this."

Everyone nodded in agreement that they too would go.

Then Terel, the fierce looking one, asked, "Why do you think we've all shared the loss of suicide? It's universal among us."

Gabriel stood. "It is believed that the enemy both despises and relishes in the lost humanity like your loved ones." His voice was sweet and as soothing to the spirit as gentle music. "People of the Lamb, who take their own life, forfeit their chance of immediate redemption, but they're not erased from the book. The best description is that they're kidnapped - much like a good child on earth. He loves his parents; they say 'don't talk to strangers.' Then one day a stranger comes, and he lies, coerces, and manipulates that child to get into the car with him. Then the child is gone. Lost into a world of pain for their own bad choice that they knew better not to do, but they're never gone from the parent's heart. They would take the child back any day they could get them away from the lying one. Your mission is about bringing a few of them home. This mission is only the beginning."

"Do you think we'll do it? Bring them back?" Haydn asked with his thick English accent.

Gabriel looked sideways at Michael and growled a bit. "I do not presume to know the plan of the King for this mission. I know you are sent by Him, and that gives you all the chance any of us could ask for."

The room fell silent as the gravity of the mission sank in.

"The enemy also takes no chances with these stolen ones," Gabriel continued. "He doesn't send them on missions to the World of Flesh as he does the other lost, for fear that we would steal them back somehow because we have a legal claim to them. The fallen one keeps them together in a camp for the 'lost redeemed'. That's good because we know where the camp is, roughly anyway, and bad, because the camp you seek is very near the center of all evil. It's rumored to be deep within the bounds of Hades, the decrepit capital city of the lost realm. The Lamb has the keys, and its gates are forever open, but you'll not be going in the front gates of hell. That will be when we invade on a full scale. No, you're sneaking in the back door." Gabriel paused.

Elion gave a wry smile and said, "We're testing the waters, so to speak. We'll determine many things with this mission. How effective are redeemed humanity in hell? Can we get around undetected and perhaps actually make it back? Not to mention if we actually set our captives free? I'm sure we'll discover how easily a demon can be subdued and killed or how easily a redeemed human can be lost. Any of this will strike fear into satan's twisted heart! I can hardly wait. I was created for this purpose! I can feel it!"

"Let us break from discussing the kingdom of darkness," the archangel Tanael said. "Michael, shall we fit their armor?"

"Yes. They'll definitely need it." Michael stood and stepped back from the table. His size was impressive and imposing as he turned.

"Follow us." Tanael stood and led the group down another hallway opening at the back of the room. The hall was narrow at first, and then it widened out immensely. The room expanded until it seemed to have no bounds.

"Guardians," Tanael said. "Take our guests to their armor."

S.C. SHERMAN

X
The Armor of God

Hollow footsteps echoed through eternity. Elion followed Karial up a flight of metal stairs taking them two at a time. He trotted down a suspended catwalk continuing for quite a distance. The angel quickly glanced at the number and letter sequence near the top of the racks. Row after row of racks containing a special armor filled the room as far as Elion could see.

"Ah, here we are," Karial said with a hawkish growl. He dodged in between two racks.

"This is the armor of God?" Elion asked.

"Of course," Karial said as he kept walking. "Who else's would it be?"

"What's it for?" Elion asked, somehow sensing the silliness of the question.

"For the war, of course." Karial smiled.

"I thought that was only a metaphor in the Bible about being strong. I didn't think there really was *actual* 'armor'." Elion said incredulously.

Karial stopped in front of a particular suit of armor. "That's what most humans think. They like the fantasy that war doesn't mean war, or it's not real. It's easier to swallow as a metaphor for those that need soft food, but the meaning is literal - armor. Armor is used for protection during the battle against evil. The armor of God exists for one reason alone, war. No metaphor." Karial couldn't contain himself and hissed a bit, his hair-feathers bristling.

Elion looked at the suit Karial was admiring, and he noticed etched on the hanger, *Elion*.

"These are specific to specific people? Not just small, medium or large?"

"Of course, you want it to fit. Do you not?"

"Yes, custom fit would be grand. I shouldn't even be surprised." Elion smiled.

The charcoal grey suit was not really shiny, but not dull either. The material had been trimmed with a simple, yet elegant style. The armor appeared functional, yet regal due to the ornamentation. The cloth portions were of a royal burgundy fabric trimmed with a shiny gold thread.

"Let's get you fitted for battle my friend," Karial said.

Elion smiled at that.

Karial took a slinky chain mail material and raised it over Elion's head. Elion put his head through and found that it slid down over his body perfectly. Once on, it felt as if it was not even there. It shimmered in the light like a fragile, breakable crystal.

"This is a lightweight mail tougher than the toughest ever created on earth. It goes underneath the armor. The mail alone should protect you from many of the lesser demons or the evil animals you may encounter."

Next Karial strapped the breastplate around Elion. After buckling it in place, a warm, comforting, sensation enveloped Elion.

"I feel something," Elion said.

"Righteousness; it will give you an inner peace and strength," Karial said with a smile.

"Now buckle that about your waist." He handed Elion a belt. The clasp was made of a matte metallic substance that felt like strength. The belt itself was a dark, leathery type of material with metal diamonds inlaid. It clasped into place with a perfect fit. An ancient symbol was embossed into the metal made up of three oval-shaped leaves with the points touching in the center; the shape was one continuous line.

"It's a triquetrous," Karial said as if reading his mind. "Three parts as one, the belt of truth."

Karial handed Elion the next item. A pair of shoes, Elion sat and strapped them on. They felt like shoes made for running, but looked as if they were a military marching boot. They also fit perfectly, and Elion could tell they would not require breaking in.

"You're fitted with readiness. If you must walk, these are the only way to go into battle. They'll never wear out and your feet will not tire." He handed another item to Elion.

"Your helmet, my lord."

Elion pulled it on his head. It was nothing like he'd ever experienced. It fit well even without a strap and felt comfortable all the way around. It was the kind of helmet that made you stand a little straighter once you had it on.

"That helmet may one day save your head. Now last but not least." The angel held one item in each hand. In his left he held a shield. It was a shield of the same dense yet lightweight material as the breastplate. The shield was intricately engraved and inlaid with a silver silhouette of a warlord lion. Karial handed it to Elion.

"What material is this?"

The angel smiled, "Its dragon scale, hewn from the very creature you seek to destroy. The only substance ever created that his claw cannot penetrate, and his fiery darts harmlessly deflect. Praise our King!"

Elion reached his left arm through the circular strap that came to rest on his forearm as his hand gripped the second strap. He pulled the shield to his chest. The feel of it filled him with courage.

"I've never used one of these. We had flak jackets and bulletproof vests."

Karial's eyes widened. "Ever used one of these?"

The icy sound of a razor-sharp sword being pulled from the confines of its scabbard chilled the room. It flashed like lightning and dazzled the eye. The blade had strange writing on it. Elion couldn't read it even though he had knowledge of every language present in the World of Flesh. These letters were much older than that. The angel handed the hilt of the sword to Elion while letting the blade rest in his open palms.

"Your sword, my lord."

Elion slid his hand into the grip to find it was molded to his hand in such detail that his fingerprints were actually melded into the metal. Upon examination it looked as if Elion had grasped the metal while it was being forged to make it uniquely his.

Something within Elion ignited as he held the sword in his hand, and he felt the strength and guidance of the King flowing through his every fiber.

"The feeling is from the Spirit of the Lord which you now grasp," Karial spoke as if he knew what Elion had been thinking.

"I've never used one in battle, but I get the idea." Elion finally pulled his eyes from the sword and looked at Karial. "Why don't we get some rocket launchers, hand grenades? A machine gun would be nice, especially since we're so inadequate against the evil one. That would be more like what I am used to."

A grin came over Karial's face. "Sorry, only the armor of God will pass through the Lake of Fire. All of those things were created by flesh. This armor was created here. Where you're going, you're better off with just this. Either way, it's all you get."

"We'll have to do our best." Elion put the sword away and clipped it to his belt.

"You'll do marvelously," the angel said as he leaned in closer. "You're a hero of humanity. You're special because of your desire and your relentless pursuit of someone other than yourself. It's an honor to serve you, my lord Elion, even if only for a little while longer." The angel clipped a smaller dagger type knife to the back of Elion's belt.

"Karial, it's been an honor to get to know you. I feel as though we've been friends for ages, and I might just surprise you. I might make it back, you know." Elion put a hand on Karial's strong shoulder.

"Thank you, my lord. I've been with you since you were created. You just never knew me until you came here. I'll miss you when you're in the darkness. I wish I could go with you, and protect you."

"I'll miss you as well, my friend," Elion said.

With a sigh Karial looked away. "Let's go find the others.

You're armed."

They found the rest of the group making their way back to the war room. Elion noticed everyone walked smoothly, as if they'd always worn armor. It was surprising; there was no awkwardness at all, perfect.

"Nice armor," Elion joked to the others. "Where did you find it?"

"It was just lying around," Jubal said with a smile. "Fits alright I guess."

Elion drew his sword, and in one motion swung it over his head and downward with force toward Belak's helmet covered head. Belak struggled to draw his sword in defense, when suddenly Elion's blade stopped sharply with a loud clang.

Everyone looked with surprise as they saw that Bethalia had drawn her dagger and stopped Elion's strike with her blade. She'd stopped Elion's blade inches above Belak's head. Everyone began to laugh.

"Praise the wisdom of our King for choosing Bethalia for our mission!" Belak said. "I knew it from the first moment I saw her."

The squad chuckled as they followed the guardians.

The armor was something to behold. No two were exactly alike in appearance. Each suit fit the wearer perfectly and enhanced everything about them, giving them a strong look of readiness.

Michael and the other archangels approached. "We've some more to share with you," Michael said. "And then you'll go to your homes and wait for the call that it's time." He motioned back to the stone table. Everyone found their seat while the guardians positioned themselves behind.

"I'm surprised I can sit in this stuff and it feels so comfortable," Terel said.

"You must remember to stay together at all times," Michael said, ignoring Terel's comment. "Do not split up. Keep your armor on at all times. As far as I'm concerned, you should leave the sheath for your sword here. Never, never, let it out of your hand, I'm not kidding. You'll be weaker, slower, and much less merciless than your enemy. Your only hope is to stay concealed as long as possible. I must warn you that the enemy does have spies. Especially within hell, he's always watching, but he's not our King. He does not know all things. He can be in but one place at one time. He may discover your identity by whatever means, and that will jeopardize the identity of whom you seek."

"We, the angels, are stepping everything up to high alert status. We're going to be running diversionary missions on earth. These maneuvers will distract the enemy, and he'll be forced to focus on us. He's always watching for our attack, and we will let him think its coming. Earth's where he's committed. With every birth, the King creates a new life. That spiritual and everlasting being is an opportunity to the enemy. That's where he battles. The more lives he can steal, the more guardians he transforms into demons. It's as simple as that, and it's his only hope. He'll not be watching for an attack from within. That's your biggest asset, surprise. Once that's gone, run. If you can't run, then stand, knowing that you've done all that you can, so stand your ground with the full armor of God. You'll have a chance. Fight with the Spirit of the King within you, and whatever happens, you'll have no shame."

"You didn't say we'll have victory," Bethalia stated.

"Victory, what is victory? Victory for you or victory for the war? If you don't know the entire story, how would you know? Always, be alert. Always, always. The city of Hades is on a large, circular plain surrounded on all sides by mountains. The city sits directly in the center, as if at the bottom of a giant hole. The closer you get to Hades, the darker it will become. Everything you'll find there is the sick manipulation of one who wants to recreate Heaven for himself. Therefore, most things are reversed from here."

"Beware, there are many doors. You may see demons going in or out. These are doors to the World of Flesh. People from earth open most of them as an invitation for the enemy to enter their lives. Demons are forever going back and forth. Whatever you do, don't go through a door. You'd most likely disappear from all knowledge. You'd be neither here nor there. Never do it, never. Understand?"

"Yes," everyone agreed.

"Also, we've had great experience with demons. They're weak remnants of what they were. They're deceitful in all ways. They lie to each other or to anyone. All beings in hell are corrupt and will seek any self-serving angle. They're all rebellious and coveting. If you capture one, he'll tell you everything with very little torture, but little of it's trustworthy. The truth is always buried within their lies. Most of them claim to be the devil himself, though they're only his minions. They'll betray their own kind or you in a blink. Never, never trust any of them, or what they tell you. Never!" Michael paused and looked at Gabriel for a moment, as if they were speaking without any sound.

"We'll take you as far as we can," Gabriel said. "We don't know exactly how far that will be. Somewhere short of the Lake of Fire to be sure. The storms around the lake have worsened, and we cannot fly directly over it anymore. We'll drop you, and then you must find the Lake and plunge yourselves into it. This will seem rather suicidal, ironically. However, you're not flesh, you're redeemed humanity. Death has lost its sting. Do not ever forget that. You can survive the time in the water no matter how deep, and you'll come out on the other side in hell. When in doubt on which way to go, go downhill. Hades is at the lowest point in all realms, the depths of depth."

"Do not dally. Once you've found your targets, make your way back to the Lake of Fire and get them through. Don't attempt to rescue any others beyond those who you're sent after. It will be death to you, I assure you. Your lost loves will fear the lake, but assure them they'll survive it as they've already experienced the first death as well, and the Kingdom of Heaven is on the other side. That should be enough to convince any of them."

"Lord Elion is your Captain," Tanael said. "Follow his leadership and trust that the King selected him. His second is Commander Belak. If Elion should fall, Belak will be the lead. From there if Belak should fall, you may select your own leader or it may not matter by then."

"Now go say your farewells, we'll come for you when it's time," Michael said. "The King will see you again before you go.

He has planned a feast in your honor. We will go and begin the diversions on earth. May the strength of our King be with you!" Michael stood as did the others and he dismissed everyone.

The archangels left through a side door of the room. The seven and their guardians walked out of the Hall of Angels silently, each in their own thoughts. Once outside, the bright, joyful light of the White City surrounded them, but their thoughts were of dark and evil places.

"We must return inside and help prepare the way for you," Karial told them. "We'll come for you when it's time." The guardians walked back into the Hall of Angels, leaving the newly formed group alone for the first time on the steps.

"I look forward to our mission," Elion said as he turned to the group. "I'm honored to have you with me. Long live the Kingdom of Heaven. I'll see you all soon." He ambled down the steps toward his home, alone.

As Elion walked, he thought of his daughter Kelly and the few happy memories he had of her when she was young before he lost her. The sweet smell of baking bread impressed itself upon Elion's senses, and he admired a lovely bakery with a café and chairs. He found a chair and sat watching the people walk by. A young lady brought a basket full of an assortment of fresh, warm breads. She also left a plate with several different spreads and a little butter knife. A clay glass, full of a sweet smelling red wine, sat sparkling like champagne on the table as well. As the bubbles popped, sparkles glittered up into the air for an inch or so before disappearing.

The woman left her special breads in a basket covered with a cloth napkin and disappeared as if she knew Elion wanted to be alone. He picked a soft bun and applied some honey butter. It melted in his mouth making it almost unnecessary to chew. As he lifted the cup to his lips, he envisioned Kelly sitting across from him. A smile came to his face as he tried to imagine her at her perfect age sitting here smiling at him. They would share a roll and laugh. He wondered what name the King would have for her. His smile disappeared as the sadness of missing her slowly eased back into his emotions. A gentle tear dropped on his cheek as he said out loud, "Soon, very soon, baby girl."

He stood and moseyed down the busy street, so consumed by his own thoughts that he felt rather alone, as if he was deaf amongst the noise of the crowd. Elion quietly entered the front gate of his mansion and made his way to his room, settling in his favorite spot on the balcony. The waves repeated their never-ending cadence upon the golden sands of Heaven.

"The calm before the storm," he said to himself.

There came a knock at the door. He opened it to find his parents. "Please come in."

"We heard you were back," Elberon said.

"I was just sitting out here listening to the sea. Would you join me?" Elion asked.

Lovilia grabbed his forearm and they walked back out on the balcony, shoulder to shoulder.

Elberon followed. "How did it go? What did the King say?" They both sat patiently waiting for the story to come.

"The King has given His blessing upon the mission," Elion began. "He also added several others. We've a team of seven, we're leaving soon. We went to the Hall of Angels and discussed the mission with Michael and the others."

Lovilia looked surprised. "You were in the Hall of Angels… with Michael?"

"Yes, with Michael and Gabriel and Tanael. I'm leading the team into hell with Belak, Haydn, Terel, Bethalia, Tarkio, and Jubal, I'm their Captain. We all have someone we are going after."

"I've never heard of anyone going into the Hall of the Angels before," Elberon said. "This is something big. This could be part of the fulfillment of the prophecy. This could be the beginning of the last war."

Elion looked out to sea. "I don't want any more wars. I just want to bring Kelly home. Here. That's all I want. I'll help the team bring theirs back too."

Lovilia looked sad. "As you long for Kelly, the King longs for all who are lost. I will miss you, Elion. You'll do what you must.

I love you, my son. Make sure you come back to me. Understand?"

"I love you too, Mother. If I don't come back, then pray that the prophecy is starting."

They spent the night just talking and sharing in each other's sweetness. After they left, Elion spent the next period of time on his balcony, reading and thinking.

News of the mission spread like wildfire across the Kingdom. Much to Elion's dismay, not everyone thought of it as a great idea. Everywhere in the White City the mission was the source of conversation.

As Elion wandered through the great hall of the mansion, an old member of Elion's line came to him in the grand entrance and asked, "What do you think you're doing?"

"What do you mean, sir?" Elion answered.

The man stared directly at Elion, not hiding his disagreement. "What're you doing? Are you a troublemaker? Even here in this place?"

"No, sir, I mean no trouble. The mission is to invade hell and to retrieve my Kelly, and nothing more. The King has approved."

"You should just leave well enough alone. Probably all you'll do is make the enemy angry!"

"Forgive me, but the enemy cannot hate you any more than he already does."

"Going in there like that, what's the point? All you're going to do is rile him up. The enemy has left us alone for ages, and now you're going to stir things up. Why do you want to do that?" the man snapped, obviously quite bothered.

"I don't want to stir him up at all. I just want my Kelly back, and I'm sorry but the enemy hasn't left the World of Flesh alone. It's tough there, maybe you've forgotten," Elion said.

The man scowled and waved a dismissing hand at him as he walked away.

Elion shook his head in disbelief. A man who'd been reading a book by the fire approached Elion and said, "Don't listen to him. You're a hero. I lost someone…they're where you're going. If you get your daughter back or bring the prophecy nearer, you're a hero.

Don't you ever forget that! May the King bless your mission." The man returned to his seat and picked up his book.

Elion nodded his head in thanks and quickly ducked outside.

"A little sunshine and fresh air might do me well," he said.

Strolling along the quaint streets and experiencing the abundance of the Kingdom brought joy to his heart. Around every corner came a new sight to be seen, a new smell, or a new taste. Suddenly, he found himself trudging along the golden, cobbled street along the sea. Without a care, he took off his shoes and stepped into the sand. As it wiggled between his toes the sand sparkled as if made of gold and silver flake. Elion continued right into the sea up to his thighs. The water was surprisingly warm and the scent salty sweet. He closed his eyes and tilted his head back to the sky.

"Thank you, Lord. Thank you for creating this place. Thank you for my life. Thank you for letting me go after her."

A big wave smacked against his legs and splashed up onto his shirt soaking him entirely. With a laugh and smile, he wiped the sweet waters from his face and ran his fingers through his wet hair. As he turned back to the beach, the force of the receding water pushed firmly against his legs. He lay in the sun on a small jut of rocks. Dolphins jumped and sea birds dived for fish. Two men walking on the path behind the rock ledges spoke loud enough Elion overheard their conversation as they passed by.

"I can't believe the King has allowed it," one man said.

"Isn't this Elion content to be in the White City? Everyone has loved ones who are not here. You don't see us trying to cause a war," the other man agreed.

"I don't understand how he could be here and not be completely fulfilled."

"I just don't understand it. The ones that are lost will get a second chance in the prophecy. They made their choices in the flesh life. Why does he think he is so special to go after his, uh, daughter I think I heard it was, now?"

"Exactly, and the facts are facts. If she's there and not here, she chose it. She was not loyal to the King."

Elion craned his head in an attempt get a look at the men. He saw the side of them and then their backsides as they disappeared down the path.

Elion shook his head. "Not backed by unanimous approval I see." He smiled and threw a small rock out into the approaching waves. The sound of the sea calmed him and sent a surge of reassurance through his spirit. Combined with the smell, it was intoxicating.

"My lord, it's time. I've come for you. Are you ready?" The now familiar voice of his good friend, Karial, said from behind.

Elion closed his eyes tightly for a moment and whispered to himself, "My girl, I'm coming. God give me the strength," then he said louder. "Yes. I'm ready. Let's go."

Elion dusted the sand from his feet and slipped his city shoes on. He put his hand on Karial's shoulder. "We must stop by my home to tell my mother and father goodbye and gather my armor."

Elion decided to put the armor on. No use in carrying it. He went to his mother and father's room. At the sight of Elion in his armor, Lovilia caught her breath and put her hand to her mouth.

"Already, it's time?" she asked.

Elion nodded. They both came and hugged him and gave him their blessing, showering their love down upon him.

When he pulled away, Elberon looked Elion in the eye and said, "I look for the day that Kelly will be here with us. I'm proud to have been a part of your life, my son. Praise the King and may your journey fulfill His will."

"Yes, Father. Thank you. I love you."

Lovilia wrapped her arms around Elion and wept onto his shoulder. "When you find her, tell her we all wait for her and we've not forgotten her."

Elion looked deeply into his mother's tearful eyes and nodded. "Goodbye Mother, I love you."

"I'll not say goodbye," she said as she smiled and placed her hand on his lips. "I love you, my son."

Without another word, he turned and walked out the door with Karial following close behind. He wiped his eyes on royal fabric. As they wound their way through the streets of the White

City, the sight of the armor caused everyone to pause and stare. Some looked away immediately, while others cheered.

"Bless you, my brother!"

"May God grant you victory!"

As they walked, a woman with red, bouncy hair and a sweet face stepped in front of Elion. She placed a strange multi-colored flower in his hand that was scented like lilacs.

"Thank you, my lady," Elion said.

"I have someone I love over there. This is the beginning. The realms will be united. May the King be with you."

Elion took her gift. "Thank you, my lady."

They left her behind and continued on toward the grand courtyard, pausing in awe at the sight of it.

With their sharp eyes they could see several of the others in their armor already down on the paths walking past the Tree of Life. Elion and Karial made their own way down into the sweet brightness, alive with exhilaration. New arrivals made their way to the steps of the Throne Room. They admired Elion in his armor and stared in wonder.

"If they knew where I was going, they'd really stare," Elion said to Karial.

"Yes, if they knew that, they would say, *I didn't think there would be crazy people in Heaven!*" Karial laughed and clasped his friend on the shoulder.

Belak and Jaxim waited for them at the entrance of the hall. When they reached the top, the two men hugged and slapped their hands roughly on the back of the other's armor.

"It's good to see you, my brother," Belak said.

"It's good indeed!" Elion agreed.

The others made their way up the steps; Elion and Belak waited patiently for the friends to join them. Suddenly the steps were empty other than the team. The seven and their guardians stood alone, but then as Elion and the others looked out over the courtyard, they discovered a great multitude of the redeemed humanity and angels. They silently filled the valley floor extending well past the tree. There came a clear beautiful sentinel, as from a horn. At the call, the multitude began to cheer and praise the King. The great doors behind the seven opened with the sound of stone on stone. A refreshing aroma filled their nostrils and a longing to enter rode the sound of the trumpets call. The seven and their guardians turned from the cheering crowd and entered the Throne Room of the King.

Once they passed by the great doors, they closed in behind them. The seven entered as one and found the room had been prepared for them. It was full of flowing tapestry bathed in light. Delicious smells and glorious sounds of Heaven permeated the atmosphere. The seven went and stood before the great throne. The King sat on his throne with the four and twenty kings in their thrones. The Lamb, who was the Son, stood as a man to the right of the Father. Sweet music filled the air as slight smiles of love were on the king's faces.

"Come." The Lamb motioned for the seven to approach the throne.

The seven redeemed approached humbly. They stopped and waited at the bottom of the steps to the throne.

The King stood. As He did, the room shook and the sound of thunder echoed through the hall, while lightning dazzled the glass sea that was the floor and ceiling.

"Come up, my children." The voice of the King pierced the room, even the thunder and lightning obeyed.

The seven proceeded up the steps as the King descended down toward them. When they came together the seven knelt on the stair before their King.

He looked slowly and deliberately at each of them. "Rise, my sons and daughters, you are well with me."

The words were sweet to the spirits of the seven, and they stood with a tingling sensation throughout their bodies.

The Lord returned to His throne. "Gift Bearers, bring the gifts for the seven."

From the back of the room, seven angels began walking forward in single file. The sound of their marching snapped loudly a defined cadence. The Gift Bearers were so similar in appearance Elion could find no differences from one to the next. They were the same class as guardians and their hair-feathers were white as snow. They appeared in white uniforms accented with black belts and a tight black sash across their chests.

The seven stood shoulder to shoulder in a row across the middle step up to the throne. They instinctively knew the order in which to stand: first Elion, then Belak, Bethalia, Terel, Haydn, Jubal, and Tarkio.

The first gift-bearing angel approached Elion. He stopped directly in front of him while the others waited on the floor. The angel removed a chain from around his neck and placed the chain around Elion's. As the weight of it settled around Elion's neck, he looked down to see a vial that was like the ones he'd seen before. It hung on a golden chain, and upon the chain hung a small glass vial surrounded by gold metal latched with a lid, so it could be separated and the contents poured out. Elion's vial appeared to be full of a crystal blue liquid.

"Elion," The Son of the Kings' voice rang out. "Your vial contains water from the river of life. It will provide sweet coolness and bathe your spirit. It will quench your thirst in the never-ending desert."

The next angel took two steps up and faced Belak. He nodded his head as he took off his chain and placed it around Belak's dark neck.

The Son spoke again, "Belak, your vial contains food from the Tree of Life. From it, you will feed the hungry, and it will sustain you in your weakness and famine."

The second angel returned to his position as the third approached Bethalia. The angel removed his chain and vial, placing the beautiful gold and glass around her dainty neck.

"Bethalia," The Son proclaimed. "Your vial contains the blood of the Lamb. From within woman is life. The blood of life will heal the wounded and raise the dead."

The fourth angel approached and placed his chain around the neck of Terel. His brow wrinkled as the vial fell around his neck. His contained an orange substance swirling like fire.

"Terel, your gift contains fire from the wrath of God. It is all consuming and will provide warmth and comfort to those who love Him and burn all who have turned."

The next white angel went up and placed his gift around Haydn's neck. The vial on the end of the gold chain sparkled with a dazzling light.

"Haydn, your gift contains the light of the morning star that is the Spirit of the Lord. It will be light to you in the darkness and will lead your steps."

The next angel approached and placed a vial that was tan and grainy as if filled with desert sand.

"Jubal, your vial will make what was wet, dry. With it the flood will be no more."

Then the last angel approached and placed his gift on the neck of Tarkio. His vial appeared to have lightning zigzagging from side-to-side within the glass.

"Tarkio," The Son called out. "Your gift is the sweet breath of Heaven. It will give you thunder, quake, and storm. These things will be your strength when all hope is lost."

The seven white gift bearers turned and marched away from the seven redeemed, leaving the Throne Room with their mission accomplished.

The King raised his arms. "Turn and receive my blessing."

The seven turned and faced their Lord.

"You are my beloved. You are chosen for such a time as this. Enter the darkness as one body. Use these gifts as needed in support of one another. My blessing be upon you in the face of the defiant one. May you find whom you seek and bring them home. My strength be with you, and always know that you are citizens of the Kingdom of Heaven. In you I am well pleased. Go now. Go with the angels and feast. Enjoy the sweet nectar of Heaven, and then go with my blessing. Go and make war on my enemies. I love you, my children."

Silence filled the hall as the kings stood looking with love upon the seven elect before the King. Then the music became louder and rejoicing filled the air. White doves flitted about the room, and the seven guardians approached the steps. The seven redeemed descended and proceeded back out of the Throne Room.

Elion and Karial led the group as they filed down the center of the magnificent room, shoulder to shoulder. A shower of white blossoms blew in the gentle breeze. The crowd had not yet dispersed, and they cheered and parted to make way for the seven and their guardians as they walked to the Hall of Angels. The closest ones peered in wonder at the redeemed in their armor walking in the boldness of the King.

Holy pride emanated forth as they marched in glory, strength, and power. Elion was humbled and honored, and as he walked, the Lord's Words echoed through his spirit. The vision of Kelly appeared in his mind's eye as the sounds of the crowd once again faded away, and he felt alone among the multitude.

"Thank you, my Lord," he whispered to himself.

Karial heard him and put his hand on Elion's shoulder for just a moment. Elion looked sideways at his friend as a single tear fell from his eye.

At the sight of it, Karial bellowed forth a roar like none Elion had ever heard. It was like the roar of a lion as well as a hawk. At the sound, the other guardians roared as well, casting an eerie feeling over the crowd as the angel's ancient battle cry issued forth.

The seven marched on and left the throng behind, as they entered the streets of the White City they found them quiet and empty. The steps were full as many angels waited in front of the Hall of Angels. They roared and cheered as the group walked through the grand entrance.

Once inside, a gray angel said, "The feast is in the war room. They're waiting for your arrival."

Karial nodded. The war room had been filled with tables and foods of all kinds. Angels of every class stood about in their battle gear, and with the arrival of the seven, they roared, hooted, and beat their hands against their chests.

After a time, Michael rose above the crowd and said, "Welcome, our redeemed seven. You're the first humanity to join us in our war feast. Soon you will join the ranks among us as warriors against the fallen one. I welcome you as willing servants of the King in the acts of war."

The crowd interrupted Michael intermittently with hoots and hollers. He waved his hand and waited for silence before continuing.

"Soon we depart for the Lake of Fire and the dark realm. Let us rejoice, valiant warriors. Eat and drink to your mission and the victory that is in the Lord of Lords, our King, the Most High. All praise and honor and glory be to Him that is and was and will always be."

Elion nudged Belak as they listened to the speech. He nodded to Belak to look at Michael's feet. They were conspicuously not on the floor.

Belak's eyes grew wide.

Elion smiled back with a wide grin.

Michael finished and settled back to his feet. The room filled with music, and a soft glow of light danced across the ceiling. The angels and the redeemed took whatever food and drink struck their fancy. The array was a splendor unto itself, complete with succulent steak and meats, main dishes, sushi and fish, and salads of every type, including fruits and vegetables, breads, pastries and desserts. Nothing had been left out or ignored. There were servant angels walking around filling cups with red wine while laughter filled the hall as story after story was shared. The angels never tired of telling stories of their great adventures for the lost. They seemed especially fond of stories of the earth where they'd vanquished some demon, and how the human they were protecting had seen the light and had some measure of victory.

Elion joined in with stories of his battles and foes conquered. The angels made both Elion and Belak tell and retell what they'd seen in The Forgotten City. Even with the heightened interest, the story of The Forgotten City left the angels feeling a sense of loss, as if better times had been behind. With a sigh, an angel slapped Elion on the shoulder.

"To your mission, may it be a beginning to things new!"

Then with a hearty drink a new story would begin, full of laughter and drama.

Every now and then, Elion would catch the eye of one the

others of the seven from across the room. They'd maintain eye contact for a moment and nod with a knowing smile as if to say, "Soon, soon all this will be a memory."

Time passed and the feast was ending. Small groups sat together talking quietly as the noise and music faded away.

The seven found themselves sitting together gathering their strength and talking about the old world. Just old stories of the flesh, things long gone, pretending like they didn't matter anymore. Then just as it began, it ended, as Michael and the others stomped up to them.

"It's time, my lords, we fly," Michael spoke with purpose and a fire glowing in his ice blue eyes. Without waiting for a reply, he turned and walked toward the open hall with the glass ceiling.

Elion immediately followed Michael, and the others joined as well.

"All is as we've instructed, there is nothing more we can say," Michael said. "Go with courage and do great deeds. We'll wait for your return. Rely upon each other and trust no one else. May the blessing of our King be upon you!"

Each guardian stepped up next to their respective human.

Karial leaned over and whispered to Elion, "It has been an honor, my lord. I pray that we meet again, here in the Kingdom."

"It has been my honor, I call you my friend." Elion smiled at his guardian.

With a shattering cry, Michael sprang forth and left the ground. He exploded upward with great speed like a fighter jet off of a carrier.

It had begun.

Karial reached his arms around Elion, and without a word they were off the ground with the same burst of speed, falling into formation with Michael. Elion looked to the side and saw all seven of the group followed in the shape of a 'v' like geese, with Michael in the lead position. They punched through the opening in the roof of the Hall of Angels and soared above the White City. In a flash, they were over green fields and plains with new arrivals and Vandilons appearing as dots on the surface. The forests and mountains came and went, and then more plains. After a time Elion forgot how far they'd traveled, as it was farther than he could comprehend with the speed at which they were traveling.

Suddenly, in the distance clouds began to build. At first they were white and fluffy and then they began to darken. As the darkness grew, great bolts of lightning shot from one cloud to the next, and the winds began to increase. The angels were adept at catching a current and wrapping around this cloud or that to increase their movements with ease. The storms increased and loud cracks of thunder began to accompany the bolts of lightning that weaved among the clouds.

Then it began to rain. Water pelted their bodies with a force that belied how fast they were moving. Wind swirled about as if they'd entered a giant hurricane. The force of it was awesome to behold, and it literally sucked the breath from Elion's lungs. He felt Karial grab on a little tighter so as to not lose his grip. The angels had lost the ability to maintain the 'v' and were now just trying to stay together. Suddenly, with the light from a lightning strike, Elion realized that they were close to the ground. The surface looked mountainous, covered in prickly brush and jagged rocks.

Michael headed down through an opening and they landed roughly on the ground. He turned and saw everyone had landed behind him. Michael leaned close and shouted to Elion.

"We can go no further! You're close. Keep to these bluffs and follow the ridge down. You should be directly above the lake. You will smell it! We'll wait for your return down by the water's edge. The storms won't be so bad there. May God bless you!" He grabbed Elion by the head, stared deeply into his eyes, and nodded a look of strength. Then he let go and was gone. Karial and the other guardians followed into the clouds without a word.

The group pulled in tight around Elion. He screamed into the wind and their faces. "We must walk until we find the Lake! Stay close to each other. I'll lead. Belak brings up the rear. Lose no one. Let's move out!"

Elion faced into the storm, following the natural ridgeline. They descended slightly, and struggled with the unstable ground of loose shale made slippery from the rain. Several times they fell and helped each other back to their feet, pressing onward. An awful smell filled their senses, even through the great storm. The stench was nasty and rank like rotten eggs, the unmistakably foul smell of burning sulfur. Elion knew this meant they were close to the Lake of Fire. They stumbled a little further and Elion brought them to a halt on a rock ledge. Occasional lightning strikes allowed Elion to see a wide-open area with steam rising up from it.

Elion motioned to Belak to come close and look. "I think it's the Lake of Fire, but I can't see it for sure through the storm and the smoke. What do you think?"

Belak strained his eyes and waited for another lightning strike. He leaned close to Elion. "That has to be it. The smell and the smoke, do you think we're above it from this point?" he asked.

"Yes, I think so." Elion nodded affirmatively.

Belak smiled and with his eyes wide he yelled, "Then I guess this is it, Cap'n! After you!"

Elion huddled the group in close. When the lightning flashed again, he could see the faces of his friends. He smiled as he felt a bond of kinship toward them. Elion squinted his eyes against the rain and wind.

"This is it," he yelled. "The Lake of Fire is just ahead. I'll jump first. Follow me in. Once on the other side, don't leave the shore until we have everyone accounted for."

Everyone nodded their agreement.

"I'll see you all in hell!" he hollered with a crazy smile on his face.

With that as his final words, Elion stood erect against a lightning backdrop. He ran full speed off the rock ledge. His feet continued running after the ground was behind and his body fell toward the evil-smelling, fuming darkness. He couldn't look to see if the others were following. It didn't matter if they were.

Elion held his breath against the foul smelling fumes and hit the water hard. The impact knocked the wind from his chest and he was under with a choke. He gasped only to have his mouth fill with sick tasting water. The awful pond was dark and hot, like a bathtub of crude oil. In a panic, he struggled to swim to the surface to grab a breath, but he couldn't tell which way was up and the once lightweight armor was sinking him like a rock. He slid down further and further into the abyss of darkness, choking on the black-water, eyes wide and arms flailing. Hopelessness enveloped his thoughts, and somewhere in the deep, he lost consciousness.

PART III
THE REALM OF HELL

S.C. SHERMAN

XI
The Lake of Fire

    Elion flailed through the surface and gasped for air. Wild-eyed, he stood in waist deep slime. He waded to shore and crawled up a muddy bank collapsing to his hands and knees. His body violently heaved attempting to remove the vile mix from his lungs and stomach. The excrement that spewed from his mouth was a brackish, black substance much like a newborn baby's first bowel movement. Waves of gut twisting spasms left a pile of the black scum beneath him. He wiped the back of his hand across his mouth; the vomiting had passed. Elion fell over to his back in the mud regaining his breath and his senses.
    A yellow light cast eerie shadows around the rugged and rocky terrain. Elion's head snapped to the left as he heard coughing through the fog or steam, or whatever it was coming from the lake. He struggled to his feet and stumbled toward the sound. The air smelled awful, but the taste in his mouth was worse. He pressed on until he discovered Terel struggling to his feet with the black vomit dripping from his chin.
    "Terel!" Elion yelled. Terel turned and waived his acknowledgement, while Belak and Jubal emerged from the smoky abyss behind him.
    "You guys alright?" Elion asked.
    "Whew! What a ride! That puke was the worst part," Terel said, his eyes scanning as far the intermittent smoke would allow. "So this is hell, huh? It reminds me of Nevada."

"We have to find the others," Belak said. "They've got to be through by now."

"Let's head that way," Elion said, motioning toward the direction from which Belak had come. He led off with the other two following. They hadn't gone far when they found Tarkio and Bethalia, both looking a little shaken.

"You alright?" Elion asked them.

"Yes, Captain," Bethalia said in English.

Tarkio nodded his agreement and asked, "Where's Haydn? He was right with me when we hit the water."

"We gotta find him," Elion said. "Now let's move." He struck out again with the rest following along behind. They skirted the edge of the disgusting sulfur lake, enduring the stench for a solid half-mile. The ground was rough; covered in black rocks and mixed with rotten creeks and little hills. A scrubby type of brush with long thorns and a few gnarled trees were the only sign of vegetation. Suddenly, Haydn staggered from the fog.

He smiled enthusiastically when he saw the group. "I'm glad to see you gents. Hell is rather rank and I didn't like the idea of being alone here. This place smells dreadful and tastes worse!"

"Yeah, it's bad. See anything?" Elion asked.

"No, but I'm sure I heard a wolf howling," Haydn answered with his English accent just audible over the wind.

Elion drew his dagger. The others did the same. "Let's get away from this nasty lake and see what we can see." He didn't wait for agreement and led off with the decisive authority of a true leader. The troop of seven followed along without resentment or question. Belak brought up the rear.

Marching was difficult on the loose rocks as they continued up a modest slope. Finally, the angle leveled out on a large plateau which made for easier hiking. The fog dissipated and Elion realized they'd left the Lake of Fire behind. The air tasted bad and burned the nostrils to breathe, much like a sauna sometimes does. Even so, the dead air was not as rancid as the air near the lake. A large wall of steam rose up behind them, concealing the fiery lake. An occasional howl cut through the fog like a knife delivering prickly fear to the invaders.

Elion focused away from the lake. A series of rugged, treeless mountains, covered in nasty brush that looked like black sagebrush, extended away from them. The queer light grew somewhat brighter as the lake disappeared, but never exceeded a dusky sort of experience.

Elion pointed to the expanse, "A wasteland, very bleak."

He eased down the most obvious path to the wasteland below, mountains in the distance. He frowned as thoughts and feelings assaulted his sensibilities. Elion's emotions followed a path he'd not felt in a long time. Feelings not found in the Kingdom of Heaven, but thoughts that ruled the World of Flesh. One by one, these impressions entered everyone's mind; fear, worry, anger, and doubt. Some even began to wonder why they'd volunteered for this God-forsaken mission anyway. Sweat poured down the bodies under their armor and the marching was miserable. The horizon promised nothing but more of the same. A deep depression set in, leaving a black mood over the group.

Tarkio slipped on some loose gravel, and his shin skidded across a sharp rock. "Son of a bitch!" he screamed.

Tarkio sat on the ground examining the jagged gash. "There's something about this place. I'm sorry, I haven't sworn like that since I was flesh. Sorry."

"Don't worry about it," Elion told him. "It's this place. We've all heard it before. Well maybe Bethalia never has heard it before." Everyone chuckled.

"I've heard it," Bethalia said indignantly.

"Remember how wonderful the Kingdom is? Like a shining star, our precious jewel?" Elion said. "This place is the opposite. It affects everything. We must stick together in every way to survive this. We're not here for us. Always remember why we're here. Agreed?"

Everyone nodded agreement.

"We'd better keep moving," Belak said, looking around as if expecting something evil to pop out at them any moment.

"He's right, can you walk?" Elion asked Tarkio.

"Yeah, I'm fine," Tarkio picked up his dagger and stood to

go.

"Good, let's move," Elion led off at a brisk pace. A gusty wind assured him their sound could not be heard, so he didn't bother trying to be quiet.

They proceeded into the foothills full of low valleys and high ground. Certain views promised a never-ending sea of mountain range after desolate mountain range, surrounded by bleak nothingness.

The seven were forced to stop every so often to rest as they tired quickly. It alarmed Elion, they all felt so weak.

Then as they sat resting, Bethalia pointed off in the distance, "Look!"

A line of fiery torches moved along the other side of the valley in the growing darkness.

"Now who do you suppose that is?" Terel asked.

"Welcome Wagon?" Tarkio said sarcastically as he smiled. He chuckled to himself, but the majority of his humor was lost as everyone watched the small band of the enemy disappear around the mountain.

"Well, I don't think they noticed us," Elion said.

"We're in the valley of the shadow of death, and now we're in the presence of our enemies," Haydn said with narrowed eyes, keeping a close watch where the torches disappeared.

"Let's keep moving." Elion stood and waited a moment for the others to rise. There was no clear path to follow so Elion just picked the easiest route that seemed right.

Haydn looked tiredly at the backside of everyone as they followed after Elion, like baby ducks. He shook his head to himself, wishing he could rest a little longer. He soon realized the others weren't going to wait for him. In fact, they were walking off without even realizing he wasn't following.

"They'd just leave me here," he whispered, feeling sorry for himself. "They don't even miss me. If I sat here they'd just keep walking."

He finally realized they were getting farther away. His self-pity was interrupted by shock of fear. If he didn't get going, soon he'd be alone.

Haydn jumped to his feet and started off at a jog to catch up to the others. As he passed a large boulder, he saw a flash of movement out of the corner of his eye. At the same moment he heard growling and snarling. He stole a peek over his shoulder to see two giant wolfish dogs racing towards him, teeth bared. They moved fast with thick muscles covered in wiry, black hair. In a split second he calculated they were closing in too fast for an escape. He drew his sword and turned to fight, tripping in the process.

"Ahh, help!" he screamed out as he hit the ground.

The wolf dogs were on him instantly, slimy teeth sank deep into the arm holding the sword. The metal blade clanged against rocks as it fell from his grip. The wolf's awful breath smelled of decayed flesh as they snapped and snarled. Haydn instinctively held tight to his shield, protecting himself as much as possible.

Haydn's cry turned the others. They saw the hounds attacking their comrade and charged to his defense.

Belak drew his sword as he ran, raising it high above his head. He slashed downward with all his strength. The blade split the foul air, and in one smooth motion severed the head of the wolf that held Haydn's arm.

Terel plunged the deadly steel of his sword completely through the rib-cage of the second animal. The wolf-dogs, or whatever they were, lay dead on either side of Haydn. After helping Haydn to his feet, everyone stared at the dead animals.

"They're bigger than in my dream," Elion said as he sort of cocked his head. "But other than that they're the same."

"Dream?" Tarkio asked.

"Oh, I used to get a lot of dreams…near the end. I've seen these wolves before."

"Captain, please come see?" Bethalia called out. She displayed Haydn's wounds. Blood ran out from several puncture wounds. Haydn held his arm close to his body, pain racking his face into a tedious expression.

Elion looked at the wounds. "He'll be fine, wrap it up," he said brusquely.

"I don't think so, Captain. Look." She motioned for Elion to look more closely. The wound was torn and bloody.

"Captain, in the Kingdom this would already be healed. Look at the blackness surrounding the puncture - and the smell," she said.

"We quite obviously aren't in the Kingdom," Elion said matter–of–fact.

Bethalia cracked the seal on her vial, tipping it to allow the contents to drop. A deep, beet-colored liquid dripped out, slow like molasses in summertime. She quickly turned the vial upright, allowing only one drop to fall onto Haydn's wounds. All eyes focused on the little red drop as it fell through the air as if in slow motion. Then inevitably it landed on skin and immediately began to fizzle like hydrogen peroxide. Elion stared in wonder. The fizzing ended and Haydn's face grew into a smile. He wiped his arm clean and the wound was gone. It had completely stopped bleeding, and the skin was all healed over. There was a distinct, dark, purple scar where the punctures had been, but other than that, it appeared fine. Haydn stood up and rubbed his arm with his good hand.

"It still aches, but it's alright," Haydn said as he continued rubbing his arm.

"Good," Elion declared. "Then shall we proceed? Do I need to remind everyone to stay together? Lagging behind may be dangerous. Tarkio, hide those carcasses under some brush or something. I don't want them just lying there dead like that, for all to see. No need to attract attention."

Tarkio and Terel grabbed a hind leg and dragged them up under a bush. Elion and Belak stared at the bleak horizon.

"What do you think?" Belak asked.

"I have no idea. It all looks the same," Elion said out of the side of his mouth.

They both stood in silence for a moment.

Finally, Elion pointed to an ominous looking dark mountain. "That way looks particularly evil. Let's try that way."

"Sounds good to me, Cap'n." Belak nodded in agreement. "I like your navigation. Find the most evil looking thing and head toward it, makes perfect sense." They shared a smile.

"Nothing makes sense here. Nice job with the wolf dog, too," Elion said.

"Thank you, sir. Do you think there are more wolves following us?" Belak asked, his eyes glancing about.

"No way to know, but I'm sure all sorts of evil things may be hunting us, if not yet, then soon enough. Be ready." Elion raised his voice to the others. "Let's go."

He struck out again and this time everyone fell in step immediately. Depressed or not, no one wanted to be left behind.

They headed out onto another small plain separating two mountain ranges. The ground was a chalky alkali substance that puffed up white dust with each step. Every now and then a wet, bubbling place would appear and discharge a gas with a distinct odor. The foul odor was something akin to the smell of raw sewage. The stench grew so strong it forced them to place their hands over their noses as they walked. The twilight continued getting darker, but the air did not cool. In fact, it began to feel hotter. There was no way to know how far they'd gone. Time, distance, and hope were now things of the past. They pressed forward committed to going all the way, whatever the consequences.

The light-colored basaltic ground generated the only noticeable light as cracks glowed molten. No stars or lights of any kind penetrated the darkness ahead of them. Despite the blackness, Elion kept driving on. He rarely looked back, and just kept walking as if his Kelly was just up ahead. The others remained stalwart and did the best they could.

Somewhere in the middle of the darkness, Elion heard a wafting sound like wings flapping overhead. He raised his right arm in a ninety-degree angle and knelt to one knee without looking over his shoulder. The others followed suit and knelt, quietly waiting for whatever would come. Nothing did and the sound disappeared. Elion finally stood.

"Did anyone see what it was?" he asked.

No one answered.

"It was something winged. I wonder how long we can keep our presence here secret. We have to get into some cover, or we'll be discovered sooner rather than later, if it ever gets light," Elion said and then pressed on.

Ever-so-slowly the darkness waned to a pre-dawn half-light. They'd become accustomed to such sepia, that even the small amount of light felt like a sunrise. No sun could be seen in any direction.

"It looks like pine trees over that way." Tarkio pointed.

Everyone looked, and without a word Elion led off toward the shadowy trees. As they drew closer, they could see they were a kind of scraggly spruce tree, bent and sick. They were celadon-green with many rusty dead spots, but they would provide some cover.

"I can't wait to be off this flat, it's sick," Terel said to no one in particular. "The mountains and the trees are my favorite, no matter what Kingdom I'm in."

Once they stepped into the scrubby trees, Elion zigzagged amongst them. He didn't stop until he found a nice secluded spot, then he turned back toward the group and sat on a black boulder. Everyone else fell about on boulders or on the ground, exhausted.

"I don't know how far we've come or even if we're going the right way. I must remind everyone after that thing in the air and the wolves, we have to stay close together. No lagging, no wandering off. Understand?" Elion ordered.

No one answered, but everyone agreed by nodding their heads.

"I plan to keep us moving in that general direction toward that dark peak over there." Elion motioned toward an ominous mountain off in the distance. "These trees will help us, but we must be prepared for an attack at any moment. Keep your dagger or sword in your hand at all times --"

"Captain Elion, I think something is wrong with me," Bethalia interrupted his speech.

"What is it?"

"I have a pain here," She put her hand on her stomach and sort of doubled over. "It's a hollow, sick feeling. I think I'm going to die. I'm sorry, I've failed you!"

Elion smiled and shook his head. "You won't die, you're just hungry. I've been hungry for a long time myself. We're close to the Old World, so we're feeling weaker, fleshier, and hungrier. Karial told me the angels thought we shouldn't eat or drink anything from this place. They didn't know what it would do to us, everything here is evil."

"Then we just starve?" Terel asked his eyes wide.

"Starve? Not with our King," Belak stated with a smile. "I carry the food of life. Who wants to try it?"

Everyone sat up at attention because they all were gaunt with hunger.

"My Cap'n, you go first?" Belak asked Elion.

He held out his hand. Belak poured a brown liquid from his vial, very much like the red liquid from Bethalia's vial. As the brown drop landed on Elion's hand, it did not run, but sat up and made a perfectly circular little mound. Belak snapped the vial back upright as everyone watched.

Elion eyed the little drop for a moment, and then put his palm up to his mouth and licked it clean.

Everyone stood waiting and watching.

"Mmm, very satisfying. I tasted nothing, but my hunger is completely gone. Beats an MRE!" Elion smacked his lips together, "Praise the King!"

After all had partaken, they sat back down as if they were stuffed from a Thanksgiving feast of old. The food renewed their strength, and it wasn't long before Elion stood again looking at the terrain, selecting their route.

"Ready? Everyone up." Elion ordered.

The group stood and stretched for a moment, checking their gear and donning their helmets.

"Let's go, then," Elion said.

The air remained still and hot among the trees, but Elion felt more comfortable due to the illusion that the trees provided safety from evil eyes. The rough ground undulated with bluff-like swales.

The seven suddenly found themselves on a bluff of sorts looking out over a valley, surrounded on three sides by scrubby flat-top mountains. Elion immediately flattened his body to the ground so as not to outline himself against the gray sky. The group did the same, lying on the sharp rocks, awed at what they saw.

The valley floor was alive with activity. People trudged in forced rows, some worked with pick axes, and others toiled with shovels. A large sculpture of sand-colored rock had been carved into an awful face of some monstrous creature. The mouth swallowed people with its darkness, as they disappeared below ground.

Creatures shaped like men, sat upon dark horses. The horses themselves were skinny and sick looking, and their heads were not beautiful as a regular horse. Their heads were enlarged and drool dripped from large exposed teeth, no lips or muzzle covered them. To add to the horse's foul appearance their eyes glowed red and their riders were concealed in black cloaks. Occasionally, one of the riders would draw back an arm and snap a very long whip at one of the people walking on the ground.

It was obvious to Elion that this was some kind of penal colony. There was another hole at least a half mile from the 'mouth' entrance where people came out of the tunnel, pushing heavy carts of huge boulders. They'd dump the cart, and send it back into the dark hole. Then they would get back in line and return to the depths of the first entrance.

"Slaves," Belak whispered.

Elion nodded his agreement. "Looks like thousands of them. They look like people."

"What do you think they're doing?" Jubal asked.

"It's a mine or something," Terel whispered. "Or maybe they're tunneling, bringing the spoils out over there." He pointed to the exit shaft.

Just then four creatures flashed across the sky traveling fast. They circled the valley and then landed. Immediately several of the cloaked riders rode over to them.

"Demons," Elion said. "Fallen angels."

Everyone stared horrified at the sight below. The flying creatures were hideous in every way, but if Elion looked hard enough he could identify some similarity veiled in shadow. Each one had some feature of the angel they once were that remained unmarred by deformity, albeit an eye, a tuft of hair-feather, one hand.

The demons obviously commanded authority. The men in robes dismounted and knelt before them. One of the demons viciously kicked one of the robed riders hard in the face, sending him flying backwards. No distinguishable words could be heard other than yelling and arguing. The demons took off from the ground and quickly vanished into the gray sky. After they'd gone; more arguing ensued amongst the cloaked riders. Finally they mounted their animals and returned to vigorously whipping the slaves.

After a time Elion leaned in gathering everyone around him. "That's enough motivation for me. Did you see how many of these workers are old? People here are the same age as when they died. No perfect age or redeemed bodies in the realm of hell. I don't think our people are here. This is not the pit of Hades. That's where Michael said they'd be. We should backtrack and go around this place. Does everyone agree?"

The seven looked from one to the next and all nodded in agreement.

"Then let's get back." Elion belly-crawled a safe distance from the rock ledge before he stood upright again. Once everyone was ready, they started out by falling into the formation that had become a habit. Elion took the lead, followed by Jubal, then Bethalia, Terel, Haydn and Tarkio, with Belak bringing up the rear.

The twilight and the thick heat remained steady. They hiked around the base of the mountain the slaves were digging into, only to discover another work camp identical to the other one. Elion was forced to pull back even farther to get around a different way in order to remain undetected.

After hours of trekking without any breaks, Elion noticed the trees getting larger and thicker until they found themselves in a dense forest. It was unnerving because there were no noises like woods they'd known before. No birds, squirrels, or virtually any life at all. There wasn't much undergrowth, and mixed amongst the thick evergreens were many full-grown hardwood trees, long dead and lifeless. It looked as if the forest had at one time been teeming with life, but that time was long past. There were many steep bluffs of black shale-like rocks, jagged and especially vicious.

The group found themselves in a horseshoe-shaped gully surrounded by the shale bluffs on three sides. Elion turned to head back as this was an apparent dead end when he paused.

"Let's take a rest. This is a good spot for it. The evergreens are closed in tightly, creating a ceiling above us. We shouldn't be detected here." Elion sat down and leaned against a tree.

Everyone found a spot and took a break.

"The angels weren't kidding about these boots," Jubal commented. "My feet feel better than when we started. Other than that, I'm completely exhausted. I don't think I was ever this tired, even when I was flesh."

"It's too quiet for me." Elion glanced all about him. "That usually means death, but this entire place is death."

"How far do you think we've come?" Tarkio asked. "Or how far do you think we have left to go?"

Elion picked up a stick and began shaving the bark with his dagger. "No way to know anything like that."

"How are we going to go back through all of this if we find our people?" Haydn asked. "What if we have to carry them? They could be weak."

"None of you were in the military were you?" Elion chuckled.

"I was an Air Force pilot," Tarkio offered.

"See any combat or ever get shot at or shot down?"

"Well, no."

"I thought so. It's different on the ground. No one wants to admit it, but somebody has to take the ground. That's what we're doing. This enemy's already defeated because of the Lamb, he's already lost this war. That makes him very dangerous, like a mortally wounded animal capable of anything." Everyone stared at Elion. "Don't worry about how we're to get back yet. We may not all have to make the trek…back." He smiled slightly as he continued working at his stick.

"You weren't very good at inspiring your troops, were you?" Belak said.

Everyone smiled at that and some chuckled out loud.

"Very funny," Elion said as he glared at Belak. "No, I wasn't good at blowing smoke up their asses - if that's what you mean. This is the reality."

Haydn rubbed his scars as his eyes closed slightly. Rest came to all and time didn't exist for a little while.

Elion snapped awake, and in one motion rolled onto his side, his dagger in his hand. He melded into the edge of the woods as if part of the landscape. Belak and Terel both sat up just in time to see Elion disappear into the woods, and they both followed him into the trees.

As they approached, Elion put his forefinger to his lips. "Shh!"

He heard it again. It sounded like voices and a humming. Elion leaned in close and whispered, "Let's sneak on down and have a look. Everybody else is still sleeping?"

Belak and Terel nodded. Elion moved stealthily down the valley until the source of the noise was discovered.

Several people stood around in a circle as if they were holding a regular conversation. An occasional ember of a cigarette glowed as one of them inhaled. It appeared they were just waiting for something, as nothing seemed to be pressing them to do anything.

Behind the little group stood a perfectly rectangular object shaped like a door. The frame rose up from a flat rock and looked like twisted iron. Across the opening where the door would be, a wall of sparks and lightning cast a blue glow over all who stepped near it. The door hummed a steady buzz, heightening with lightning bolts.

Then it happened.

Those who stood in their little circle barely turned their heads to look. The event was evidently so commonplace to them. The electricity intensified into the center of the door, and with a burst and a flash, one for each person, two people stepped out from within the door. The door was free-standing, and there was no back to it to allow for anyone to appear from anywhere.

"It's a door to the other world, like the angels said," Belak said in a hush. "These people are tormenters."

"Look at their clothes," Terel said. The tormenters were dressed in many incongruent styles. They looked like soap opera actors in dumb costumes, but this was no mindless theatre.

Suddenly, Elion remembered Karl Albrecht, the soldier who'd visited him just before he'd died. Elion wondered what became of him and imagined him standing around just like this, waiting to go through the door, to visit old Joe.

People started coming faster now through the door, one, two, three, and then four and on and on. Once through the door, most of them immediately walked down the valley and out of sight.

"It's definitely a door," Terel said. "We better get back and tell the others. We have to get out of here. This is too hot for us."

They slinked back toward their makeshift camp and quietly gathered the others, escaping back through the forest.

XII
The Woman in the Wilderness

Hell seemed to have one thing that remained constant. It was hot like a fever. After traveling what seemed an entire day, they half-slid down the steep trail. Finally, they landed at the bottom covered in dust and sweat. They discovered they were in a dried-out riverbed, dusty, sweaty, and miserable.

"This looks like it once had water," Tarkio said with cracked and bleeding lips.

"It's been a long time gone." Terel pointed down the riverbed.

"Let's follow it," Elion said. "It has to lead somewhere out of these woods."

The riverbed provided a nice path for marching. With a solid distance behind them, they discovered a circular depression where water had once pummeled the ground leaving bare rocks.

"Used to be a waterfall here and a pool," Jubal said as he examined the signs.

Elion sat on a fallen log, "Let's shade up a bit."

"Shade up?" Haydn asked.

"Sorry, let's take a break in the shade," Elion enunciated the words carefully.

"It's no cooler in the shade here," Terel complained.

Bethalia noticed a vine growing along the back wall and climbed over some boulders to examine it. The men were in the bottom of the old pool resting.

She leaned close to the vine. It beckoned her senses, almost

The greater angel marched to the front of the hall and stood off to the left of the throne of God. Four creatures followed him. The first appeared to be a lion, walking silently on padded feet with a majestic black mane draping from his shoulders to the floor. His tawny skin, stretched tightly over muscle upon muscle rippling with each step.

Next came a young calf, he appeared small and weak, as his little hooves clicked upon the glass floor. His hair was fluffy and reddish in color. The calf walked up and lay at the feet of the lion, which stood proudly next to the strong angel.

The third strange animal to follow the great angel looked like a beast, except that his face was that of a man. He was mostly brown in color and appeared to be tough and agile upon its four-hoofed feet.

Following the beast, there came an eagle, roughly the same size as the lion. This enormous raptor had the coloring of a golden eagle of the old world, with a sharp, yellow beak and razor tipped talons. The eagle flapped its wings and floated into place next to the lion. Underneath its great wings, Joe noticed many eyes.

Then, in one voice all the kings, elders, and beasts stood and said, "You are worthy, our Lord and God, to receive glory and honor and power, for You created all things, and by Your will they were created and have their being." In one fluid motion, they all placed one knee to the floor and bowed their heads in honor of the one true King.

The low, earthy sound of thunder again began to grumble and continued emanating from unseen origins. The music fell into the background and bright flashes of lightning streaked across the alter. Joe stood in wonder as something that looked like snowflakes drifted in above the throne. The flakes sparkled as they flitted down; one side shined like mirrors and the other, clear like glass. As the shards neared the throne they knit themselves together like a puzzle, and then suddenly it was as if He had always been. He was just there - standing before His throne.

Music filled the hall again, but this time it came from within each person and creature present. The worship of all beings thanking audibly calling to her. She squinted and noticed little pink flowers on the vine, no larger than the head of a pin, but they were there, intricately beautiful, delicate...wonderful.

Bethalia's heart leapt with excitement as the speck of sweetness filled her with a sense of hope. She glanced over her shoulder to the others and reached to pick a flower.

Elion noticed her glance, and watched in horror. As her fingertips touched the vine, the ground beneath her feet opened in a flash, her weight dropped into the earth, and she was gone.

"Bethalia!" He screamed as he jumped to his feet and ran to the spot where she'd been standing a moment ago. The ground had solidly closed, showing no opening or passage. Elion stomped hard on the spot, but nothing. He focused on the vine, his dagger in his right hand. With his left, he reached up to touch the vine, and with a flash he fell into complete darkness. He hit solid ground with a thud. Dust settled around him as he rubbed his eyes, trying to establish his night vision. Light emanated from somewhere down a long hallway, but they remained in shadows.

"Captain Elion," Bethalia said from where she sat near him. "I'm sorry. The vine had little flowers on it...did you see them? They were lovely."

"What's this place? It's not a natural cave. Look at the carvings."

Suddenly, the others fell out of the darkness and hit the floor in a pile. Everyone gathered themselves, brushing off the dust.

"Cap'n," Belak said in a firm voice. "You said not to go off by ourselves, so we followed you. Where are we now?"

"Let's follow this tunnel and find out. Bethalia said there were flowers on that vine," Elion said.

"Flowers, here?" Haydn questioned.

"They were beautiful," Bethalia contended.

Elion headed down the dark hallway toward the light. Several open doors lined the hallway, each of which led to darkened rooms or other halls. With caution, Elion kept on toward the brightness. He slowed as he approached the doorway that was the source of the illumination. He hesitantly glanced back at the others with a wry smile. Elion inhaled again to be sure of what he smelled. His nose hadn't tricked him. It was a fresh and sweet fragrance that reminded him of the Kingdom.

He stepped into the room and at the sight of it, his eyes widened, and his guard dropped. The others followed their leader and they all stared, equally amazed.

A huge cavern expanded before them with a rounded stone ceiling much higher than the tallest tree. Light from an unseen source danced and reflected off of a clear, cool, pool of water.

The stone passage gave way to soft, velvety, green grass. There were plants of all kinds and thick oak trees lined the pool. Birds sang and flitted about, landing on stone pavers which led off into the lush abundance surrounding the pool.

No one spoke for a long time.

"Are we dead, again?" Jubal finally asked in awe. "Are we back in the Kingdom?"

Elion looked over his shoulder to make sure the dark door was still behind him, and it was. "No, we're still in hell, but I'll take it." He wondered at the reality of this place.

"Where are we?" Belak asked.

Before anyone could answer they saw her.

She walked out of the garden along the path past the pool. She strolled with a smoothness and poise that matched her royal attire. Her gown glowed as if the sun had provided the stitching, glistening with richness. Her lovely face had a sweet smile on red lips.

Elion felt warmth within as she neared. Her auburn hair bounced in ringlets laced with jewels. A crown laced with gold and silver bands graced her head, and Elion thought she was the most beautiful Queen he'd ever imagined. The crown gently peaked twelve times with a dainty black pearl seated upon each point as if the little balls perched directly on the point of a sword.

"If we're not dead, are we dreaming?" Tarkio asked.

She settled upon a seat near the pool, and motioned to them to come forward. No one moved as if they were frozen in awe like statues.

"Come and sit," she said to them in a gentle, alluring voice.

Elion shook his head to clear his thoughts, her voice almost startled him back to the present moment. He made his way down and found a bench, still staring at the woman. The woman patiently waited for them.

Once the seven were seated she spoke, her voice sweet like a lullaby on a breeze.

"You are dressed for battle. Has The Great War begun?"

"Not The Great War," Elion said. "But we're on a mission from the Kingdom."

"Not The Great War?" the woman looked confused. "What sort of mission are you on?"

"We're searching for people that we loved. They were lost and we're here to find them."

"All who are here are lost, except for me. I'm exactly where I've been placed. I have been here for a time and many times after that. However, I will remain until the prophecy is fulfilled. You must be a harbinger to the end. None others have ever come to me in my time of concealment."

"You are imprisoned?" Bethalia asked.

"A type I suppose, I prefer concealed in waiting. The great dragon has pursued me for the ages, and this place was made for me. I flew here on the wings of an eagle, and here I remain forever out of his reach until the time is gone. I do the will of my King and Lamb willingly, and these bonds are not heavy," the woman spoke kindly to them as if they were children.

"Do you know about this realm?" Elion asked her.

"Yes, I know things." She looked at Elion with golden-brown eyes. "Ask what you like."

"Do you know where those that would've been redeemed, but were stolen here by death at their own hand are located? Michael thought they might be together in Hades."

"Ah, my sweet Michael, yes, they are kept near Hades, more accurately - under Hades, in the catacombs."

"In the catacombs?" Terel said with his brow wrinkling.

The woman nodded. "Yes. They are forever digging here,

digging to find me, digging to get deeper and deeper down, insatiably. The dragon uses the tunnels as prisons. They are dark and forgotten places that need no guards. No one could escape."

"Could someone get in?" Elion asked.

She smiled. "Yes, merely walk in, but once in, you will not come out. There will be a cell awaiting you."

"How can we get in and get out?" Elion frowned.

"Would you like a map?"

"Yes, of course." Elion looked at his friends and smiled. "You have one, how?"

"Some of my little birds like to escape to stretch their wings and we keep up with what the enemies of our King are doing, no harm in that. I have prepared it for The Great War that is coming, but I can give it to you since the King has sent you. This must be the beginning, whether you know it or not."

"We saw work camps and a door," Terel added.

"There are countless work camps, torture camps, isolation rooms, education chambers, and below all that, endless tunnels, and rooms upon rooms full of holes. The fallen star forces the lost to work; and then he tortures them, then he forgets them, and back and forth, forever. He even tortures his own demons if they show any weaknesses or threaten his authority. He is continually sending demons and lost humanity on missions into the other world to gather more unto him, the never was, but is and is not."

"How far is it to Hades?" Haydn asked.

"My dear, it is all the way. Now, rest by the pool for a time, you'll need your strength. When you awaken, you will find your map waiting, and then you must leave. My time here is not finished, and you have an errand to attend to. Praise to the King of Kings."

The woman stood and proceeded to walk back down the path from where she'd come. She left behind her a memory of poise, grace, mystery and lonely patience. The woman embodied a peaceful sadness; the kind of ongoing self-sacrificing only mothers can know.

Everyone watched as she glided deeper into the garden and out of sight.

The seven lay down their heads and rested by the cool,

still water. They slept a deep, peaceful sleep and found that they all awoke at the same time. One by one, they sat up and stretched their muscles back to usefulness. Elion stood, went to the table, and picked up the map lying open. It was hand-drawn with dark, black ink on a tanned hide of animal skin. Elion spread it on the table as the others gathered around.

There were no distances or north or south coordinates. The map contained only simple descriptions of landmarks to be used as guides through the unknown. For all of its vagaries, the map was boon to the endeavor. It showed the Lake of Fire to be virtually surrounding the land mass.

"Hell is an island within the Lake of Fire?" Tarkio said, his voice laced with uncertainty.

"It looks that way," Elion answered. "Look here - mountains with a dry river. We must be here." He pointed his finger to a sketch of mountains near the edge.

"It doesn't look like we're very far in." Haydn didn't try to hide his disappointment.

"No, but if we follow this dry river, it will lead us right to the pit of hell and the city of Hades."

Belak and Terel nodded.

"Then we have to find access to the catacombs," Jubal said.

"Well, let's get to it." Elion spoke again like a seasoned commander. He rolled up the map and handed it to Jubal.

"Why do you want me to carry it?" he asked.

"With me leading, my chances of not making it are pretty high. Belak bringing up the rear - not good chances either. You guys in the middle, slightly higher. I'd hate for the best thing that's happened to us to disappear with me."

Elion walked toward the dark doorway. He paused and took one last sweet look at the woman in the wilderness.

"Eden lost," he said. What a sweet memory it would make.

He strode into the shadowy hallway examining each room until he found a ladder that led up a pitch-black shaft. They climbed a long while and finally a dim light showed they were in a cave. They weaved through the stalagmites as the passage was damp and narrow. It forced them to crawl and climb several times squeezing through tiny holes, but slowly light grew and they stood at the mouth of the cave. The heat assured them they were still in hell.

Elion noticed they were further down the riverbed than where they'd gone in. The high bluffs of the old waterfall could be seen standing stark, dry, and dead. Elion put them to his back and continued to follow the old riverbed.

Slowly they descended, and the thickness of the woods returned to sporadic trees and brush mixed with erratic rock formations. The ground grew unstable, and huge mounds releasing obnoxious fumes were becoming more common. They paced on for many miles, or at least it felt like a great distance even though there was no way to gauge it.

Elion carefully edged up onto a crest of rocky knoll and motioned for the others to come up and look. "Be prepared for what you'll see," he cautioned them. "It must be a torture field."

Elion knew the warning didn't prepare the others for what they saw. Tears welled up in Belak's eyes as he looked out onto the awful plain. The desert-like ground contained only random dead trees. The enemy had constructed a wide-ranging labyrinth of metal framing that went on for miles. Scores of people hung in box cages hanging from the metal frames. Still others hung by ropes or on hooks, even some appeared crucified. The people in the cages struggled every now and then, and without the occasional movement, Elion would've thought they were all dead. In fact, they were all alive, even the ones hanging by their necks. The hope of death no longer offered any comfort in eternity. Several large animals strolled among the rows and growled and snapped at those being tortured.

The beasts tramped on padded feet like a grizzly bear, and their size was muscular like a bruin. But they had spots and a long tail like a leopard and a shaggy mane over a snarling face with deep-set eyes and sharp, exposed fangs. They were awful to behold.

"Guards, I suppose?" Elion said.

Belak slid down to the ground, his head in his hands.

"Anything I can do, brother?" Elion asked him softly.

"Thank you, Cap'n. No. Remember the window below the

amphitheatre in The Forgotten City?"

"Yes."

"That is the place." Elion suddenly remembered the thin arm in the cage. "This is where she was. My Marie was there!" Belak choked out the words.

Buzzardy black birds circled overhead, watching and waiting.

"Do you think we should go down and take a look?" Elion asked.

"No," Belak answered his cheeks still wet. "For some reason I don't believe she is there. I know it. Let's go around."

"You sure?"

Belak nodded. "Yeah, she's in the catacombs, with the rest, I can feel it. Let's keep moving." He stood up and wiped his face, gathering his composure.

Elion led them back down the bluff and around the edge of a huge rock wall that went on for what seemed like miles. The ancient river followed the rocks when it had flowed here, leaving the bedrock exposed. The riverbed turned sharply this way and that. Following it so closely was forcing them to turn back on themselves more than necessary.

After the third big return where the path was shaped like a giant 'S', Elion said, "We have to get out of the riverbed. It's easy walking, but it's lengthening the trip. We can go cross country and keep it in view."

He climbed up a rocky bank. The little short bushes had been replaced with large thorny ones. A long branch of one of them ripped across Elion's forehead as he pushed his way through. He stopped and put his hand to his head and found blood on it when he pulled it back. He didn't stop long or ask for any sympathy. The blood dried on his forehead and turned black. It stung as sweat ran into the cut. The others all received cuts of their own from the evil bushes. Some scratches were on forearms, hands, calves and anywhere that flesh or cloth left an exposure. The only remedy was to remove the shields from where they were slung across the backs of the seven and use them to block the vicious, little thorns from doing their work. The sword could be used to cut with the other hand to chop a way through the bramble.

The sky was darkening with a swirling mass of gases and clouds. The center of the swirl hovered over a place just up ahead and out of view. The colors were an ominous mix of black, gray, red, and purple.

Bethalia pulled the tip of a thorn from the back of her hand.

"As terrible as this thicket is, it's our last cover before we reach the Plains of Esdraelon surrounding Hades," Elion said. "The site prophesied for Armageddon. There'll be no cover there. I still haven't come up with a plan yet as to how we'll cross that open expanse."

"Somehow, we'll find a way," Belak said with confidence. "The King is with us in our hearts."

Elion noticed Belak's words strengthened the spirits of the group. It gave them a glimmer of hope in the midst of everything that appeared hopeless.

"Ready to keep on?" Elion asked. "I think I see an opening or something up ahead."

He continued forward while the little band of warriors followed along as they were now accustomed. The ground slipped away and the little opening that Elion had seen was a depression where the brush didn't grow. The open space was surrounded on three sides with the brush and contained a large rock spire rising high above.

"Maybe we can find a trail down through the rocks and avoid this brush." Elion inspected the rocks at the base of the spire and discovered boulders piled as if from a slide. However, a cleft in the face of the rock appeared to be a trail. It disappeared into a maze of rock walls reaching high above their heads.

"I don't like it, but it's the only way," Elion said.

He was uneasy being so tightly confined. The passage was narrow and kept the column to single file.

"Good place for an ambush," Elion added. He continued marching keeping a wary eye about the surroundings.

Elion froze, leaning against the rock wall. The group did

likewise, eyes strained forward and loft searching for evil. Elion quietly put his dagger away and drew his sword. The others did the same. Slowly, Elion inched forward, sword ready. Soon, everyone became aware of what had alerted Elion.

It wasn't anything he'd seen or heard; it was a smell. A sweet aroma, alluring, like French perfume, mingled with a slight wisp of wood smoke. Elion rounded a corner and entered a room what looked like some sort of Bedouin's lair.

The others stepped up beside their leader, and one by one sword tips rested on the ground, as well as the jaws of every man. Their blood began to pulsate a little quicker and their breath came shorter as their eyes feasted on the scene. The roof was draped in deep plum and scarlet fabric with edges tasseled in gold. Little pots of something like incense burned along the walls, which were covered with beautiful tapestries. The ground of dirt and stone ended directly in front of them. If they were to take one step further, their feet would fall on rich-looking rugs of animal skin sewn together in one giant piece like a carpet. The sweet aroma permeated into their very beings, lolling them into a dream-like state, their bodies tingling with excitement. The scent of a woman lingered in the air, promising a sweet dream of ecstasy. Platters of fruits and open casks of wine were spread upon a banquet table to one side. Sheer fabric hung delicately around a large oval bed covered in silk and spread with fine pillows.

The scene was intoxicating as feelings of flesh long since lost to these redeemed suddenly burned within them and demanded satisfaction.

The sound of water splashing caused every head and every eye to turn. Almost unnoticed, off to one side sat a golden claw-footed tub with a woman in it. She had her back to the group and steam rose from the water. She continued to bathe as if she were alone. No one spoke or moved as they watched. Thoughts began to race through Elion's mind, and judging by the looks on the other men's faces, they too were being enticed by the woman.

She said nothing with her mouth, but then in one graceful motion, stood from the tub, keeping her back to the men, and letting the water beads roll down the curves of her body. She arched her back and shook the water from her sultry red hair that fell to the middle of her back. Elion expected her to reach for a towel, but she didn't. She carefully raised her leg and stepped out of the tub. She stood silhouetted for a moment before she placed a thin robe over her shoulders. The robe clung to the woman's wet body and hid nothing. She tied it low around her hips, allowing it to hang open, displaying the smooth, white skin between her breasts all the way down to below her navel.

The woman stepped toward the men as if she was a ballet dancer minding each lovely step, graceful as a deer. Finally, she stopped and placed her hands on her hips and coyly cocked her head, as if innocently realizing she was not alone. Her face was beautiful with pouting lips and long eyelashes, accenting eyes of brilliant green, sparkling like emeralds. Her gaze shifted slowly, looking each man directly in the eyes, still speaking no words. It was as if she knew them all, and was inviting each one individually.

She gave Bethalia a slight glance, and then her eyes settled upon Elion. The woman spoke to him in low and sensual tones as if they were alone.

"Come a long way, Joe. Remember Thailand? Did you tell anyone about that?"

Elion remained silent, but all the color drained from his face. She walked a couple steps to an ornate table with many bottles and a few chalices. She picked up an open bottle and poured a burgundy into a golden cup. She licked her lips before she took a small sip.

After she swallowed, she selected Tarkio, like a lioness picks a prey. "It's good to see you again, Jeffrey. It's been too long. I've missed you. Would you like a…" she paused and looked directly at him in a way that left no room to doubt her meaning. "…a taste."

Tarkio took a step forward onto the rug, and one side of her mouth curved up in a smile, as if, it was all too easy.

Bethalia was the only one clear-headed enough to notice the look, and she began to chatter in Chinese. "Tarkio, no, no, no, come back, she's a devil! She'll kill you!"

Immediately, the eyes of the woman flashed at Bethalia full

of rage.

"Virgin! Say not another word, unless you would like to come and discover what you've missed?"

Bethalia's desire flashed with a twinge of lust for the first time, leaving her confused and in silence.

The woman handed Tarkio the golden cup, and he raised it to his lips for a drink. The other five men stood in dumbstruck awe. Their lust and desire soared to new heights, only rivaled by jealousy as they watched the woman take Tarkio's hand and lead him behind the sheer fabric to the bed chamber. She placed his free hand on her breast, and embraced him, pulling him close. She breathed sweet, hot, breath on his neck and wrapped one delicate foot around his leg.

After a moment, she pushed back. "Take off that dreadful armor!"

Without hesitation, Tarkio reached down and unlocked the breastplate, allowing it to fall to the floor. The sound of the King's armor hitting the ground echoed through the realms. Next, he unbuckled his belt and let it drop next to the shield that already lay at his feet. As his blade hit the floor, Bethalia looked sideways at the other men to find them all still completely enraptured with the vision before them as if in a trance.

"What's all this worth to you?" the woman purred. "Jeffrey, nothing is free, you know that?"

"I have no money," Tarkio said. "What do you want?"

The woman batted her eyes and let the robe fall open for only Tarkio to see. "I'll take that necklace as payment." Her eyes fell to the vial hanging at his chest.

Tarkio closed his eyes as he bowed his head, removed the chain from around his neck, and placed it in her hand. Her fingernails looked like claws as they wrapped around his gift from the King. Tarkio bowed his head to her bosom and as he began to kiss her body, she stared coldly at the others; the smile completely gone from her face.

"Captain!" Bethalia said in a forceful whisper. He did not respond.

"Captain!" she said again, louder.

Elion blinked his eyes twice and shook his head. He looked over at Bethalia.

"Captain, she is a devil!" she screamed.

Dreadful reality and reawakening came too late. The woman held Tarkio's vial in one hand and his dagger in the other. Blood dripped from the corner of her mouth as she spoke, ever so slowly, in a sensual whisper, "Oh, Jeffrey, oh yes, how *is* your wife?"

Tarkio stopped what he was doing, and a flash of painful realization flitted across his face. He attempted to push her away as she slammed the dagger forcefully through the center of his back very near the backbone. She did not stop until the hilt was resting on his bare skin.

Blood splattered everywhere - all over his back and front and all over the woman as well.

"No!" Elion and the others yelled in one voice.

Their swords all jumped to service as they rushed her. She still held Tarkio's limp body, and with her foot she deftly kicked back the rug on the floor. In a flash, she dropped into darkness and was gone. Tarkio's blood covered armor was all that remained.

Elion carefully pulled back the rugs to discover a round hole in the rocky ground just large enough to accommodate a body. Just inches within the hole; darkness reigned, black as night.

Jubal sat down on the bed and put his head in his hands, not crying or saying a word. Haydn looked nervously at everything. Terel kicked the golden tub completely over, spilling the water out.

"Ahh! You whore! Devil-woman!" he yelled.

Elion knelt beside the hole and peered into it, his mind racing.

"Let's get up on that rock. I need to know if we can see Hades from here. If we can, this might be an entrance to the catacombs. If not, it could be any kind of tunnel. According to the map we should be getting close," Elion spoke his command like any other. As if they hadn't just lost one of their own.

"Captain, Tarkio is gone!" Haydn said.

"I still need to know where we are!" he answered.

Terel and Belak took off, climbing straight up the rough face like expert rock climbers. Once they were on top, they stood for a moment and turned a full circle looking at the distance.

"What do you see?" Elion asked. "Is it Hades?"

"Yes, Cap'n," Belak yelled down. "It's dead ahead, across a vast open plain. It sits in darkness, but I can just see it."

Elion waved them back down.

When they'd found their way back down, Elion asked them, "So what did you see? How did it look?"

Terel scowled wrinkling his forehead. "The bowl starts just ahead and to the other side of these rock spires. It gets darker all the way to the bottom, but it does look like the city is in the center at the bottom. It was hard to see much as it's completely dark there, but I could just make it out."

"It looks old and dirty," Belak added. "Like an old medieval castle in ruin and decay. The walls were dark and fires burned all around. Strange flashes of light came up from within the city."

"We've failed our brother, Tarkio. He is lost." Elion looked at the others.

"Will we not find him?" Bethalia asked. "We can't leave him here."

Elion shook his head. "Tarkio is not why we came. We must assume that as we speak our identities are being hand-delivered to the enemy, along with the body of Tarkio. If we get the opportunity to save Tarkio, of course we will do it, but we must focus on our task. It's very probable that the dragon will figure out what we seek once he knows who we are. We must act quickly. We must get our people as soon as possible, because the enemy will move them if we tarry and he will come against us."

"What do you plan?" Jubal asked.

"We enter the catacombs right here. We follow the great harlot and begin the search. Traveling across the Plains of Esdraelon isn't a good idea unless we want to join Tarkio. The catacombs are our best hope."

"Once in the catacombs, how will we find them?" Belak asked. "The map doesn't outline the tunnels."

Elion looked around, his mind a blur of activity. His eyes settled on the vial around Haydn's neck. "The gifts of the King will lead us. We must rely on Him and not ourselves," Elion pointed to Haydn's vial. "Haydn, your gift contains the light of the morning star that is the Spirit of the Lord. It will be light to you in the darkness and lead your steps."

"Let's get on with it," Terel said. "Time is suddenly against us, time for the two minute offense." He peered into the dark hole, then reached over and wrenched a metal pole holding a small container of oil with a wick loose from its base. Terel opened his vial, allowing one drop to fall onto the wick. He closed his vial and everyone watched as the little wick sparked, flickered, and lit on fire.

"Fire from the wrath of God!" Terel smiled wide. He didn't wait for Elion and returned to the hole. He held the light in his left hand and his sword in his right, shield across his back. With one look at his friends, he stepped directly into the hole and dropped out of sight. The others looked into the hole to find that Terel stood no more than ten feet down on a paved floor.

Elion and the others jumped in after him one at a time.

S.C. SHERMAN

XIII
The Catacombs

Amber-colored light pushed back against the midnight shadow as the little torch illuminated the immediate area. They were in a round chamber shored up with timbers. Three doors offered only darkness and nothing else.

"Which way?" Jubal asked.

"Look!" Terel said as he held the light to the floor. Drops of blood disappeared into the abyss of the left doorway. "She took Tarkio that way!"

"She'll be taking the quickest route to the city to inform our enemy. Follow the blood of Tarkio, as his gift to us. The Lady in the Wilderness said below the city, it's our best hope," Elion said.

"Let's go," Belak said.

Terel handed the torch to Elion and he led the way through the dark tunnel, keeping track of the blood-trail. The tunnel was simple, only seven or eight feet tall and wide like an imperfect square. Occasional rocks and boulders littered the floor; some piled high and forced them to climb through tiny holes as if there'd been cave-ins. The passage seemed to angle subtly to the left and then to the right, sometimes up and down, but there was no real way to gauge anything in the depths.

Elion froze in his tracks. He placed the lamp near the floor and stared at the dirt ahead of them.

Terel and Belak stepped up and peered at the ground.

"No more blood?" Terel asked.

"Nope," Elion said, his eyes searching for his telltale sign.

"There've only been a couple of doors leading off that we've passed up till now," Terel said. "This has to be right, but from here on, we're on our own."

"Let's keep going until we come to another door." Elion waited only a second before Belak and Terel nodded, and he started off again at a brisk pace. An intense sense of urgency drove them now more than ever.

Quite a distance passed with no doors, and then they came to a crossroads. It was a perfect fork in the road. The two passages displayed no distinguishable differences from left or right.

Elion stopped and everyone puzzled which to take.

"I've an idea," Haydn said.

He stepped before the diverging tunnels and carefully cracked the seal on his vial. Nothing visibly escaped from the little glass container. No floating gases or smoke, or sticky liquids, nothing at all. Haydn snapped the lid shut a very satisfied look upon his face.

"Without doubt, it's to the right," he said.

Elion didn't question his validity and hastened immediately to the right.

They traveled for several miles, with each step, inching ever nearer to the center of hell. They came to several more crossroads and a few shafts that crisscrossed up and down, creating a labyrinth of tunnels. Haydn guided them with utmost confidence.

Movement on the ground caused Elion to jump sideways. The torches shined light upon the thing and it glistened.

"It's a little frog," Jubal said.

"What is a little frog doing down here?" Haydn asked.

"They like the heat, I guess, but this is more like a desert. Doesn't make any sense to me," Terel added.

"Let's keep on then." Elion kept walking and eventually the presence of frogs became commonplace there were so many of them. Something about them slowly began to work on Elion, making him nervous, perhaps it was because they were absolutely silent.

"I could hear the sound of night frogs on a good fishing pond when I was a boy. Man, they sang to the stars like a symphony.

What's wrong with these ones, mute?" Terel said.

"Everything is wrong here," Jubal said.

The heat was stifling like a steam bath, and the sweat rolled off each of them. They continued marching along, when suddenly the tunnel opened up around them, and they found themselves standing in a cavern.

Elion held up the light. It grew as if on command to illuminate the room a bit more. All along one wall of the cave were holes no bigger than four feet around with bars across them. The wall was riddled with them. It looked like birds had dug nests into the side of a cliff so often that the holes virtually touched, but no birds could have done this.

"Oh my Lord, have mercy," Elion said in awe. "It goes on as far as I can see, what are these holes?" The room was quiet, and no one stirred. Somehow, instinctively Elion knew the holes were filled with lost souls.

Concealed in shadow, emanated a low, evil growl and a sort of hissing sound. No amount of heat or humidity could stop the icy chill that ran the full length of Elion's backbone.

What sort of evil is this?

At the sound of the growling, the room exploded into motion. The group spun on their heels, swords raised and eyes attempting to locate the peril. Three wolf hounds leapt through the air, teeth barred with snarling slime and mud caked to their hides.

Belak slashed one wolf completely in half as it flung itself at him.

Another wolf leapt at Haydn, causing him to fall backward on the ground. His sword impaled the creature as it jumped atop of him.

The third one knocked Bethalia sideways with a glancing blow, and as it spun, Jubal stabbed his sword through its neck, killing it.

For the briefest of moments the conflict felt like an easy victory as the wolves lay dead at their feet. Then from the shadows, eight eyes, glowing yellow in the firelight, appeared. The creatures approached the group without fear.

Three were smaller, but no matter their size, they were foul. Their scaled, wet skin covered what may have been a human frame at one time. Now it was bent over, and the knuckles and joints were large and swollen. These vial creatures' eyes protruded slightly, and their heads held only a small amount of hair. They had strong-looking teeth covered in dark spots, not really fangs, but rather squared off. The three weren't identical and could be easily distinguished from one another, but seemed to be the same species.

"Goblins," Jubal said disgusted.

The last set of eyes stepped into the light, and he drew everyone's attention. He was much taller and more formidable than the others.

"Now that would be a demon," Terel said, balancing himself, and gripping his sword tightly.

This demon was nearly the size of a guardian. Half of his face and body was shriveled and scarred as if it had been badly burned. The other half of the creature was covered in flaky skin or perhaps a very fine scale. It was too hard to tell in the poor light. He snarled viciously. No one even noticed the Goblins now. Only half of the demon's mouth actually worked, but the glistening fangs were enough to command respect.

"What are you scum doing out of your cages?" the demon demanded. There was a hissing sound to his language, probably from the injury to his mouth. "And where'd you get those swords?"

Elion immediately caught on to his confusion. "We found them back there in the dark."

"I don't care where you found them," the dark demon slurred. "You're going to pay for killing my dogs! Are you new arrivals? Drop the swords and down on your knees! Now!"

Elion did as commanded, but didn't toss the sword away. He rather sat it just to his side as he knelt and put his hands behind his back, grasping his dagger. He held it in his hand, waiting. The others did the same, displaying their explicit trust in their leader.

Once they knelt, the disgusting Goblins approached to pick up the swords and secure the prisoners. Their nonchalance showed Elion they did not fear them, nor did they expect an attack. The lead

Hell & Back

Goblin bent to pick up Elion's sword.

"Would you mind terribly if I kept that?" Elion said with a smile.

The Goblin looked confused as he pondered the question. Elion quickly drew the dagger from behind his back and deftly split the Goblin from privates to brisket, spilling his putrid, green guts everywhere. The others pulled their daggers and easily killed the other Goblins.

Elion jumped back to his feet just in time to feel the shoulder of the demon hit him and send him flying backward. The demon moved so quickly that he almost couldn't be seen - almost.

In a flash, the demon sank his teeth into Terel's shoulder. His jaws clamped down and his clawed hands slashed at Terel's soft underbelly. Without the armor Terel would've been killed instantly, which is most likely what the demon expected. He released Terel and paused cocking his head, much like an angel, but with a confused look on his face. He was evidently trying to understand why Terel was not dead. Anger filled his face and he unleashed it back on Terel.

Terel slashed with his dagger and covered himself with his shield as he was hit again. This time the force of the blow knocked him down, and he cried out as he felt fangs sink deep into the back of his thigh. Elion and Belak slashed across the demon's back. The demon disappeared into the shadows. Both Belak and Elion noticed black blood on their blades.

"It bleeds," Elion said. "Therefore, it will die!"

Terel lay on the ground, not moving, and Bethalia knelt over him.

The four remaining warriors stood back-to-back, awaiting the attack. It came in a rush from above.

The demon hit Jubal with full force of motion, weight, and viciousness. He was knocked to the ground, and blood spurted from the lacerations to his face and neck. Once again, the demon fled back to the corners of darkness.

"This is it boys! We've got to kill it now! Kill it on this run!" Elion said with determination.

Bethalia pulled out Terel's vial and cracked it open, pouring out a drop right on the ground. As the drop hit the dirt it exploded into fire - a big fire! The battle anger in the room kindled the flame that was the wrath of the Lord. The flame greatly increased and illuminated the large cavern and it happened just as the demon was making another run.

This time he zipped straight for Belak. In a thousandth of a second, Elion swung his dagger up and held it tight in both hands. The force of the demon aided in burying the dagger deeply into the chest. He tumbled out of the air and crumpled up, hitting the floor with a thud. He was absolutely dead.

Elion, Belak and Haydn stood over the demon in death. Elion swung his sword hard and cut off the demon's head. The others looked at him strangely.

"Just to be sure."

Bethalia had already remedied Terel with the blood of the Lamb, and he was rubbing the new scar tissue on his leg, which was obviously producing some pain.

Bethalia and the others went to Jubal. He looked much worse. His face was ugly with deep cuts, and his throat was fairly shredded. He appeared to be lifeless. Elion shrugged his shoulders, not knowing what to say.

"You might as well try it," Belak encouraged them. "The Lord heals and raises from the dead."

Bethalia smiled with the encouragement, poured several drops into the neck wound and stood back. They watched as the wound covered over in a fizzing gel-like substance, and then hardened into a dark, purple scar. The wounds to Jubal's face scarred over as well, and then everyone waited for what seemed like a long time.

"It was worth a try..." Belak said as he hung his head, defeated.

Suddenly Jubal gasped loudly and then coughed up frothy blood, spitting it to the ground. Everyone jumped back, startled by Jubal's life. For a moment no one helped him, and then Bethalia stepped up and patted his back, lifting him to his feet.

"How do you feel?" Elion asked with a smile.

"My throat hurts," Jubal said, barely above a whisper.

"I should think so," Elion said. "Good thing you don't talk much anyway. You should keep quiet for awhile and let that heal further."

Jubal nodded his agreement.

"I am ready. I'm alright, Captain." Tercl stood straight and strong.

"Then let's keep on. Haydn, which of those exits do you like?" Elion asked, pointing at several dark openings around the cavern, leading off to the unknown.

Haydn cracked his vial, waiting for his direction from the Spirit. After he closed the vial, he said, "That extremely dark opening second from the right would be the one, Captain."

"Grand, beats a GPS!" Elion picked up the torch and his sword.

They soon discovered it was another tunnel that went a short distance, and then opened into another cavern full of a multitude of more lost souls in their dark, lonely prisons. They went through several more of these caverns, passing by one after the other. Every now and then a bleak-looking face would peer out through the bars as they walked by, but the group still heard not a sound from any of them. No crying or wailing, just deafening silence like an orphanage at night. Full of lost and abandoned souls bereft of crying, pitifully knowing that weeping would bring no solace.

Sadness was so thick; it felt like a presence that kept the group moving fast.

"Keep together, avoid overwhelming thoughts of home," Elion said. "We've been sanctioned, by the King. We must find our loved ones only, nobody else."

S.C. SHERMAN

XIV
THE WOMAN AND THE DRAGON

The putrid smell of decay clung to the air like fat on meat. No one seemed to notice the half-clothed woman sneaking up the black rock stairway. The stairs led up to a castle that looked like it had been under siege. Broken, cracked. and burned out what was once glorious. Random fires lit the sky with wavering reddish light and smoke. The woman carried a heavy load, but it did not seem a hindrance, despite her diminutive appearance. She reached the top step where two guards stood, both large and nasty-looking demons. As she approached they crossed their spears to stop her progress.

"Who comes to the throne of the one king, satan?" a demon's voice growled.

"I am Mystery, the great whore. Let me pass," she said quietly and kept walking as the guards removed their spear barricade.

The demons stared at her as she disappeared into the castle carrying strange cargo. Her bravery or foolishness was a surprise to them. Her eyes were well adjusted to the darkness as though she were an animal of the night. Firelight danced across the ancient walls of the ruin. Strange sounds resembling music emanated from a nearby room. It sounded like rhythmic chanting with a low drum beat, and the occasional rattle of a rattlesnake, or a hoot and a howl. Unafraid she walked directly into the hall of demons. She'd been there many times, but never with a presentation like this.

Demons stood all about the room, arguing with each other and talking loudly. They were all mangled and burned to the core.

Their very souls black with malice, shadows of what they once were. Beautiful flesh now blackened by flame, scaled, and rotting. They spoke filthy things and hated one another. The woman ignored them and walked past two demons, punching and snarling, locked in mortal hand-to-hand combat, clawing and biting.

Ordered seats remained as ancient rows on both sides of the hall. All heraldry and regal pride covered in grime. The thrones appeared long since abandoned and it was obvious no one sat in them anymore. Discarded crowns hung on chair corners, remnants of glory, forgotten like the kings who once wore them. All power and authority abdicated; allegiance handed over to the evil one. Chaos ruled.

No one minded the woman as she marched to the front of the room. She sashayed up the steps and tossed her package through the air. The dead weight of Tarkio's body landed with a meaty thump and slid across the worn rock floor coming to a halt directly in front of the seat of darkness.

"Great king!" the harlot screamed. "Look and see we are under attack!"

The noisy room quieted down immediately. Demons gathered around to see what the woman was talking about. Her robe was pulled tightly around her and was entirely scarlet, dyed red from the blood of Tarkio, and it did a poor job of covering her body. No one cared about her half-naked appearance. The demons despised her, and all attention was focused on the dead man at the foot of the throne.

Satan slowly stood with his eyes fixed upon the corpse. It looked as if he was examining a carcass to determine its cause of death or where would be the best place to start eating. His head cocked sideways, and twitched involuntarily every now and then. The devil's appearance was twisted by evil so that nothing remained of what he had been created to be, the Archangel Lucifer. Evil had changed him in every way, both physical and spiritual. His nose and mouth area protruded out into a snout displaying wicked teeth, smoke pulsing between them with each breath. Sunken sockets held eyes glowing as embers of hate. Skin of thick, black scale covered most of his body, but around his face it looked more like red leather. It was as if his appearance had been scarred or burned and never really healed, continuing to ooze and seep. Vicious claws that had once been retractable were now always out. The skin around them pulled back tightly. The razor-sharp points glistened in the firelight as he knelt over Tarkio, inhaling his scent. His head twitched side to side like a cat waiting to pounce.

The throne itself was constructed from the dirty, black, coal-like rock that appeared to be everywhere. Anyone who'd ever seen the throne in the Kingdom of Heaven could immediately see this throne was a pitiful copy.

The lord of darkness raised his head and roared with the sound of a dragon, spewing fire from his mouth, enraged.

Once satan stopped his awful roar, he violently kicked Tarkio's body, flipping it onto its back. The king of hell looked away.

"Who is this disgusting human? Why should I not kill you for bringing him before me?" the devil said in a low guttural voice so raspy it was difficult to understand.

"He's Jeffrey Collins," the harlot screamed with a mixture of contempt and fear. "He was under my control for many years," she stuttered, afraid to continue.

"So throw him back into the pit," Satan roared his words at her and small tufts of flame occasionally slipped between his teeth. "The very sight of him and you disgusts me! Whore, you will now pay for bringing him into my throne room!" the dark lord rose up with claws extended as if to strike.

She gathered her courage and continued. "My king, you don't understand. We lost him years ago. He had a daughter who prayed for him constantly, the little maggot, and eventually he went the other way when he died. He's not one of ours. He's redeemed! Look at him. Do you see your mark? He's from Heaven!" She cowered, fearing that the devil's wrath would fall on her for bearing the news.

"He's never been here before, but he's been there?" He spoke slower now to be sure that he was clear.

"Yes. He's one of the elect, the redeemed, and I killed him with his own sword," she said straightening her back in pride.

The demons enjoyed that part of the story and beat their chests, growling war cries thrilling their vicious hearts with her tale of death.

The devil half-snorted and silence fell again over the room. "Whore, where did you kill him, was he alone? How did he get here?"

"I don't know how he got here, but they walked into my lair in the wilderness. I'd no choice, I had to kill him, and they were dressed in the armor of the Lord. They were prepared for battle. It has begun, my lord, The Great War is upon us!"

The demons screeched and shouted out, growling, crowing, and cackling echoed throughout the hall.

Again the devil snorted and silence fell upon the room. "You said 'they'. How many were there?"

"Seven."

"Seven? How dare they come here?" He spoke slowly as if calculating each word. "Did you see the White Rider, the army? How strong are their numbers?"

"I didn't see any others but these seven, which are now six. I left them in the woods, and brought this one straight to you, my lord."

Satan rose a foot taller barking out commands to his minions. "Draka?"

A very large demon stepped forward, somewhat at attention. He was larger than the other demons and had an especially wicked look to him in his military uniform. Most of the demons in the hall wore uniforms, but none of them matched. They were from different time periods and different countries, confiscated from some lost soul leaving the World of Flesh behind. Draka was ugly even for a demon, as his nose looked like it had been bitten off, and his face was a myriad of scar tissue.

"Take a squad through the catacombs. Go to the whore's den and seal the entrance. Then track the six humans. Kill or capture them. Report back to me anything you see. Look for the White Rider and the army. They'll be marching for the plains of Esdraelon, where we will crush them once and for eternity."

Hell & Back

"Yes, my lord." Draka accepted his orders, abruptly leaving the hall to go about his business.

The devil called out to him as he left. "Tell the goblins to flood all the lesser entrances and seal the catacombs."

"Yes, my lord," Draka said as he continued on his way.

"Cank!" Satan snapped.

"Yes." A particularly small demon with much less heft stepped forward. His skin was blotchy and not as scarred as the others. He looked more sickly than imposing.

"Gather all forces on the plains and prepare the defense of the city," Satan howled.

Cank looked side to side with the shifty eyes of disrespect. "My great lord, it would be easier to defend the city if we could lock the gates." He sort of hissed and snickered, looking for some others to join in.

Satan left his perch, and in a flash he'd crossed the room and pinned Cank to the floor beneath the weight of a clawed foot. The devil lowered his head and blew smoke into Cank's face.

The little demon put a hand up to protect himself. In one quick snap, razor sharp teeth removed Cank's hand at the wrist.

The demon cried out in pain, which made the other demons wickedly laugh and hoot.

"You are such a fool," Satan's words came slow and deliberate. "You little scum. Don't ever talk to me like that again! Understand?"

"Yes, my lord. Forgive me, sire. It will be difficult to defend the city. The vast majority of our forces are deployed in the World of Flesh, sir, recruiting as ordered."

The devil released his prisoner. "No need to recruit anymore. This is it. Call them all back. Call them now! We need all our soldiers here! We will crush them, here and now! Then we will take back Heaven!" the king of darkness roared fire and cackled at his own victory.

The drums in the other room beat louder and faster, in anticipation of the coming war. Outside, fires sprang up all around the ruins, giving the appearance the entire city was burning.

Satan moved like a shadow and stood over Tarkio's body. He hooked one claw on Tarkio's body, and with a flick, the body flew to the floor next to the harlot.

"What would you have me do?" she asked.

"Get out of my sight! Take this flesh and leave my presence before I change my mind and just kill you now."

Mystery picked up her prey and slinked out of the hall with no words. She smiled slyly with one last look at her dark lord. Satan noticed her glance and roared fire at her. She screamed as her hair sizzled and smoked. "Why did you do that?"

"What are you hiding from me? I won't ask again," Satan said.

Mystery lowered her head as a scolded child. She produced a vial hanging on a chain and tossed it to the evil one, not wanting to go closer.

Satan caught the chain with his claws and examined his spoils with an awful smile. Mystery gathered Tarkio's body and disappeared into the dark.

❦

Elion raised his arm as he froze. He said nothing, and everyone held their breath, eyes and ears straining for clues as to why they'd so abruptly halted.

Sounds bounced off stone and traveled on stale air.

"It's voices," Bethalia said. "I hear screaming, yelling, people crying out."

"I hear metal machinery, clanging, and straining," Jubal whispered.

They crept forward carefully and silently. Firelight flickered on the cave walls, while shadows kept low. Elion snuffed out the wick on their light and proceeded, using the darkness like a friend.

The cave opened up on one side, as if they were on a balcony overlooking a coliseum. With backs pressed tight to the wall, horror gripped them and refused to relent. Peering from the shadows the scene was breathtaking. Open flames deposited a blue haze throughout the cavern, busy with people, demons, goblins, and other awful creatures with no names. Some looked like giant bats with human arms, while others were wolf-like creatures that stood erect, snarling and snapping their vicious teeth wherever they went.

Several demons that appeared to be in charge sat on an elevated platform in the center of the room, overseeing the torture. A giant circular shaft led upward presumably to the surface. Demons of all shape and size continually dropped down from the shaft like bees carrying in bits of debris for their queen.

"Look, they're carrying people," Elion whispered.

"New arrivals," Belak whispered back.

The looks on their faces told a great tale. Some were angry and kicked and bit at the demon carrying them, while others just hung their heads in defeat and loss. Some looked around with great wonder as if absolutely surprised at what was happening to them.

Haydn leaned over to Bethalia and whispered, "They are all believers now."

She just nodded, both cheeks wet with tears.

The crying and wailing rose and fell like the sea. The awful sight of new arrivals standing in lines waiting for their turn, almost as surprised as a new arrival in the Kingdom. First their clothing was removed and handed over to the goblins, and then it began. The torture room looked like an assembly line factory. The lost just moved on down the line receiving some new hell with each station. There was no goal to extract information or any lofty subterfuge to justify such behavior. It was done out of sheer unadulterated hatred and in every evil way that a human mind has ever conceived of and some still as of yet unthought-of.

They used every manner of tools to effect their torture: sharp things, pointy things, things that chewed flesh, things that peeled, things that grind, things that pull and stretch, things that chop, things that burn, things that pound and many more things that don't sound or feel or smell very well when forcefully applied.

Finally, toward one end of the room, the wounded and broken were rather piled upon each other as if they were dead. Goblins pulled them from the pile and placed them in an ordered row waiting their turn. The ones standing in rows appeared to stare into nothing. All memory of hope had been abandoned and they hung their heads waiting for the final screw to be turned. A demon was applying a hot iron to skin and branding the lost souls forever with the eternal mark of the beast, the three sixes. There was no doubt that this was the utter pit of hell.

"Let's follow this way around, keep to the back wall. We don't want them to see us now." Elion spoke in a whisper. He started off again, and the others followed, mimicking his every movement until they'd gone half of the way around the awful chamber of torture.

Suddenly, the wall behind them faded back until they noticed a dark, little, side cave. Rocks and debris had been discarded as if it was of no concern. Elion noticed Haydn staring into the darkness of the little room. That in and of itself would've been no reason to pause, but for something else, Haydn's vial pulsated with a blue light.

"Maybe we should take a closer look, don't you think?" Elion put his hand on Haydn's shoulder.

"I think yes." Haydn agreed.

They stumbled around in the darkness, their only light coming from the vial. Nothing seemed particularly special about the little closet.

"Aha, here we are?" Belak said.

He pushed some scraps of wood out of the way.

"Look here, it's a hole!" he said. The hole was no bigger than a couple feet in diameter. Haydn knelt holding his glowing, little vial near the opening, letting the soft blue light shine in. Nothing could be seen, and the light disappeared into the deep. Terel leaned over and poured a drop from his vial into the darkness. As the little drip fell away it ignited and burned brighter the further it went. Twelve eyes watched intently as it kept distancing itself, second after lengthy second. The walls of the hole appeared to be a perfectly circular shaft much like the shaft of a well. Along the walls in no sort of pattern there were large metal stakes stuck into the rock to allow for climbing.

Finally, the little ball of flame hit bottom and hissed as it immediately went out.

"Water at the bottom," Belak said. "It's nothing, maybe a well or something? Do demons get thirsty?"

"I'm going down," Haydn announced, not asking anyone else what they thought about it. "I can feel something, very strong. It feels like the spirit in my vial." By the time he finished speaking, he'd already begun to descend into the darkness. The little vial provided enough light for Haydn to see a few feet around him.

As soon as he was down a few feet, Elion turned around and stuck his feet into the darkness feeling for the first peg.

After Elion had disappeared into the hole, Terel relit the torch and climbed in.

"I guess we're going down the well," Belak said, less than enthusiastically. The torch provided just enough illumination for the others to see the pegs as they climbed down.

Haydn had gone several hundred feet down into the dark shaft, when he suddenly couldn't find another peg. His legs thrashed around as the walls of the shaft were gone. Haydn couldn't see a bottom and finally could no longer hold his own weight with his hands.

"Aahh!" he screamed as he fell a few feet and landed in ankle deep water.

He laughed out loud at the lack of a terrible fall, and held the vial away from his chest in an attempt to see where he was. The constant sound of water dripping and the team climbing down was all he could hear. Haydn shuddered and held perfectly still, watching a deathly-looking black snake swim around his right ankle.

Just then Elion let go of the last peg and splashed as he landed in the water next to Haydn.

"There are snakes in here."

"Really, what color?" Elion asked.

"Black, what does that mean?"

"That you probably won't see it before it bites you," Elion said, all humor lost.

Just then the little cavern lit up as if a switch had been

flipped. Terel dropped into the water next to the others. He waved his torch around, and everyone's attention was drawn to the single, dark opening. Elion strained his eyes against the dark in an attempt to see anything.

Terel handed the torch to Elion. "After you, El Capitan." He smiled, obviously not wanting to go into the dark opening first.

Without any discussion, Elion grasped the torch and sloshed through the black water passage, extending the fiery light ahead of him. The water funneled into the opening, and meandered into a small stream bed, crisscrossing a sort of trail. The ceiling was short, forcing them to hunch over as they walked. The torch flickered as a slight wind blew from somewhere ahead.

They stepped into another large cavern even deeper in hell than the pit of torture.

"Just how deep does it go?" Bethalia asked. This cave was similar to the others they'd seen, but it seemed more isolated, even more forgotten, absolutely lost.

The walls contained a myriad of dark holes. These holes had no bars. Only the lower ones would need them anyway. The higher holes where so far up that it was obvious whoever would put someone in the upper cells was capable of flying. If the captive were in a weakened state, the height alone would deter attempts to escape. Escape to where, anyway?

Bethalia started to cry – so hard, that she covered her mouth with her hand, but the sound of her weeping echoed into every hole.

"What is it?" Belak put his hand to her shoulder.

"They're here," She inhaled a difficult breath and struggled to speak. "I can feel it. My mother's in here somewhere."

"She's right," Jubal also fought to speak "I feel it too, we've found them."

"Watch yourselves then, there should be some guards." Elion looked around the room with trepidation, holding his sword at the ready.

Nothing happened, and after a moment of silence, they felt very alone. There appeared to be no guards, and only sounds of water running over stones could be heard.

Haydn suddenly yelled out, "Mary!" with all that his voice could muster. Everyone jumped and Terel and Belak readied their swords. First Haydn began walking, and then trotting along in the ankle-deep water hollering, "Mary! Mary Ward! Mary! It's me, Samuel. I've come for you! Mary!"

No one moved, the others watched hoping that he was right, wondering if they should do the same or if he was wasting precious time. Then suddenly, a quiet voice called out from one of the holes.

"Samuel? Here I am! I'm here!" A woman with see-through skin and looking like a living corpse stuck her head from a hole halfway up the wall and waved her long thin arm.

Haydn burst into action, climbing up to her by using the other holes or cells as a ladder of sorts.

Emboldened by Haydn's success, the other five spread out and began hollering.

Elion cupped his hand to his mouth and yelled, "Kelly! Kelly!"

"Abe! Abe! Mack! I have come for you!" Terel shouted.

"Laura, Laura Kensington!" Jubal tried to yell, but his voice wasn't working well yet. "It's James! Laura!"

"Mother, mother, mother!" Bethalia called in Chinese.

Belak joined in calling out his wife's name.

"Marie, Marie, where are you! It's me, my love! It's John."

With all the commotion and yelling going on, bedraggled expressions appeared in almost all of the holes. Empty, hollow eyes peered out from the darkness. The room seemed to go around forever. Elion could see that Haydn had reached his wife, and they were embracing as their bodies were racked with wailing.

Elion continued to call for Kelly. One by one, Elion watched as every member of the group found their loved one.

"John? John, I am here!" Belak's wife called to him from her hole, only four rows up. He ran to her and was up to her hole in a flash. He grabbed hold of her, and literally jumped to the floor with her in his arms.

"James? James Kensington, is it really you?" Jubal's sister called out.

Elion could see she looked thin, tired, and down to bones. When Jubal saw her, he didn't call out to her due to his voice. He simply ran to the wall and began climbing toward her hole, which was a great distance up. Jubal moved swiftly and reached her prison casting his arm around her with loud sobbing. He pulled her out of the hole and onto his back. She clung tightly like a child to its father's neck. Carefully, he descended the cliff until they were safely on the ground.

From across the hall, a man's voice called out shakily, "Gene? Is that you?" Terel ran to the voice. He knew the sound of it as memories long buried arose again. He climbed up to the hole where what remained of his father-in-law was detained. Once they reached the floor, Terel carried the old man to where the others had gathered.

Bethalia's head snapped to the left as faint Chinese could be heard.

"Child, child, child, I'm here," she heard.

"Mother, mother," Bethalia cried as she ran to her. She grasped Bethalia's hands, climbing from the hole and was carried to the others.

The reunion was full of weeping, hugging, and smiling into one another's eyes. Words could not contain the emotion flowing from one to the other, each knowing the great sacrifice to risk coming to a place like this. Fear for the predicament they were all in left little room for words.

The lost were so weak they looked like concentration camp victims, gaunt, hollow, and dirty. Their scarred skin and marred states left them hardly recognizable. They walked as skeletons with skin pulled over bone frame.

"Bet you're surprised to see me," Terel said to Abe.

"Not really," Abe answered with a smile. "The way you lived, I thought you'd be my cell mate."

"All that changed after..." he stopped himself. "Well, everything changed after you left."

"What are you doing here?" Haydn's wife asked.

"We've come for you. We've come from the Kingdom of

Heaven. We're taking you home. You'll come with us before the King, and you'll leave this awful place…and…"

Haydn's voice trailed off as he realized a short distance away Elion fell to his knees alone and wept into his hands.

"One moment, my love," Haydn said as he stood. "None of us would be here if not for our Captain Elion. Wait here." He approached Elion. Jubal and Terel followed along.

Bethalia stayed behind with the weak. She opened her vial and applied a single drop of the blood of the Lamb to her mother's tongue, as a bird feeds its young. One by one Bethalia administered her healing drop to the others.

Bethalia's mother's eyes lit up as the drop of life's blood immediately filled her insatiable hunger and thirst. The aches and pains lessened and her skin actually tightened as weight added to her ghastly frame. Color returned to gaunt faces and eyes began to dance with excitement as the King's gift nursed them.

Terel, Belak, Haydn, and Jubal closed in around Elion. Elion did not look up as he spoke. "I'm happy for you. I truly am. I was sure they'd all be here, but where is my Kelly?"

"Maybe she's in the next cave," Terel said, trying to sound hopeful. "I saw an opening down at that end." He motioned to the left and everyone looked and saw the dark passage.

"Cap'n, we will find her. I know it," Belak said.

Elion wiped his face with the back of his arm, from mid-forearm to wrist. He strengthened himself and said, "Well, she is not in here. Let's move out." He walked back to the group that was sitting with Bethalia. "Can any of you walk?"

They all nodded that they could. Bethalia's gift worked healing wonders on them, strengthening their minds and bodies. Wounds were still visible and weakness weighed heavily on them, but a newfound energy had taken root. Belak's wife's wrists were no longer red with blood, but rather sealed over in jagged scars. Abe's neck that had been entirely black and blue was returning to a more normal skin color.

Elion turned and headed toward the dark opening. No one spoke as they followed him. The sadness of not finding Kelly with the others reminded them they were still within the borders of the enemy.

"Come on. You all have to keep up," Elion said sternly.

"Cap'n?" Belak spoke from behind him. "Keep up? Where are we going and what about Kelly?"

"She's not here," Elion said, trying to contain his anger. "They must've moved her. Maybe the enemy knew she was mine, I don't know. You *all* have your people. I have to get you out. It's only fair, we can't linger, but I'm staying. I won't go back without her, and you can't all go looking around for her with me. Let's go." Elion turned his back and walked off through the dark doorway.

As they passed through the doorway, the light from the torch spread itself thinly across echoing darkness. It was another cavern just like the first one and all the others, with walls covered in holes that were cells. The sheer quantity of holes and the never-ending number of caverns was unnerving to say the least.

This time, no one looked at the walls or the holes. Every eye was focused on the spectacle in the center of the cavern. A metal rack stood about ten feet off the ground. On it hung the unmoving shape of a single man, his back to the group. They slowly walked toward him, and could see he hung upside down and his hands were bound to a large rock that lay on the ground beneath him to restrict him from swinging up and unhooking his feet. Angry blood flooded Elion's head as he realized the man's feet weren't tied at all.

They were bare and bent sharply at ninety-degree angles while the toes were curled tight. Metal spikes, each about an inch in diameter, had been pushed through the skin just behind the Achilles tendon, and all of his weight hung unmercifully upon those two points.

Elion held the light towards the man and it roused him. He startled and attempted to pull his arms up to protect himself, but his bonds would not allow it. His red eyes squinted as he attempted to focus, then his face changed to bewilderment as he could see that those before him weren't demons at all.

He stared directly at Elion and said in English with a thick German accent, "Joe? Is that you? Joe Rellik?"

"Karl Albrecht," Elion said as he recognized the man. "You seem to be in a predicament."

"Well, yes, and it's your fault!" Karl said. "As everything that happens to me is."

"My fault, what'd I do?" Elion snapped.

"Draka put me here after losing you. He said it was my fault we lost you. Apparently, not to build your ego too much, your guardian, Kari something, is highly regarded and would've been quite a prize for capturing you. We had you all set to kill yourself and wham! You up and die on me."

"Sorry," Elion said with an edge of sarcasm.

"I'm sorry too. I've been here ever sense as punishment for losing you. No more missions for me." Karl looked over the group suddenly realizing the oddity of the crew. "What are you doing here?"

"Where is my Kelly?" Elion asked, ignoring his question.

"You promised me once that if I told you that, you would take me with you," Karl reminded.

"You tell me where she is, and I will get you down from there. How about that, for starters?"

"Deal! Get me down!"

Elion nodded at Belak who stepped up to help. They grabbed his skinny, little body and slid his feet off of the spikes. The feet stayed grotesquely bent. The feet had obviously been positioned like that for quite some time and didn't return to their right place. They carefully sat Karl on the ground.

"Where is she?" Elion demanded. "Or your time is over!"

"You can't threaten me with that you fool," Karl pointed to the darkness behind Elion. "She's in a worm pit. Ever since you left the flesh world, they couldn't punish you, so, they punished…"

"Jubal and all of you stay here," Elion said. "Keep your eyes alert and yell if you see anything. Belak and Terel come with me." He tramped off into the darkness in the direction Karl had pointed, and they soon found another hallway. This one was different because it didn't open into another a cavern, but continued on like a mine shaft. About every fifteen feet or so there were open air pits in the floor of the cave.

Elion held the light into the first pit and stepped back with a gasp. After a moment he looked again. The pits were no more than ten feet square with walls of solid stone. The floor looked like it was mostly covered in water. Along one wall there was a three by five section of muddy land. Lying on the drier spot was a man curled up in a fetal position. He was covered in mud and looked sick as he coughed and shook violently.

Elion went to the next worm pit and looked in. He kept on until he came to the fourth worm pit. He bent his head and focused his eyes to see the person in the bottom. Suddenly, the person in the pit rolled onto her back. The sight of her face was almost too much for Elion to bear. Covered in mud, blue eyes flashed the firelight.

"Kelly!" Elion left the others behind and jumped into the pit with his daughter.

"Daddy?" She spoke softly and quietly, almost mumbling. "Is that really you? What are you doing here?"

Elion picked her up in his arms, rocking her lightly. "I have come for you. Just like I said I would. Let's get out of here." He stood and reached his hand up out of the pit. Terel and Belak each grabbed on and pulled them up. They hurried out of the dark passage and headed back to the cavern with the others.

When he reached them, he sat down with Kelly on his lap. She was unresponsive like she'd passed out. He wiped her scraggly hair out of her face, vaguely aware of the group who stood watching the scene. Her clothes were dirty, wet rags. The white skin of her arms and legs was covered in thin, red lines in a random pattern as a web. Elion rubbed his hand against her skin, puzzled.

"Look at her skin. What is this?" Terel held the light closer. At the end of every red line there was a slight bump in the skin.

"They are water worms," Karl said from where he sat nearby, massaging his mangled feet. "They live on the water from the flesh just under the skin. They get in you and burrow around like a mole, growing and laying eggs. No amount of scratching will get them out; they will just burrow deeper in until you leave them alone. It gets so you can sit and watch them dig through your own body."

"How do you get them out?" Elion demanded, barely able to control his anger.

"You don't. They don't really come out - ever. Unless you spend time out in the sun, then they'll mostly leave you, but otherwise, no way to get rid of them. Welcome to hell." Karl's face showed a thin smile.

Elion pulled his vial from under his armor and cracked the seal. As he opened Kelly's mouth and poured in a drop, he called on the Lord.

"My dear, Lord and King, I call upon the power of your holy water and gift to me. Enter this body and cleanse it of all evil. Kill these worms that seek the water of hell. May your water of life be death to them. Thank you, in the name of the Lamb."

Kelly shuddered a bit.

Suddenly, the little bumps started wiggling around under the skin. Their movements increased, and then one on her leg broke the skin with a small drip of blood. Elion watched as a little, one-inch-long worm that looked like a dark brown mealworm emerged from her. Elion grabbed it and threw it off into the darkness. The little worms were popping out all over her now, driven out by the holy water. Elion continued to throw them as they exited her body.

There were too many for him to keep up with, so Belak knelt and helped pick them off of her. Eventually, no more worms exited her body, and Elion checked her over carefully.

Kelly was still out cold. Bethalia stepped forward and placed a drop of the healing blood into her gaping mouth. Once that fluid mingled with her body, color began to return to Kelly's skin, and the wounds from the worms sealed over, leaving red dots behind.

Her eyes violently moved back and forth under the lids, and then opened with a start. Kelly tried to sit up as if she didn't know what or where she was.

Then, she focused on the young, strong face of her father. Without any words, she gingerly reached her fingers to his face and gently touched Elion.

She looked astonished as she continued to touch Elion. "I've had dreams of you. Is this a dream? Are you really here?"

Elion wept onto her as he pulled her close to him. "Yes, I am really here, baby girl. I really came for you. I am so sorry…" He wailed from deep within his soul.

Kelly also wept. "I am sorry Daddy, so sorry…I shouldn't have…"

"Shh! I know, I know," Elion said soothingly. "Don't be sorry to me, I love you baby girl."

An ominous sound like a large metal gate slamming shut startled everyone. Then a cool breeze sucked its way through the passages.

"What was that?" Terel asked.

"Do *they* know that you're here?" Karl asked. "Because that sound means they're preparing to flood this section of the tunnels!"

"Let's get out of here!" Haydn shouted.

XV
FROM THE PIT

Elion scooped Kelly into his arms as if she were a child. She clung tightly to his strength. The others readied themselves on their own two feet, each holding the arm of the one who came for them, both out of love and stability on wobbly legs.

Karl sat on the floor alone in his misery, still rubbing his feet mangled beyond repair. Elion led off tromping back the way they'd come.

"If you go that way you'll be drowned," Karl called out to them.

Elion brought the column to an abrupt halt. "How do you know? And how can we trust you? You're an agent of evil."

"If I didn't have bad luck, I'd have no luck at all." He shook his head, disgusted. "Take me with you and I'll lead you. You've no idea what they'll do to me now, especially after this," Karl said hopeless and dejected. "If you don't take me with you, then put me back up on the spikes. Please?"

Elion stomped back to the little German and pointed the torch at him.

"If you lie to me or trick us, these demons will seem nice compared to what I will do to you."

"Forgive me if I don't shudder." Karl looked away. "Nothing you could do would be worse than what you have already done."

"Oh poor you, show us the way," Elion snapped.

"There is the matter of my feet." Karl pointed at them with

a grimace.

Bethalia approached and offered her precious liquid. He opened his mouth and absorbed the healing power. His wounds began to cover over with scar tissue, and his bent feet relaxed as he continued to rub them. He smiled and laughed out loud as the blood returned to his toes and he could move his ankles again.

"Thank you, my lady, thank you." He stood slowly and gathered his balance.

"Where to guide dog?" Elion said without patience.

"Cap'n, Michael said to trust no one?" Belak reminded.

"We don't have any choice and we are running out of time," Elion said. "We have to get out as quickly as we can."

"Yes, Cap'n," Belak agreed.

"This way," Karl said as he led the group the other direction and out a different tunnel. He hobbled along, half jumping every now and then in order to go as fast as possible.

"We must hurry! It won't take long and these passages will be filled up to the top." As if to accentuate that he was telling the truth, the once small trickle of a stream that ran the length of the tunnels suddenly swelled to a new width, growing in intensity.

"How far till we're safe?" Belak asked.

"Not far," Karl said over his shoulder. "We will escape up to a higher level, but we can't stop there. Who knows how many levels they will flood!"

Jubal carried his sister, and Elion carried Kelly. Haydn's wife kept up pretty well, as did Abe, Terel's father-in-law. Bethalia and her mother followed close behind, hand in hand.

Elion knew they had a long way to go to get out alive, but for a moment, he relished in the fact that he accomplished something no human had ever done. He'd gone to hell and found his sweet Kelly. Her breath; hot on his neck as she clung to him for dear life, was a sweet victory. Now, the task remained to escape.

Hell & Back

War Cries-Hades

Satan paced on a parapet atop his castle, looking out over the vast wasteland that was the Plains of Esdraelon. The evil creatures operated under a pale, greenish sky, like a tornado that bathes everything in green sepia. The fallen star growled and puffed smoke as he watched the scene.

The plains buzzed with activity; already an innumerable amount of demons stood in rank formations. Encircling the battlefield stood many doorways sparking with flashes as demons poured forth from the other world to prepare for the great battle. The doors flashed like lightning with each demon's passage and they came quickly, one on the heels of the other. They were dark, awful creatures, full of malice, both in countenance and appearance. They were all coming home with one purpose; to conquer the army of God. They fought and growled, slashing viciously at one another as they found their places in a carefully balanced hierarchy. Demons and other evil flying creatures flew over the field, like flies over a carcass. Each landing and falling into formation to wait for the war to come to them.

Draka, the head demon, approached his lord, satan, to oversea the growing army. "We have many more than last time. We've done well."

"Have we located the army or the White Rider?" the great dragon growled with a booming voice. "Are they approaching?"

"We have not located them as of yet, my lord. The catacombs are being flooded as we speak. This will be the only way into Hades. They will have to cross the Plains to enter the gate."

"Did you place guards at the exits of the tunnels in case we flush out the six the whore discovered?"

"Yes, my lord, I posted goblins and warlocks at the entrances, leaving all the best demons, for the great battle here."

"Good, good," the devil nodded his approval. "Let him come. He will pay for his arrogance and the Kingdom of Heaven will be mine!" He arched his head back and roared. Red flames shot forth from his mouth for several feet, ending it with a puff of smoke. The fallen one coughed and double-blinked a second eyelid, his snake-like tail twitching behind him in anticipation.

The White City

Michael waited patiently as loud footsteps echoed against the hallowed halls. Karial and Jaxim marched across the War Room within the Hall of Angels, excited looks on their faces.

"What is it, my brothers?" he asked.

Karial began speaking very rapidly. "Something big is happening! It must be Captain Elion and the others. All of the demons are retreating back to their realm of darkness. They are fleeing - like never seen before."

"All of them?" Michael asked. "They are leaving none behind on earth?"

"None that we can see," Jaxim answered. "They are lined up at their doorways and jumping as fast as they can. They are most excited to be going. They will not engage with us at all. Their only aim is to get back to hell."

Michael smiled and let his claws extend just enough to roll them along the stone table. "I must tell the King immediately."

"Tell me of the demons flight," the familiar voice of God spoke soothingly as He was suddenly beside His archangel.

Michael and the guardians immediately bowed to one knee in honor of the King.

"Yes, my Lord," Michael said. "The demons are fleeing to hell of their own accord and with the utmost haste."

The King smiled and stood in front of the table. "Our adversary has lost none of his pride. He is preparing for the last great battle, our invasion."

"But we aren't invading," Michael said.

"He has mistaken our seven as a great army. So foolish, he knows the book, but not my Spirit. Michael, send every guardian and every angel that can be summoned. Send them all. Send them to the world of men, and destroy every door you can find. By the Spirit we will reap souls with a great harvest. For a time there are no tormenters to oppose us, no opposition at all. The opportunity is great," The King smiled. "Prepare the way for their return is soon." The King's visual presence smiled and was gone.

"Karial," Michael said. "Take the guardians to the Lake of Fire. Be ready, for the warriors will be coming. They will return as heroes of the Kingdom. Go! Fly! Fly now!"

Karial and Jaxim exploded into action as their feet left the ground. Karial let out his mighty hawkish cry as they broke free through the roof of the Hall of Angels. It was not a random cry, and every angel within the Kingdom knew its meaning. The shining sky suddenly filled with angels. Karial rallied the other six guardians on the steps of the Hall of Angels, each anxious and with teeth barred and muscles tense in anticipation of their mission.

"We're commanded to return and await our redeemed by the Lake of Fire," Karial told them. "Each of us will take another to carry the lost souls they found. We are ordered to fly. Fly now! Let us go!"

In one motion they took to the sky, each going a separate way and then falling into a formation over the meadows surrounding the White City, each with another guardian. The fourteen guardians streaked overhead as a great multitude of angels were backed up in long lines at the stairways leading down to the World of Flesh. The air sizzled with excitement, as the Spirit of the King was falling toward the people of the Earth.

***

The Catacombs

The little German stopped suddenly, searching for something on the ceiling. It took a bit of searching. "Ah, there we are." He climbed up onto a boulder that leaned against the wall of the tunnel and reached to the low ceiling, straining as he unhooked a latch Elion would have never seen. Finally it clicked free and a trap door swung down, covering Karl in a cloud of dust.

He coughed and quickly scampered through the hole. Karl's head popped back down the opening. "A shortcut to a higher level, what do you think of that?"

"Great," Elion said. "Let's get up fast. The water is coming!"

They could all hear it. An ever growing sound bubbled from the darkness behind them. Belak climbed up into the next tunnel and Terel began handing the weaker ones up to him one at a time. First Belak's Marie, then Elion handed Kelly up, then Jubal's Laura, then Bethalia and her mother, followed by Haydn and his wife. Abe went next, with Jubal and Terel pulling Elion up behind them. Elion reached down and drew the trap door shut, latching it tight.

The light showed them that they were in another tunnel almost identical to the one they'd just left behind. However, this one seemed to be angling in a direction roughly forty-five degrees upward from the first tunnel.

Karl headed off into the darkness, not waiting for the light or permission. Elion grabbed his shoulder and stopped him short. "Where exactly are you taking us?"

"I'm taking you to the surface the quickest route possible. Some demons don't even know these short cuts. I had a goblin show me once," Karl said with a smile.

Terel frowned at him. "How do we know we can trust you? You could lead us anywhere in here."

"Remember what Michael said about trusting them here," Belak added.

Elion stared at Karl, assessing as to whether they should trust him. He looked like a weak, little boy masquerading in his father's old army uniform. The dark spot on his chest drew Elion's gaze, and he remembered inflicting the wound that sent this boy to this place.

In a moment of diversion, Elion softened around the eyes. "Karl, why did you end up here?"

Karl shook himself free from Elion's strong grip and straightened his tattered uniform. "I'm sure you remember killing me," Karl snarled, informing everyone of their shared history.

"I mean, why did you not enter the Kingdom?"

"Religion was frowned upon in my country," Karl mumbled slightly as he averted his eyes downward from Elion's stare. "We were getting rid of the Jews for their beliefs and I came from a long line of atheists. I had no beliefs at all."

"And now?"

"And now?" Karl stammered. "What, are you crazy? I've seen things- I would very much like to see the other place. I'd change everything if I could live it over again. I'd do it all different."

Elion looked Karl squarely in the eye. "There is a prophecy that the dead will be judged by their deeds. Karl, if you do right by us now that is a very good deed. Our lives are in your hands. Karl, I trust you, with my daughter's life. Can I trust you?"

Karl looked confused and stuttered as if he didn't know what to say. He finally looked into Elion's eyes. "Yes, you can trust me."

"Then take us to the surface as close to the Lake of Fire as possible, and the safest exit as possible. I'm sure they're guarding the exits by now."

"This place I'm taking you is a good exit. It's in the woods. I've used it many times. There is a door nearby. I used it to go on my *personal* missions."

"Then let's get on with it!" Haydn chimed in.

The sound of water rushing past roared through the trap door beneath them.

"It's quite a distance," Karl said. "We'd better hurry." He turned and started off at a trot. Everyone fell into a line and followed along.

Terel lit a stick he'd found and handed it to Elion, who was bringing up the rear. He kept his own light near the front. They trotted for what seemed like hours. It became commonplace to come into large open rooms full of holes in walls containing thousands of lost souls. They entered room after room after room. The group didn't know that for every soul they passed in the lost darkness, a demon in Satan's legion was taking his place on the plains above, preparing for the great battle.

They continued on and on. The newly-recovered captives tired easily and now had to be carried. Their weakness and frailty allowed them to be packed easily on the backs of the strong warriors. Even Bethalia had no trouble carrying her mother. Karl led on as if he knew every rock and corner of the labyrinth. They suddenly stood on a balcony overlooking an abandoned torture room, shaped exactly like the one they'd seen operating. This cavern was even more disturbing for its total lack of people and the fact that the entire room below them was a swirling pool of rising water.

"Don't worry about the water," Karl said. "We're going to make it easily now. We're well into the upper levels. Just a short distance more to go and we're there."

After a brief pause to look at the water, they continued on, following Karl through dark holes and winding tunnels, until he stopped suddenly. He motioned for everyone to remain quiet, and held his breath, listening for something. Elion and the others gathered around him.

"What is it?" Belak whispered.

"Nothing," Karl said. "I don't hear anything, but the exit is just up ahead. Can you see the stairs?"

Belak and Elion both nodded. Elion put Kelly down and slung his shield around to the front. Metal on metal lanced the air as he pulled his sword from its sheath.

"Leave our loved ones here," Elion said. "They're too weak to fight. Let's go up there and take this entrance. No one must stop us. It's our only way out. They'll defend it dearly. No matter what, we must pass. Is everyone ready?"

Swords and shields readied as the wide-eyed captives stared in awe.

"Ready, Captain!" Jubal whispered with his raspy voice.

Elion held his sword out, and every member of the group touched his sword to the center in a show of allegiance. Elion nodded his head for a split second, and then turned with purpose. He exited the doorway with the other five members of the squad marching right along. They stepped boldly into the greenish light, inhaling what should've been fresh air, but it wasn't.

Elion paused momentarily while he and the others surveyed the scene before them. They'd exited right into the middle of a camp of sorts - obviously the camp of those sent to guard the exit.

Six goblins sat on the ground. They were round, greasy, and disgusting. They each had a small sword, but they weren't holding them. The goblins were lying on the ground as if they hadn't seen any action in a long time, and didn't expect any. One goblin leaned over the dice he'd obviously just rolled onto a blanket.

When the goblins saw them step forth from the darkness, their mouths dropped open in astonishment. With squeals that sounded like pigs, the goblins all jumped up to hurriedly gather their weapons.

Elion stepped into the center of their little gambling party and stuck the dice man clean through with his sword. The other warriors each had their way and in the blink of an eye, the six goblins lay dead. The air curdled with their rank-smelling innards, and the ground covered in their green and blue guts.

Elion spun about searching for any stragglers. Suddenly he was slammed from behind. The force of the impact knocked him to the ground where he quickly rolled searching for his adversary. The dark-winged creature was a large bat-type nightmare. It circled up high above the trees and dove in for another pass.

The winged hellion let out a piercing cry and swooped down at Bethalia while both Terel and Jubal waited patiently with swords drawn like batters waiting for a pitch. The bat creature angled its sharp claws to gouge at her. With its evil intent, it came in hard, apparently not noticing the two men waiting for its arrival. Eyes focused, timing their attack perfectly with quick, slashing movements, the two men mortally wounded the creature. It screeched and dropped straight to the ground in a heap of steaming death. One wing virtually cut off and a long slash through its body.

"There goes another one!" Haydn cried out and pointed to the sky.

They watched as another bat creature ascended through the treetops, escaping to the sky.

"Well, good news travels fast around here," Elion said. "We have to move. We have too far to go to fight every inch of it. Let's get the others up here and get going."

As he turned back to the opening that led to the Catacombs, six men stepped from the edge of the forest. Elion saw them and could tell right away it meant trouble.

"I'll take the big one in the middle," he said quietly to his companions as he readied his sword in his right hand and adjusted his shield on the left. "Everybody pick one and kill him."

"I'll take the one in the army helmet," Belak said.

"I'll take the short one on the left," Bethalia said.

Jubal spoke next, his voice still raspy and low. "I got the one on the right end."

"I'll take muscle man there with no shirt." Terel smiled as he readied himself for battle.

"That leaves the one in the prison-orange jumper for me," Haydn replied.

The six men were an ugly, surly-looking crew, with teeth missing, scarred faces, greasy and dirty. They had a deathly look to their skin, and glared as if eager to do battle.

The one in the middle was a large, strong-looking man. His big head fit nicely on his thick neck. His hair was long and stringy, and he wore dirty rags for clothing which looked like they'd been stained with blood before this encounter.

Elion was not intimidated. He stared his man in the eyes as they approached, carefully watching.

"Did you kill these goblins?" the big man asked. Elion surmised him to be the leader of the goblins.

"Yeah." He looked over at where they lay. "But there's room enough for you too."

The leader held up a club with spikes in the end, and in his other hand he wielded a long knife. He looked sideways at his cohorts who were similarly armed with knives, clubs, and chains. "Kill 'em, boys, and we'll have liver for dinner!"

The dirty band of fighters growled and snorted their approval of the plan.

Elion had seen their kind before, common thugs, bravery in a group, cowardice in isolation. He knew they might be bluffed into foolish action.

"You look like men. Why would you fight for the dragon when you're his prisoners?"

"We were prisoners, but now we're in management," the

leader laughed loudly and his cohorts joined in.

"You're fools. Even now, you chose death," Elion scoffed. "You're traitors and enemies of the King. It is our sovereign duty to kill you, but we'll let the bugs eat your livers."

"You'll be dead soon and we'll be heroes!" the leader snapped.

"You're worm bait!" Elion retorted.

The leader couldn't contain his anger any longer and it drove him to charge. He ran straight at Elion with his arms over his head, screaming. His gang charged behind him.

Elion stood perfectly still, coolly waiting, and the others followed suit.

As the leader neared, he swung his club at Elion, who easily blocked the blow with his shield and sliced viciously across his back. The man stumbled out of balance. He cried out in pain as his back was laid open. Slicing, kicking, screaming, and gouging; dust rose around the fray as the two factions collided.

The leader turned and lunged at Elion with his knife. Elion brushed it aside with his sword blade and hit the man squarely in the face with his shield. His nose exploded and blood poured forth like a faucet. The leader saw the blood and became enraged even more as he charged at Elion again. The man did nothing to defend himself and ran wild-eyed at Elion, flailing his knife around.

Elion held the sword over his head, again patiently waiting. When the timing was right, he swung the blade downward as hard as he could. It slashed the base of the man's neck, and he fell to the ground instantly. The blade had penetrated and lodged in the spine, severing it. The leader was dead before he felt the pain.

Elion spun and looked for another adversary and discovered his partners in various stages of victory. He watched as Bethalia withdrew her sword from the short man's chest. She looked formidable as her hair was flung about her with blood and dirt smeared on her face from the battle. The dead man fell at her feet.

The others were dead as well, as the mercenary band of thugs were no match for the redeemed. Haydn had gone a little white as he slumped to the ground. The others gathered around him. A growing pool of blood seeped from under Haydn's armor.

"Where is it, man?" Belak asked. "Where's the wound?"

Haydn half-raised his right arm and blood was everywhere. He'd taken a knife from the side. The blade had penetrated just under the armpit; the only place on the torso not covered in armor.

Bethalia didn't hesitate. She popped the lid on her vial and poured a single blood-red drop into his mouth. He sat waiting like a little bird with his mouth open.

Elion didn't wait to see the miracle. It was a foregone conclusion. He went to the catacombs and found the others cowering in silence. They looked somewhat stronger and Karl paced anxiously.

"Come on, let's go," Elion demanded.

Everyone stood as commanded preparing to go, but Karl seemed uneasy and didn't move.

"What is it, Karl?" Elion asked.

"I can't go any further," Karl said, looking away back into the tunnels.

"Why not?"

"Because you'll not succeed in escaping this place. No one does. I'll be tortured for all eternity if they catch me helping you. I'm sorry, but I must turn back into the tunnels. I can say you tried to kill me and I escaped. Maybe I'll just lay in a hole for awhile, a long while."

Elion walked over to Karl and embraced him. When he released him, Karl looked embarrassed and astonished at the show of affection from his killer.

"Go into the tunnels. Know this, if we do escape, it was only due to your aid. That will not be forgotten, and we'll tell the King of it."

"Thank you, Karl," Kelly said quietly.

Elion turned and smiled proudly at her. Every member of the group stared at Karl, aching that he would chose the darkness, but knowing it was his choice.

Karl gave a thin smile, obviously uncomfortable with these feelings. Then he turned and headed back into the caves.

Elion and the others proceeded into the pale light of hell.

They stood over the corpses of men and goblins that lie dead from the skirmish.

"All of you former captives," Elion said to them. "Look around here, and each of you find a knife that these gentlemen have so unwillingly provided for us. You may need it to defend yourselves should that become necessary."

They all did as they were told.

Belak, Elion, and Terel stood side-by-side, looking off in one direction. They could see a great darkness that flashed with what looked like bombs exploding. The sky rumbled with thunder and clouds swirled a mass of dark colors centered on one location.

"That must be Hades over there," Belak said as he put the storm to his back and pointed. "Then that way must be the Lake of Fire."

Elion and Terel both nodded in agreement.

Elion struck out down an obvious path to escape the catacombs and press deeper into the woods. The rest of the group quickly grabbed their things and followed Elion. It didn't take long before they found something unusual. Elion brought the group to a halt to examine what they'd discovered.

Six large animals patiently stood tied to trees in the woods. These strange creatures looked vile and smelled worse. The warriors approached with swords ready until they realized these creatures wore bridles and saddles for riding.

"Are they for riding?" Haydn asked.

"Have to be, look at the saddles," Terel answered.

They were as large as a Clydesdale horse, but mostly looked like a giant bug because they had wings tucked away like a grasshopper. Four very muscular legs culminated in human-like hands covered in tough leathery-skin and sharp claws. The body was long and sturdy and the saddles were strapped tightly in the center of the creatures' backs. Each saddle seated two riders complete with handles on both sides.

The creature's heads were shaped much like the head of a giant squirrel, but they had no hair other than a long mane that flowed from a spot directly between the short, rounded ears. The manes were long and flowing, and each animal seemed to be identical to one another in every way, other than the color of the mane. The animals head movements gave them a quirky nervous appearance. They seemed friendly enough as the group approached them, and they began to make a sort of clicking noise that in some way was inviting.

"I think these creatures belonged to those dead men," Elion said.

Terel unhooked the reins of the one with a long, black mane. "Then we just inherited them. Praise be to our King, let's mount up."

Elion felt a little uncertain of the creatures and looked at the others for assurance.

Terel tossed his leg over and found his seat easily. He offered his arm to Abe, who slid up behind.

Belak shrugged and went to the creature with the blonde mane. He placed his Marie in the back seat and climbed aboard.

"Alright then," Elion said to no one in particular. "Let's commandeer these animals." He untied the one with a brown mane and put Kelly in the back seat as he climbed aboard, holding tightly to the reins.

He waited as Jubal, Haydn and Bethalia settled in on their creatures. Once they were ready, he called out to everyone, "Keep the dark storm to your backs, and we should eventually see the fog of the Lake of Fire ahead of us. Let us go as fast as these animals can carry us. Try to stay together, it is our only hope. Ready?"

"Ready!"

"Yes, Cap'n, ready!" Everyone, in turn, called out his or her readiness.

"Then here we go!" Elion shouted. He gave his creature the slightest of kicks from his heels and soon discovered why there were handles on the saddles. The speed and roughness of the ride would have been exhilarating if it wasn't so terrifying.

The creature between Elion's legs gave a leap with a burst of power that left Elion breathless. It burst virtually straight up from the trees, and then coasted for what seemed at least a half a mile. As it drifted back to the ground, the wings flitted off to the side and behind them as they glided. They were still in the rocky, forested areas, and Elion feared they would crash. His fears were laid to rest as the creature deftly grabbed a treetop with its hand-feet, and then pushed off with a renewed burst of strength and speed. The clicking noise had a cadence as if the animals seemed to be communicating to one another.

Elion could feel Kelly's head buried against his back as she hung on tightly. After several more of the jump and coast combinations they'd covered much distance quickly. Elion praised the Lord for their good fortune as he realized the agonizing hours it would've taken them to hike that distance with their loved ones in their weakened state.

The ground grew barren as they entered the wastelands. The vast nothingness was disheartening in it size. However, even amongst the bleak expanse Elion noted huge swells, rock formations, bluffs, and mountains.

The creatures made swift time and fantastic gains through the open areas as they passed by several torture fields, full of cages. They flew over several different mines that all seemed to be abandoned.

"Where is everyone?" Elion whispered to himself. "What's going on?" He knew it didn't matter, and every moment closer to the lake was a moment closer to their escape.

S.C. Sherman

XVI
THE RACE TO THE LAKE

Row after row of demons ready for battle spread across the vast plain. Demons argued and fought with one another within their ranks; gnashing teeth and clawing against each other, drawing blood and spilling hatred. It was all the commanders could do to keep them in line at all. Satan's roar reverberating overhead seemed to be the only thing that forced these awful figures to cower.

Satan ordered them to stay on the ground as he circled above, as if to display his control. "Behold the great dragon. I am he. Do not defy me!" He clutched a jagged rock and hopped down next to his captains who stood waiting on what remained of a high tower.

"Still no sign of the White Rider, my lord," Draka said.

Satan hit Draka on the side of the head with his tail knocking him to the ground. "Did I ask for you to speak to me?"

"No, sire, forgive me?" Draka spoke without getting up.

The devil did not answer him.

The little one-handed demon, Cank, stepped up to the devil with a demonstrative bow. "My lord, I have word."

"Out with it!" Satan roared as a small puff of smoke emitted from his mouth.

Cank continued to look sideways careful to avoid direct eye contact. "We have received word that exit number twenty-two in the forest saw the humans."

Satan's claws scraped scars into the crumbling facade in front of him. "What do you mean *saw* the humans?"

"My lord, the humans escaped from the catacombs, killed the goblins and the men guarding the entrance, and are as of yet, unable to be located. They're on the move, my lord."

Satan said nothing, a low growl emanating from within, as he pondered this news.

"Were these the same ones the whore saw in her lair?" he finally asked.

"My lord," Cank said, continuing to look down. "I do not know what humans these are, but there is more."

"More?"

"When the humans left the catacombs, they had six of our captives with them."

"Six of our captives?" the dark lord's head twitched and he seemed to shudder. "Where is the army? Where is the White Rider? What is He up to?" he roared loudly and slammed his hand in anger on the tower wall, causing huge pieces of it to crumble and fall away. In his rage, he blasted fire against a boulder until it virtually melted.

"My lord, what if these humans are the only ones here? What if the army and the White Rider are not coming? Perhaps this is not the great battle?"

Satan spun and sunk his claws into Cank's right leg and held him out over the edge of the castle. Black blood dripped down his leg as he whimpered. Satan growled as he viciously shook the little demon. Draka and the other captains chuckled.

The idea settled in the evil mind of Satan. He tossed Cank back over the side slamming him to the ground. Satan stood over his wounded demon. "You are more useful than I thought."

In a flash, the dragon spun and cocked his head like a bird, watching Draka. Nothing happened for a moment as all the demons on the parapet watched in wonder. With no warning and a perfectly clean slice, Draka's head rolled off his shoulders and fell to the ground with a splat. Satan flicked his clawed foot and Draka's body flew over the side disappearing into the melee below.

"He failed me for the last time!" Satan puffed. "Cank, send the legions back to our war on the flesh! They will pay dearly for this. Find me the lost woman!"

"Yes, my lord, the lost woman?" Cank's knobby knees shook.

"Bring me her offspring. Kill them, steal them, and destroy them all! They will all pay!"

"Yes, my lord." Cank nodded his head in allegiance. Then he escaped to the air in a flash and was gone.

An enormous horn blew from some unseen source, and the demoniac army sprang to action. Doorways began flashing as long lines formed. It would take some time to return the army to its war on the flesh of earth.

"Jakl, come!" Satan commanded.

A formidable demon stepped forth from his position in the shadows. His eyes glowed like a cat's. His uniform was too small for his size, and burst at the seams. His face was mostly black as if the flesh had been burned in a fire.

"Draka's position is yours. Bring your squad and follow me. We'll put an end to this. I'll kill these humans myself!" The old dragon took to the sky, and a small detachment of demons followed him.

⚜

Elion could see a wall of smoke up ahead, and the terrain became rocky and brushy just like they remembered. Everyone knew they were getting close. The awful smell of burning sulfur served as reassurance that they were on track.

A flash of fire shot directly in front of Elion raining down from above. A great roar accompanied smoke as more fireballs burst through the sky.

He reached back and adjusted the shield on his back positioning Kelly underneath it. Elion saw that most of the group was close together, but the source of the fire bursts was nowhere to be seen. Elion urged his animal on and it faithfully kept jumping as hard and fast as it could manage, clicking continuously.

Haze from the lake sporadically covered them. They were getting close.

The smoky clouds made it harder to keep track of one another as a deafening roar broke the clouds. The sound was much closer, and despite the heat, it chilled them to the core. They were so close. Elion looked sideways in time to see that Terel's creature was off to one side, farther away than he'd hoped.

"Terel!" he called and waved to him to direct the creature closer.

Suddenly, a blast of fire struck Terel's creature on the back of the head.

Terel saw the flash as the fiery arrow went into the base of the creature's head. It was dead immediately and tumbled end-over-end, sending its passengers aloft. Terel and Abe hit the ground hard with a skidding *thud*. They landed almost on top of each other amidst some brush. Terel staggered to his feet and shook his head as the dust settled around him. His face was scuffed and bleeding from sharp bushes and landing on the rocks. His shoulder stabbed with intense pain, and his head pounded. He reached over and helped Abe to his feet.

"You alright?" Terel asked.

"I don't know? I guess so. I'm still in one piece. What was that?" Abe's lip was cut and bleeding, but he didn't complain.

"Fiery arrow, I guess. Let's take cover and keep moving toward the smoke. We are almost to the Lake."

"What are we going to do at the Lake?"

"Jump in!" Terel said with his wild child smile.

Abe looked confused as to why that would be a good thing, and Terel laughed. They trotted deeper into the fog and wound their way through the scrubby trees and brush. A terrible cry exploded from above and the sound of wings on the wind promised only death. They ducked their heads in fear and dove behind a rocky bluff. Bright light immediately captured their attention; partially covered in the brush stood a door sizzling with electricity. Lightning zigzagged across it as Terel inspected it.

"It seems to be working," Terel said.

"Gene! Look out!" Abe yelled, using Terel's old name.

A fiery arrow hit him directly in the chest. The force of it knocked him to the ground. He struggled to regain his feet gasping for air as the wind had been knocked from him. Wheezing terribly, Terel laughed out loud. The arrow lay at his feet smoking. It had not penetrated the armor of God.

"We better run for it!" Terel screamed.

Their escape halted instantly as the demon, Jakl, stepped from the mist directly in front of them. He clacked his wicked teeth, waving his knifelike claws.

"Where are the rest of you?" he hissed.

Terel didn't answer and drew his sword. Abe already held his confiscated knife in his hand. Terel turned to run the other direction only to see several other demons step into view. They were surrounded, and the demons slowly moved in. Abe and Terel were back-to-back with nowhere to go.

"You'll just have to die by yourselves," Jakl said with slurred words.

"Gene, I'm sorry that you came here. You won't ever leave now."

Terel's eyes danced as he looked for opportunities. He was unwilling to accept their defeat and his spirit fought for an escape.

The demons crept closer. The words of angels burst through Terel's memory.

Never go through a door! Never! We don't know what would happen or where you would go.

Terel chuckled as the thought flashed through his mind because he knew instantly that he would do it. "I guess we're gonna find out," he whispered to himself.

"Abe," Terel said quietly. "We're not staying here."

He spun around, threw his shield on the ground, and wrapped his left arm around Abe, forcibly pushing him with all his strength right through the door standing behind them in the brush.

The demons lunged at them and with a flash Terel and Abe were gone.

Elion saw the flash of the door from the bluff where he and the others had landed the bug creatures. They dismounted and swatted the creatures on their backsides to send them on their way. The animals obliged, and with some clicking, disappeared into the fog, hopefully taking their pursuer with them. Elion and the others started off on foot.

"What about Terel?" Belak asked.

"He's lost." Elion knew they must keep walking regardless of what happened along the way.

⚜

A blinding flash of white light left Terel and Abe dazed. A sharp, tingling sensation zipped through their bodies as if they had touched a live wire. After the flash of light, absolute darkness followed and they blinked repeatedly to regain their sight.

Slowly, their eyes adjusted to the dim light as Terel felt a sudden burst of pain to his head. He felt his scalp with his hand and discovered a cut and a bump surrounded by bloody hair.

A sparking sound to their left caused Terel to jump to his feet, staring at the door. He realized it was wide open for enemies to follow. He swung his sword violently with all of his strength at the metal frame of the door. With the impact of the sword, the doorframe bent in on itself and went completely dark.

"I think you closed it." Abe stood and rubbed his head.

"I hope so," Terel said.

The smell of stale beer filled his nostrils as they scanned their surroundings. A man stood behind a long wooden bar wiping it in lazy circles with a white rag. He appeared to be in his thirties. He looked big and strong, but somehow soft like a marsh mellow. His bald head was shaved clean and covered in an assortment of tattoos. He seemed out-of-place in his uniform, complete with bowtie and tuxedo vest. One old man sat along the front row of a stage that was the focal point of the room.

A young woman walked out onto the stage scantily dressed. She stopped next to the pole as music started to play. She didn't move or dance or anything.

"Jim!" she finally yelled.

"What?" The bartender looked up from his wiping.

"I'm not going to do this only for Old Fred," she said,

frustration showing on her face.

"What's wrong with Fred? If you don't you'll get fired," Jim yelled back.

She abruptly stomped off the stage her high heels clicking sharply.

"Yeah, right!"

"She acted like she didn't see us," Abe said quietly to Terel.

Terel walked over to Old Fred who hadn't moved from his seat. He was staring intently at his whiskey. Terel waved his hand in front of the man's face. Fred gave no reaction. Terel smiled big at Abe. "You're right, they can't see us."

Abe leaned close to Old Fred's ear. "Go home and read a book!" he whispered.

Terel laughed until his laughter turned to astonishment.

Old Fred suddenly stood up and started to walk out.

"See you later, Old Fred," the bartender called out to him.

"I think I'll go home and read a book," Fred said without looking at Jim.

"No way! I don't believe it!" Terel said as the two men followed Old Fred. The door slammed shut on Terel, and it swung right through him without touching him.

"Are we like ghosts or something?" Abe asked.

Terel realized they were standing on a sidewalk below a flashing sign.

Live Girls.

"Well, we aren't in the Kingdom. We better get out of here. Those demons will come for us. There are many doors," Abe said. "Especially in this neighborhood."

"In every neighborhood," Terel added. "We need to find a stairway."

Abe raised an eyebrow, "Stairway to Heaven?"

"Let's go to where people die. Somebody will be getting a stairway. Maybe we can hitch a ride," Terel said.

"People die in the hospital pretty regularly."

"Good idea." Terel saw a taxi coming down the street and stepped out to flag it down only to have it drive right through him.

"We could walk. Maybe they have a train or a subway or something. What city are we in?" Abe asked.

"I don't know, let's walk."

No one saw them. The world of living went about their business, never knowing or seeing the spirits of the two men passing by. A car went by, and a little girl in the back seat leaned forward and stared out her window at them as they passed.

"Did you see that little girl in that car?" Abe asked.

"No, I didn't see her," Terel said truthfully.

"She saw us. She was seeing us. I could tell."

Suddenly, they found themselves standing before a large red-brick building. The sign read, *Mercy Hospital*.

"Here we are," Terel said as they wandered the floors until they found the cancer wing. "This ought to do."

Abe easily found the lounge and slumped down in a seat to wait. The room was empty other than one person who obviously couldn't see him. She was a middle-aged woman, red-eyed from crying. She stared at the television set with her mouth open, numb.

The evening news was on, and a local newsgirl spoke in a clean, Midwestern voice. She was young and pretty with bright eyes and an effervescent nature, just what they look for in broadcasting. She stood in front of a giant white tent. Written in bright red letters was the word, *Revival*.

"Nationwide, in tents like these and churches of every sort, attendance is soaring. The story is good, old-fashioned Revival. For some time now, a growing number of people have been experiencing it. This newscaster, for one, knows from firsthand experience how much a life can change due to a faith in God, belief in a life and world to come, and hope for a future beyond this world. Countless building projects have been initiated as churches struggle to keep up with the growing numbers of people wanting to know more about how to live a life of faith. Pastor Bruce Proctor recently issued this statement, 'God is relentlessly pursuing us all. Not all of us allow Him to rescue us. If genuine revival is sweeping the world, then praise the King of Kings, all power and honor and Glory to Him. We will see His church restored!' No matter what you believe, no one can deny that something is going on in the world of faith. Aimee Grasen reporting."

Terel stood in disbelief. He looked over at Abe, and he too stared at the television, his mouth drooped open.

"What's going on?" Terel said. "Looks like some kind of revival. We gotta get back to the Kingdom before they find us here watching TV. Let's go to the cardiac wing. Somebody's gotta die there."

"I saw a sign in the hall. It's this way," Abe said.

Terel followed along, looking at all of the people of the world. So busy, missing what really matters. Going through life wrapped up in themselves, selfish and lost. Terel and Abe paused in front of some metal, swinging doors, which kept swinging right through them.

"Did you hear that? It sounds like a solid flat-lined EKG," Abe said.

Terel strained to listen, and then he heard it. "Yeah, let's go see."

They entered an operating room to see a fine-looking, middle-aged man standing beside them wearing workout clothes, watching the doctors feverishly working. One doctor had his hand completely inside the open chest cavity of the man on the table, massaging his heart. Another doctor stood by with a syringe with an incredibly long needle, while yet another held two paddles in his hands patiently waiting.

The middle aged man saw Abe and Terel.

"Hello. They're sure trying hard. I don't think I'm going to make it, though, that doesn't look good at all. My shoulder's been bothering me for months. I never told my wife how much it was hurting." The man sort of stared at the scene in disbelief.

"Quick question, sir?" Terel asked.

"Yes?"

"Would you call yourself a Christian?"

"Yes, all my life. Why?"

Terel and Abe smiled and nodded to each other. "Well, if you weren't going a certain way," Terel explained. "We'd have needed to make a quick exit. Some rather unsavory elements are looking for us. However, more than likely we're going climb some stairs with you today, if you don't mind too much?"

"I don't mind."

Just then the doctor removed his hands from the body. The doctors stared silently for a moment.

"Mark 19:08 as time of death," one doctor said as he pulled his mask down below his chin.

The man looked confused, "But I'm not dead."

"No," Abe said. "Just your old flesh."

They gazed in wonder as in intense brightness grew along the wall, and then suddenly it opened, allowing a warm, inviting light to pour in. Within the brightness, the bottom steps of a white-marble staircase became visible.

Abe grabbed Terel and hugged him tightly, weeping through laughter.

"Shall we go?" Terel smiled.

"Thank you, Gene. Thank you for this!"

"Don't thank me. Thank Cap'n Elion. It was his doing, none of us would've gone without him. The King be praised."

The three started up the stairs shoulder-to-shoulder, drawn toward the brilliantly shining door before them.

Terel motioned to Abe to go ahead as the path narrowed to one at a time. "You go ahead first. The Kingdom of Heaven is at hand."

Sweet music and pleasant aromas filtered through from the other side, inviting them to enter. After they passed through, Terel smiled at Abe's youthful appearance, as magnificence spread out before them. Off in the distance, the White City sparkled like a star. Slowly they tread the path to the jewel of Heaven.

XVII
LAST RITES

The rancid smell of the lake was enough to cause them to gag. Only now it was the smell of freedom - the smell of victory, no one complained. Elion marched hard, trying to make it over a small knoll he hoped began the downward slide to the lake. It would be even better if they could find a bluff to jump off, but there wasn't much hope for that. The group followed along single file. Elion pushed harder than some of them could handle and they straggled behind.

The clicking sounds of the giant bugs could be heard and giant flashes of light came from the same direction. Elion smiled to himself. The diversion had worked. The enemy was following the bug creatures into the fog.

They crested the little knoll and Elion smiled as it did appear to descend toward the burning liquid. Elion knew the diversion wouldn't last long. This was their one chance. They had to push on now if they were to make it to the lake without another fight.

Elion looked over his shoulder. He frowned as he noticed the group spreading out too far behind him stumbling.

"Come on. Push hard! We are almost there!" He waited a moment as they caught up to him. "I know you're tired, but we must push on hard. Now! Our enemy is very near and so is our escape. We must make it to the lake. The demons cannot follow us into it. Let's move!"

He started off again at a strong pace, breaking into a hurried jog as the ground angled downward and the others followed closely behind. They tucked into some dense, piney brush as the heat of the lake permeated everything. They were soaked with sweat, and their breathing was laborious in the thick, humid air. Elion was proud of his little platoon. He could see they were giving it all they had.

The ground leveled out a bit and everyone paused. They gasped for air with their hands on their knees and heads hanging. Elion started off again. The others fell in behind.

Swooshing sounds echoed through the clouds above them. Elion kept moving forward. He headed down the side of a slope that he thought to be the final push to the Lake.

Suddenly, there was a whirring sound as an arrow zipped past Elion and the ground just to the front and left of him exploded into flames.

"Run!" he screamed.

Fiery darts rained down from the sky igniting all around them. Elion had given his shield to Kelly, and she now carried it over her head as she tried to run. The others had done the same with their shields in an attempt to offer some protection to the ones with no armor.

Kelly hit the ground with a thud as the force of a fire-tipped arrow glanced off of the shield. Elion quickly picked her up in one arm and the shield in the other. He ran for some trees to the right and just made it as more arrows fell down around them. The others made it beneath the trees as well. They huddled together, afraid and out of breath. The last bits of energy and all remnants of hope waning away.

Overhead the dragon circled. Terrifying flashes of him could be seen as he sailed through the fog. Occasionally, great bursts of flames exploded from an ear-piercing roar. They covered their ears to block out the menacing threat. It rang chords of fear deep into their beings, causing them to slip into complete hopelessness.

Elion crawled to the edge of the trees and looked out. "I can see the lake down there," he said in a whisper loud enough for everyone to hear. "We can make it. From this little rise I can see a thin line of a creek running toward the water. We can follow that creek down."

"What about the fire? What of the dragon?" Haydn whispered back. "If we get back out there, he'll get us."

"We can't stay here," Elion said. "We have to run for it. No other choices."

"Elion's right," Jubal spoke through his wounded throat. "We have to run."

"Let's get it done then!" Belak said with a frown.

"Alright, see those boulders?" Elion pointed to the huge rocks nearby. "We can stay concealed until we round them, then we have to run the distance down that little creek in the open." With that, Elion ran toward the boulders, the others following closely behind.

After leaving the boulders, it was about a quarter mile of wide-open space to the edge of the Lake of Fire. There was no way around that part of the terrain. The smoky fog was thick at times, and then it would blow clear, providing no guarantee of concealment.

Elion stood and positioned his armor. He made sure his shield was secure with Kelly. She looked up at his face and smiled. "I love you, Daddy. I always hoped you'd come for me, but I thought I was lost to you, no good for what I did, but you came for me after all… oh Daddy, I am so sorry!" She threw her arms around him with her thin body shaking as she wept.

He lifted her up and held her in his arms. "I never stopped loving you, my baby girl. You're my sweet girl. I love you. You never left my heart and you never will. Now let's go home."

She smiled at him with big, crystal-blue eyes dripping with tears and nodded her head. "Home, okay." Her voice wobbled.

The others took a moment to savor their loved ones' embraces and to also exchange a few sweet words for 'just in case'. This last push obviously held great danger and no promises of a happy ending.

Elion drew his sword. "Everyone ready?"

They all nodded in unison and the warriors drew their swords as well.

"Ready, Cap'n," Belak said. "On your order."

"I've never served with better," Elion told them, his voice soft. "No matter what happens, I'm proud to be named with you."

A short silence fell among them.

Then Elion took a deep breath, closing his eyes as he loudly exhaled. When the breath was complete, he focused his eyes intently upon the lake. He turned his back to the group, and they followed as he crept along the thin trail through the trees and around the large rocks. They burst into a sprint as they left the boulders behind. They moved downhill at good speed concealed in a deep, dark fog. Elion kept the little creek at his feet, secure that it would lead to the Lake of Fire.

The fog suddenly cleared, and the entire crew skidded to a complete stop on the loose, black rocks. Directly in front of them stood Jakl and several other demons, blocking their passage to the Lake. Elion looked past the evil demons and saw the broiling cauldron of the Lake beckoning to him.

"So close," Jakl laughed.

The members of the group who had fallen, slowly stood and closed ranks to form a tight circle. As they surveyed the scene, several more demons flashed out of the foggy sky and formed a solid noose around what was left of Elion's mighty men.

Bethalia's mother and Jubal's sister both began crying hysterically.

Belak stood proud and tall, while his Marie lifted her chin and straightened her back holding his hand.

Kelly pressed herself tight to Elion.

Haydn shook his head in defeat as he put his arm around his wife. "I'm sorry. I tried, honey."

She put her hand to his lips to stop him and smiled at him. "Nothing they do to us will ever change what you've done. You came for me. I'll love you for eternity!"

With a great thump and a slight roar, the dragon landed in the fog and approached the captives. Satan appeared through the mist and laid his head back, roaring into the air, a sound that shook the ground. All of the demons had their heads slightly bowed in reverence or fear. The captives trembled at the sight of the devil. His repulsiveness was more than his mere appearance. It went much deeper because at the root of it; this being was the father of all sin, lies, and evil. The blackness of that soul was absolute and somehow drained all hope from those around him. He was the embodiment of every evil thing.

He cocked his head and surveyed the little band of warriors. He instinctively knew which man to address by his countenance. Elion stood straight. Assured. Not arrogant. Not resigned. Still clinging to a hope that this was not defeat.

Satan laughed, and the demons joined him out of pure loyalty, for they had no idea what was funny to the devil. Finally, satan stopped laughing and looked at Elion.

"Oh the disappointment! The Lake is just right there. You almost made it. You should be very proud of yourselves. Believe me, you will have plenty of time to think on it and relive this very moment and your failure," he spoke with a raspy contemptible voice.

"Who is this demon scum who addresses me?" Elion's shouted response surprised the father of lies.

The demons all looked sideways at each other, unsure what would happen next. Satan rose up straight and roared again.

"Who are you? You are no White Rider. Where is the vast army to fight me? You are a speck of dust!"

"If I was the White Rider I would be standing on your neck!" Elion smiled and chuckled.

Satan charged forward, but stopped just short of the circle of demons. He looked closely at Elion, turning his head from side to side and blowing smoke at him.

"You are not afraid?"

"Afraid of what? Smoke and mirrors? You are a mock king, propped up by your own pride and anger and arrogance. Anyone who has ever seen the true King could see it in a moment," Elion spoke clearly and with conviction.

Haydn looked down to see if his vial had opened to release the spirit of the King, but it had not. Elion's boldness was coming from within his heart.

Satan looked at the ones taken from his dungeons. "These you have are mine. You have no ri-"

"*You* have no right!" Elion shouted at him. "Their names are in the Lamb's Book, and we mean to take them. Step aside before I kill you!"

The demons and satan didn't do anything, but stood in stunned silence.

Elion was buying time. His mind raced as he tried to formulate a plan. Was there any possible way to get to the lake? He looked down at it and longed to feel its drowning warmth.

"You? You will kill me? Am I captured? Am I outnumbered?" satan roared.

Elion looked at his feet and saw the black water of the little creek flowing to the Lake of Fire, and in an instant he knew. His heart exploded with excitement as it birthed hope again. He began to slowly ease himself to the back of the group. He wanted to be on the high ground above the rest of them.

As he moved he whispered, "Hang on tight to one another. I will see you in Heaven." He smiled greatly as he prepared for battle.

"Where do you think you are going little man?" satan asked as he must have detected Elion's move. "Before I kill you, know that I will feast on your loved ones and hang your bodies on trees! You have failed!"

Elion reached into his breastplate and grabbed hold of his vial containing the water from the River of Life. He pulled it out and held it for a moment, glaring at the devil.

"I am tired of this game," satan said as he looked over at Jakl. "Kill them all!"

Jakl and the other demons let out their awful cries of death and wickedness.

Elion jerked hard on the chain around his neck, breaking it. In one quick motion he raised his arm high over his head, and then forcefully slammed the glass vial onto the rocky ground. It shattered into a thousand pieces and the very ground seemed to hiccup, rumbling like an earthquake.

The demons startled and spun around with uneasiness.

Satan fearfully looked to the sky as if the White Rider would burst forth upon a cloud, clothed in white with His robes tipped in blood.

Hell & Back

The ground burst upward, and in one fluid motion the tiny creek multiplied into a river ten feet wide and five feet deep. This water raged as a mighty river and swept the entire group off their feet sweeping them down the slope on its quest to empty its contents into the Lake of Fire.

Jakl and two other demons were swept off their feet and down the hill with the flowing, torrent of water.

Each member of the group held tight to their prize and let the river flow. The current was strong and they were moving quickly.

Elion held tightly to Kelly.

The dragon roared in his defeat and burst into the air. Satan dove at the river and reached his claws deep into the water as an eagle catches a fish. The dragon clasped the back of Elion's armor and raised him from the river while he still held Kelly in his arms.

Elion saw what was happening, and in a split second he released his hold on Kelly. She fell away from him toward the river, and for a moment they held eye contact. Elion smiled at her as she fell into the water and vanished into the Lake of Fire with the others. Then the river was gone.

The Lake of Fire churned as the clear water drove the team deep. They sank in deep enough to pass through.

The demons that hit the Lake thrashed and screamed as they struggled to get to the shore. Their skin sizzled as if they had been placed in acid. The ones who went in were maimed terribly and they looked even more wretched than before.

Satan landed and the demons gathered around Elion. They stripped off his armor, and he stood before the devil, naked and alone.

"Any brash last words now that you are all alone?" the devil asked.

Elion looked up to the dark sky and said, "Thank you, my Lord. All praise, all honor and all gl-"

The razor sharp claws of the devil buried into his chest and frothy blood bubbled forth from Elion's lips. His eyes fogged over and the evil one withdrew his claws, letting Elion fall to the ground in a heap, face down in the mud.

Elion breathed his last breath with this word, "Kelly…"
Satan put his head back and roared.

※

The water washed them deep into the Lake of Fire. They succumbed to the darkness and passed from one realm to another. Kelly felt ground beneath her hands and she crawled up on the shore. She stood and staggered up away from the foul lake. She coughed and spit up the thick, black liquid, clearing it from her body. She heard coughing and sputtering off to her left, so she headed toward the sound in the fog, emerging in a clearing. Belak sat on the ground next to Marie, who was spitting up the rotten lake residue.

At the sight of Belak, Kelly burst into tears, and he took her in his arms and held her as she wept.

She paused and tried to speak, "He. . . uh. . . let me. . . uh. . . go-"

"I know, I know," Belak stopped her. "I saw you fall. He wanted you to see the Kingdom, even if it meant without him. He knew that from the beginning, he told me several times. He willingly ransomed himself for you, believe it. Hold your head up."

Kelly tried to look strong.

"Higher, honor his sacrifice. His love for you is stronger than anything they can do to him. Now let's find the others and look for the angels," Belak commanded, tears dripping from his eyes as well.

"Angels?" Kelly said with an incredulous look.

"Yes angels. Welcome to the Kingdom of Heaven."

It didn't take long before they had everyone accounted for. Nothing could lift the feeling of great loss for their friends, Elion, Terel, and Tarkio.

Everyone fell in line behind Belak, while Jubal solidly brought up the rear. Lightning flashed around them with explosions of thunder and sheets of rain that pelted their skin. Belak led them up a thin trail and they hiked slowly upward along a line of trees.

Even in the midst of the storm they began to feel better in most every way. Their incessant hunger abated as well as the aches and pains they'd become accustomed to in hell. They entered a stand of aspen trees that offered wonderful protection from the storm. Belak paused and put his hand up to his face, as he suffered the loss of his friend. Marie put her hand on his back and he straightened up continuing to march. As they left the aspens they heard a loud cry much like that of a hawk.

In a moment's flash, fourteen angels descended upon the little stand of trees. Karial led with Jaxim to his right. The others were there as well, Cotton, Madrigal, Brago, Cypress, Tirzal, and the other seven that were not named.

"Is this all?" Karial asked.

"Yes, my friend," Belak answered. He motioned to Kelly. "This is Elion's Kelly."

"My lady, it is an honor." Karial bowed his head. "I was your father's guardian. May I take you to the White City?"

"Yes. That would be fine," Kelly said sheepishly.

"Praise our King!" Jaxim said. "This is a great victory. You've returned and set these captives free!"

Karial stepped up and grabbed hold of Kelly, and the other angels did likewise. Only nine of the fourteen carried passenger's home, but what had been accomplished no redeemed had ever done. The losses were a bittersweet grief.

Karial let forth his soulful cry of mourning and they took to the sky. The storm was rough for only a short distance and soon they whizzed through the peaceful skies of Heaven. They flew over rolling, green hills and beautiful mountains with many deep blue rivers flowing here and there.

"This is the Kingdom of Heaven," Karial whispered to Kelly.

As they flew two angels broke ranks and swooped down to the surface. They let out some type of cry as they went. A short time later they fell back into formation, each carrying new cargo. They had picked up the two lost warriors wandering below on the plains of Heaven. Terel and Abe hung on tightly as they proceeded to the White City straight ahead.

Kelly and the other captives had never felt so strong and peaceful in all memory. They landed in the Hall of Angels and were welcomed by a full house of angels cheering and hooting and hollering. Kelly felt different in most every way. She felt confident and beautiful. She felt like a woman. She did not yet understand that her tired and broken sixteen-year-old body had already been replaced with her redeemed body. She was fit and strong in body, mind, and spirit. The angels dressed the captives in the white robes of new arrivals, but they were anything but the usual new ones. It felt like a dream.

"The King will see you immediately. The entire Kingdom will feast in honor of your return and the success of the King's mission. You are to ride through the city on chariots to the Throne Room. They await," Karial announced.

He offered Kelly his arm and escorted her out of the Hall of Angels. In the golden, cobbled street there stood seven shining, white-chariots waiting patiently for the procession. Each bore the golden lion of Judah and the name of the warrior it carried. Vandilons pulled the chariots. Karial placed Kelly alone in the front carriage; while the other guardians helped everyone to their chariots. Belak and Marie, Bethalia and her mother, Haydn and Mary, Jubal and Laura, Terel and Abe, and one empty carriage for Tarkio.

The majestic animals pranced at a slow, steady pace through the streets lined with people who cheered and threw flowers. Some of the shopkeepers ran up to the chariots with something from their shops; a bottle of wine, a chunk of bread or cheese, gifts to the returning heroes.

The smells and the sights were almost too much for the captives, who were accustomed to constant silence and darkness. Trumpets announced the procession every few miles or so to give the parade the regal flare it deserved for such respected passengers. Everyone knew the realms had changed. After this, everything would be different.

The chariots wound their way through the White City and finally entered the plain before the Throne Room. Everyone wept at the sight of it. The tree, the river, there was no questioning the wonderful things in the Kingdom of Heaven.

The guardians escorted alongside the carriages. Karial now

helped Kelly down. "My lady, lead your ransomed captives to the Throne Room and speak with the King. You will receive your new name."

Kelly tiptoed up the steps to the Throne Room. She paused and looked back at the throng of people in wonder. She was no hero, her father was. The others followed her up the steps and into the presence of the King.

※

A time later, the girl named Kelly Rellik was now a distant memory. The redeemed woman, Cassalia, meandered through the streets of the White City stopping at a quaint café. She sat alone at a small round table. A woman with a friendly smile brought a basket of sweet-smelling breads wrapped in a cloth napkin. She also left several different spreads and an ornately-engraved butter knife. The woman returned and poured Cassalia a glass of red wine and disappeared, leaving her alone to her thoughts. The red wine sparkled and the bubbles popped as they glittered up into the air.

Cassalia smiled a sweet smile, wishing Elion was here to share this drink with her in this place. A small tear slipped from the corner of her eye. She caught it quickly with her left hand and wiped it away. She watched the multitude of people strolling by and took a small bite of the sweet bread with a touch of honey butter.

※

Deep in the darkness of the catacombs in a hole with no bars, two eyes that were closed suddenly opened. They were crystalline blue.

S.C. SHERMAN

Enjoy Chapter One of

Hell and Back
Sons of Edome
Part II

Look for it coming soon from

www.hellandbackbooks.com

S.C. SHERMAN

Hell and Back
Sons of Edome
Part II

Chapter 1
Chasing Demons

Click, click, clickety-click. The blade gently tapped against the mirror laying across Matt Rellik's knees. He methodically sliced a small chunk of crystallized rock into white powder. He smiled at the perfect line he'd created, and intently examined the fine edge of the razor blade. So sharp, it cried out for blood.

Why don't you just kill yourself? Cut your wrists and be done with it all!

Defeated, he shook his head.

"I wish I could do it," Matt whispered. "Kelly..."

Instead of slitting his wrists, he deftly licked the white residue from the blade. Tossing it aside, he picked up a two-inch piece of straw from a fast food restaurant. He leaned forward and glimpsed his appearance in the mirror. His disheveled looks startled even himself. Sparkling blue eyes ringed in red and swollen from no sleep, stared blankly. "Who the hell are you?"

Without another thought he inhaled the cocaine and with

one finger pressed his nostril firmly shut, to ensure it delivered its full kiss of power and death. He fell back in the couch and glanced around the dirty, one room apartment. It smelled much worse than it looked and it looked bad. Take out food containers and chip bags strewn about, while dishes grew mold in the sink.

Matt's attention settled on the only picture in the room. A framed color photo of a clean-cut young man in his West Point Dress Grays sat atop the TV with a cracked screen. The young soldier smiled with pride and confidence, as vibrant as his bright blue eyes. The corner of Matt's mouth curled up with pride, just for moment, and then was consumed by self-hatred. Matt wiped a tear from his cheek.

"I'm sorry…so sorry…Blake," he said out loud. He carefully unfolded the little paper pouch to find it empty.

"Damn," he swore bitterly. Matt immediately stood and stormed out the door. He didn't bother to lock it or even look behind to be sure it had shut. As he emerged onto the street he covered his eyes with a hand. Golden rays streamed down radiating warmth and brightness promising another beautiful California day.

Matt donned his sunglasses and sauntered quickly down the boardwalk. Normal people went about the business of the morning. No one seemed to really notice him as he weaved in and out of the busy sidewalk. The pounding waves of the ocean could be heard, but he'd long since lost all appreciation of its sound or fresh salty smell. Only one thing mattered, satisfaction.

After walking several blocks, he ducked into a plain looking door set between a travel agency and a bakery. The old flight of stairs creaked under his weight and he blinked to adjust for the dark hallway. Steps led up to the second floor apartment. He knocked lightly with three succinct taps, a pause, and then two more.

"Who is it?" someone yelled through the graffiti emblazoned door.

"It's me! It's Matt. Can I come in?"

"I'm closed; it's morning man, come back later!" the voice whined.

"No man. I need in now!" Matt begged.

The sound of multiple locks being unlocked penetrated to the hallway. The door opened just enough for Matt to slip in sideways. The door shut quickly and a little man with long, greasy hair and an un-kept look quickly relocked all the locks.

"Man it's too early. Did you stay up all night again?" he asked. The little fellow looked like he'd been up all night as well, with his own bloodshot eyes and disheveled appearance. He was young and slight of build, and he spoke with a nasally, feminine voice.

"I need some more blow," Matt said pleadingly.

"Just a minute, you gotta quit showing up like this," the little man said as he disappeared into a back room. Matt plopped down in a chair that rocked sideways, threatening to dump him onto the floor.

"You got some more, right, don't ya?" Matt anxiously said.

"Yeah man, just hold on." He pulled out a large mirror and laid it on the coffee table between them. He turned on the morning news with the TV remote.

"How much do you want? You're gonna run me out. You should switch to Ice, man; get into the present day, man. You're an old timer, you know, it might make you feel young again."

"Why would I want to be young again?" Matt said.

After an awkward pause, the man dumped a large pile of white powder directly in the center of the mirror. Matt stared through his puffy eyes with desire.

"Oh man, how much for that?"

"One thousand."

"I don't have that much." Matt frowned.

The man smiled at Matt and slyly winked. "You could give me what you have and earn the rest?"

Matt knew exactly what he meant. He wasn't new to this kind of scene. "Screw you!" Matt yelled.

The little man giggled, "Is that a threat or a promise?"

"Just give me whatever I can get for that!" Matt threw five one-hundred dollar bills onto the mirror and said, "You're sick and this is a sick world!"

The drug dealer pocketed the money and began cutting the

pile down and measuring out five hundred dollars worth of powder on a little metal scale. He carefully measured the powder until the two sides balanced. He generously added one more scoop and then poured the contents into a baggy. Matt greedily pocketed his desire, with an excited smile.

"You're just as sick as me, cokehead! Yeah, you sure are doing a lot to make this a better world!" the man said, obviously bitter at his rejected offer.

Matt didn't answer and stared at the TV displaying a scene from somewhere in the Middle East. Soldiers in desert camouflage were hiding behind some walls and burned out cars, obviously under fire.

"Amidst heavy fighting there were thirteen confirmed dead last night, as widespread firefights continue," the reporter spoke into a microphone as she stood in a bunker. She wore a helmet much too large for her head.

The tiny man added, "At least we're not diluted, like those poor idiots who think they're making the world safer!" Matt exploded to his feet, and slapped the drug dealer with the back of his hand.

"My son's over there! So shut up!"

The obviously startled dealer recovered from his abuse with only a tiny red spot on his cheek. "I'll bet he's real proud of you, ain't he, Daddio!"

"Nobody's ever been proud of me," Matt mumbled dejected. Matt stood to go, tiring of this little creep. He'd gotten what he came for.

"Sit down, no hard feelings right. Do a line with me?"

Matt sat down immediately, never one to turn down free stuff. "Sure, you bet, no hard feelings."

The dealer cut out two individual lines. Matt smiled at his good fortune as he saw the line this little dealer had cut for him was fat and long.

"Go on man, blow your brains out!" he motioned for Matt to partake by putting his hand to his head like a gun and pulling the trigger.

Matt chuckled and quickly did the big line. He leaned

back in his seat slightly dazed by the intensity of the rush.

"How did you get a kid like that?" the dealer asked after he inhaled the other line.

"He had a good mother…she's the only one who's ever loved me…" Matt's voice trailed off and he stared into space.

Matt rubbed his numb gums and itched his tingling nose. The unique taste dripped down the back of his throat promising more power.

"Thanks man, I gotta go." The little dealer followed Matt to the door and shut the door solidly behind Matt relocking all the locks.

Matt could feel his heart racing. "Dang, it's bright!" He put his sunglasses back on as he stepped back into the sunlight.

His destination was just up ahead and he stared at his feet as he scurried along the sidewalk. His breathing was coming very fast and he could feel his throat swelling. He'd felt this feeling many times before and tried to remain calm as he knew it would go away unless he panicked.

He whispered to himself, "That big line's killing me." He sort of shook his head in an attempt at some clarity that would not come.

"Only a couple more blocks," he glanced at the sign marking his goal. Bright red neon announced, *Junior's Surf Shop*.

He ducked in quickly, trying to remain calm. The door made a jingling sound as it closed itself. The jingles exploded in his brain like fire. Matt's senses, including his hearing, were amplified and he physically flinched at the little bell.

A woman in her twenties with punked-out hair and several facial piercings stood behind the counter and yelled over her shoulder, "Junior, there's a bum here, oh wait, sorry, it's your Dad!" she smiled a smile that meant, I detest you.

Matt ignored her. A young man with sun-bleached hair curling past his shoulders came out of the back room. He wore a t-shirt that said *Junior's Surf Shop* on the left chest and faded camouflage shorts. The girl behind the counter took it as her cue to leave. She stomped into the back room not hiding her disdain.

"Dad, dude, you look like shit. You gotta lay off that stuff. Go upstairs and crash for awhile," Junior said.

"Thanks, but I'm fine." Matt attempted a smile. His entire face was obviously numb and the smile looked wrong. He kept rubbing his nose as they talked.

"Dude, you don't look fine. Did you sleep last night? What've you had to eat man?"

Matt covered his ears as a couple teenaged boys stepped in, "That bell!" They went straight to the surf boards.

"I gotta go help those dudes, Dad, you need to go rest."

"I'm going over to Mandy's apartment, I can rest there plus it has a sweet view."

"Sweet view of what?" Junior asked as he walked toward his customers.

"Sweet view of the ocean, of course."

"Dad, you should leave her alone. You know she never stopped workin' it since you came on board."

Matt turned and put his hand to the knob. "What do I care? See you later." Mattie watched as his father walked out the door.

Matt wound his way down a side street lined with white stucco apartments and wrought iron balconies. He admired a shiny yellow Jeep parked in the driveway. It was running and just then a young man and woman burst out of the garage wearing swimsuits, holding hands and carrying bags. The girl dropped hands at the sight of Matt. She smiled coyly and bounced over to Matt kissing him on the lips.

"Matt this is Will, Will this is Matt," she introduced them.

The two men politely smiled at each other with no real fondness.

Will tossed their bags in the back of the Jeep and they both jumped in. The girl leaned out from the passenger seat. "Make yourself at home, honey; we're going to the beach for a few days. The apartment is yours. OK. Bye. Bye."

Will hit the gas and they sped away, music blaring for the entire world to hear. Matt smiled as he could just make out a lyric from a song he knew well.

Hell & Back

'there's plenty a room at the Hotel California, such a lovely place, such a…"

He shook his head side to side; his breathing was getting back to normal. He entered through Mandy's empty garage. It was obvious a girl lived here. The two room suite was neat and full of pictures. The photos were mostly of Mandy herself with a variety of different men hugging her in bars and partying.

Matt found a seat on the couch and pulled the glass coffee table towards him. He unpacked his contraband and dumped a small pile on the table. In his pocket he found his expired driver's license. He glanced at the old picture of himself and read his name out loud, Matthew Rellik. He used the card to slice up four more white lines.

Matt leaned in and did two of the lines right in a row. He sprawled back on the couch while the room began spinning a little and his eyesight blurred. Matt thought of the dumb little dealer. With a smile Matt put his right index finger to his temple and made a pretend gun noise as he fired the trigger. He stumbled onto the balcony and he lifted his hand to shield the sun. His bloodshot eyes strained to focus as the relentless surf pounded the shore.

"Is this Heaven?" The awful brightness of the sun drove him back inside. He found the remote control and began flipping through channels. He stopped for a moment on a news report. A pretty woman smartly dressed in business attire spoke succinctly into a microphone.

"Another scientist has been arrested as a worldwide hunt continues in the human cloning ring that is suspected to be part of the work of wanted scientist, Dr. A.Z. Belial. After the Coalition of Nation worldwide ban on research or attempts at human cloning went into effect, Dr. Belial, formerly of Cloning Research International, now defunct, went into exile vowing to continue his research to perfect human cloning. Despite the combined effort of many national agencies, Dr. Belial still remains at large. It is suspected that he has set up a laboratory funded by illegal drug sales. The location of that facility is still unknown."

Matt changed the channel to what looked like a documentary. He laid his head back as a man with an English accent explained about some sort of lizard. Matt drifted in and out of consciousness, no longer watching the TV, rather just listening.

"Some lizards can hold their breath for as long as twenty minutes, some can hibernate for years if need be, some can swim, some eat meat, some do not. Most have a type of scaled skin for protection from the elements and as camouflage from predators. Most prefer warmer climates and moisture free from extended exposure to direct sunlight…"

"Sounds like me, no direct sunlight. Maybe, I'm a lizard?" Matt closed his eyes and slipped into a deep slumber. A sleep no amount of cocaine could put off. He felt groggy like in a dream and he heard muffled voices that were somehow familiar.

Matt walked toward a doorway full of light. He recognized the hall and door as the Colorado house he'd lived in before he'd left home. He could hear crying and he noticed a girl sitting on the floor between her bed and the wall holding her knees to her chest and slightly rocking as she audibly wept. He knew instantly it was her. A tear slipped from Matt's eye as he recognized the girl as his sister.

"Kel, is that you?"

At the sound of the name, her head snapped up. She said nothing and stared at him through her tears.

"You got old…why'd you leave me here?" the girl asked. Matt's heart broke in two as he stared motionless at her.

"I'm sorry, Kel, I didn't know what to do so I ran, I didn't think…"

Kelly's countenance darkened, "You didn't what? Think of anyone but yourself! You left me here…all of you did!"

Matt could see her neck was torn and bruised. He suddenly realized he was in an awful dream.

"I need to wake up! That stuff must've been laced with something?" Kelly laughed, but it wasn't her sweet laugh, it was evil.

"You are awake."

"No I'm not. You died years ago, this is a bad dream," Matt argued.

"The dream that was the world is over. You're awake now

and you'll never go back. Your choices have been made," she said with an evil smile.

"What choices? What are you talking about?" Matt stammered.

"You're dead. You're ours now," she said.

"Ours? What are you talking about?" Matt asked.

Growling filled his ears and he nervously glanced down the hall behind him. He looked back to Kelly and discovered her room was gone. He saw himself lying on Mandy's couch. He looked dead. His skin was blotchy and blood had run out of his nose.

"Wake up! Wake up! This is a dream!" he yelled at himself.

Behind him a low and growly voice emanated from the darkness, "You'll soon wish it was a dream."

Matt turned slowly and horror overcame him as he saw an awful creature standing in the shadows. The monster looked big and dark as if it'd been burned. Its skin was black and seeping with eyes that were full of malice. He had teeth that were on display at all times. Matt stood motionless bound by fear. Beside the wicked creature was a magnificent looking animal full of strength and beauty covered in hair feathers and dressed in battle armor. It was on its knees, bound and gagged. The creature mournfully stared into Matt's eyes.

"Who is that?" Matt asked.

"The spoils, he was your guardian and we thank you very much. He'll make a fine demon, time to go," the dark one said with a growl.

"Go? Go where?"

In a flash, the creature hit Matt hard and knocked him to the ground. Matt screamed out as claws sank into his back. The clawed hand grasped Matt's backbone as if it were a handle. Suddenly they were flying and the guardian disappeared. They zipped through clouds full of lightning and over foreboding rivers and barren land. Rancid smells filled his senses so awful that Matt repeatedly vomited. The pain in his back was excruciating and occasionally he tried to turn and fight against the shadowy creature carrying him.

They descended into a smoky hole where Matt could hear

wailing and actually feel anguish, pain, and loss. The haze cleared allowing him to see a horrific room of atrocities. Matt witnessed people in various stages of torture as far as his eyes could see. Suddenly the realization flashed into Matt's thoughts. He hung his head and wept as he felt defeated to his core. Somewhere, deep in his spirit…he knew he was lost, forever lost.

"Welcome to hell," the demon cackled.

www.hellandbackbooks.com

Hell & Back